"MISS DIDION MAKES THE READER FEEL THINGS."

—*Philadelphia Bulletin*

"Her prose is scrupulous, exact in understatement. Yet in it our violent, flamboyant times are trapped alive, and will remain alive."

—Brian Moore

"She is an artist. How her work conveys this sense of tragic regret, I cannot quite say, but that is exactly why she is an artist."

—Frederic Raphael, *Saturday Review*

"I cannot think of a single writer whose prose matches Miss Didion's level of simple elegance, or the tremendous lyricism of passages. . . ."

—*National Review*

"Joan Didion's honesty, intelligence, and skill are wonders to behold." —*Newsweek*

JOAN DIDION
RUN RIVER

A KANGAROO BOOK
PUBLISHED BY POCKET BOOKS NEW YORK

**POCKET BOOKS, a Simon & Schuster division of
GULF & WESTERN CORPORATION
1230 Avenue of the Americas, New York, N.Y. 10020**

ISBN: 0-671-81979-8

First Pocket Books printing March, 1978

for my family and for N

Acknowledgments

"All night I've held your hand,
as if you had
a fourth time faced the kingdom of the mad—
its hackneyed speech, its homicidal eye—
and dragged me home alive . . ."
                              —ROBERT LOWELL

". . . the real Eldorado is still further on."
                    —Peck's 1837 New Guide to the West

August 1959

Lily heard the shot at seventeen minutes to one. She knew the time precisely because, without looking out the window into the dark where the shot reverberated, she continued fastening the clasp on the diamond wrist watch Everett had given her two years before on their seventeenth anniversary, looked at it on her wrist for a long time, and then, sitting on the edge of the bed, began winding it.

When she could wind the watch no further she stood up, still barefoot from the shower, picked up from her dressing table a bottle of *Joy*, splashed a large amount of it onto her hand, and reached down the neckline of her dress to spread it, a kind of amulet, across her small bare breasts: on the untroubled pages of those magazines where *Joy* was periodically proclaimed The Costliest Perfume in the World, nobody sat in her bedroom and heard shots on her dock.

Her eyes fixed not on the windows but upon the framed snapshots of the children which hung above her dressing table (Knight at eight, standing very straight in a Cub Scout uniform; Julie at seven, the same summer), Lily held her hand inside her dress until all the *Joy* had evaporated and there was nothing left to do but open the drawer where the .38 had been since the day Everett killed the rattlesnake on the lawn: the drawer in the table by their bed where the .38 should be still and where it was not. She had known it would not be.

Nine hours before, at four o'clock that afternoon, Lily had decided that she would not go at all to the Templetons' party. It was entirely too hot. She had been upstairs all afternoon, lying on the bed in her slip, the shutters closed and the electric fan on. Everett was out in the hops, showing the new irrigation system to a grower from down the river; Knight had driven into town; Julie, she supposed, was somewhere with one of the Templeton twins. She did not really know.

The afternoons always settled down this way. Late in June, after all the trouble, she had begun insisting that everyone lie down after lunch. Although on three afternoons everyone had gone upstairs, on the fourth she had heard Julie talking on the telephone downstairs ("You couldn't *mean* it. He swore they broke up *months* ago"), and on the fifth she was, as usual, alone in the house. Everett and the children had been, nonetheless, extravagantly agreeable about the plan: if there was one word to describe what everyone had been about everything since June, that word was agreeable. It had been all summer as if a single difference among them might tear it apart again; as if one unpremeditated word could bring the house down around them for good.

She got up and opened a shutter. The heat still shimmered in the air, so concentrated as to seem incendiary. After dinner she would take another shower and throw the windows open and read one of Knight's books. The floor of his room was stacked with books. It seemed to her that Knight had spent the entire summer packing, unpacking, arranging and rearranging the things he planned to take East to Princeton: he had already packed so many books to ship East that Everett had finally asked if he had reason to believe the Princeton library off-limits to freshmen. "Why leave them here," Knight had shrugged, and for a few seconds Lily had hated him, had read malice into his bland voice as she watched Everett's face take on that look of elaborate unconcern.

At any rate, she would try to read tonight, although she found concentration increasingly difficult; lately she had been able to read only books about Chicago gangsters or by oceanographers. The Saint Valentine's Day Massacre and the Mindanao Deep seemed, in their equidistance from her, equally absorbing. She had asked Knight, last week when he was driving to Berkeley, to pick up some new books in one of the paperback bookstores along Telegraph Avenue. The books could no doubt be found, Knight had informed her, right downtown in Sacramento. She did not seem to realize that there were now paperback bookstores in Sacramento. She and his father would never seem to get it through their heads that things were changing in Sacramento, that Aerojet General and Douglas Aircraft and even the State College were bringing in a whole new class of people, people who had lived back East, people who read things. She and his father were going to be pretty surprised if and when they ever woke up to the fact that nobody in Sacramento any more had even heard of the McClellans. Or the Knights. Not that he thought they ever would wake up. They'd just go right along dedicating their grubby goddamn camellia trees in Capitol Park to the memory of their grubby goddamn pioneers.

Although she did not suppose that Knight would have brought any new books about either Columbus Iselin or Mad Dog Coll, even to simply sit in the dark and watch the lights on the levee road would be better than going to Francie Templeton's, where everyone would be hot and someone would drink too much

5

and say something with a familiar edge to it; going to river parties had become unpleasantly like watching reel after reel of badly focused home movies, the prints a little frayed by wear. *Here's the kitchen and there's Joe Templeton, trying to pour Francie's drink down the sink; look, Francie's stamping her foot and it's not even midnight yet; watch now, here comes little Jennie Mason, looking in the garden for Bud Mason; remember that, because next you'll see Jennie Mason (who, in a sequence spliced out of this reel, unfortunately but naturally misinterpreted Bud Mason's presence in the garden with Lily Mc-Clellan) being comforted by Everett McClellan; that's Everett, there in the long-suffering suit.* You did not even need audio. You could count on little Jennie somebody, could count on all the same faces, all the same games; at one of Francie's parties last year, when Ryder Channing had announced belligerently that he owed money to five of the ten men in the room, it had occurred to Lily that she had been to bed with seven, and in four cases could not remember exactly when or where. They were all, now, one error in taste. Although she had not been to a river party since June, she could remember what had happened after that one with the same distorted clarity that hung about the whole of June: it had not been the first party she had deserted for a hotel room, but it had been the first party she had deserted for a room at the Senator, which she thought of, still, as her father's hotel. Her father had liked the Senator bar, and several times when she was small he had taken her there for lemonade with grenadine. (The morning after that party, clutching Everett's pillow to her stomach, she had dug her fingernails into her arm until the skin bruised, but by noon, driving to the lake by herself, she had begun again to see it all as Everett's fault. It would not have happened had Everett been at the party instead of home brooding about his sister; none of it would ever have happened had Everett been there.)

You better cut it out, Ryder Channing had said in June, that day at the lake which had been part of the trouble, and although Ryder was the last one to have said it, Ryder was right. A party could begin it all again—two drinks, someone from out of town, Everett ignoring her, that was all it would take—and when Everett came upstairs at four-thirty she told him that she did not want to go to Francie Templeton's.

"It's too hot. You go if you want."

She was brushing her hair, pulling it down over her face, trying to find the gray Julie had claimed to see among the dark. Lily could not imagine herself with gray hair: in the first place she was not yet thirty-seven and in the second place she had always imagined her style to be striking frailty. You could not, with graying hair, look strikingly frail; you could only look frail.

"Knight and Julie are going," she added.

Everett sat down by the window. Both his face and his khaki shirt were splotched with dust and sweat. "I think you should go. They're expecting you."

"I have a headache," she said mildly. "I can't help that, can I. I mean that's what anybody'd have to call an act of God, isn't it. Even Francie Templeton. You'll catch cold if you sit by the fan in a wet shirt."

"You and your mother."

"It's congenital. I read it in the *Reader's Digest.* Five New York doctors. How to Make Headaches Work for You. Anyway. You go."

"All right," he said without interest. "All right."

Everett began whistling tunelessly through his teeth. Only that and the whine of the electric fan broke the silence. Lily was aware that he did not take his eyes from her bare arms as she brushed her hair.

7

"We could go away this winter," he said abruptly.

"Go away," she repeated. "Go away where?"

"We could take a trip. We could take one of those boats that keeps going for forty-one days or something. We could go to Alaska or Australia or Europe or someplace."

"Not Alaska, baby. I mean it couldn't be much fun to go to Alaska in the winter."

"Somewhere," he insisted.

"Australia. Imagine."

"Listen," Everett said. "I'd like it. We've never done that, gone away together. For a long trip. It'll be good for you."

It was unlike Everett to want to go away. Since the war he had left the ranches only for occasional weekends, growers' meetings, funerals down the Valley; one might have thought him some agrarian Ivar Kreuger, guardian of an ephemeral empire in need of constant control, split-second manipulation. Although she had wanted him to go abroad with her and the children when they went the summer of 1957 (*There's no point if you don't go, Everett, baby, there's no use in sending me off alone, it'll only be the same when I come back, please, Everett*), he had refused.

"Could you get away?" she asked now.

"I think so." He stood up and opened a shutter. "Anyway," he added. "You and Julie could go."

"She can't leave school. She has to study for her College Boards and besides she thinks she's in love. She thinks she's going to get pinned to that Beta from Berkeley. I doubt that she could tear herself away long enough to see us off at the boat."

"You don't mean that boy she had up here."

"That's right. That very one."

"I didn't like him. You know I didn't like him." Everett paused. "He looked like a little wop in that jacket he wore up here."

Lily said nothing. The boy was six foot two, an inch taller than Everett; was almost as blond as Everett had been at his age and as Knight was now; and had worn, one day in July when he drove up to see Julie, a madras jacket identical to one hanging in Knight's closet. Everett had not liked him because he had made a drink for himself and offered one to Julie.

"Anyway," Lily said finally. "That's not the point, for me to go with Julie. I mean is it?"

"A trip would be good for you," Everett repeated without looking at her.

"It would be just like before."

"We'll see," he said. "A long vacation."

She leaned back against the walnut headboard of the bed until the carved leaves cut into her back. *A long vacation.*

Sitting down beside her, Everett took the hairbrush from her hand and began to brush her hair. When she let her head drop against his arm he put the brush down and began massaging her shoulders.

"Julie said she saw gray," Lily said.

"That's not so bad, is it?"

"She thinks it would be distinguished. She thinks it's very distinguished of you to be getting gray. Very distinguished and about time. I told her forty was not generally considered the other side of the mountain, and she just looked at me."

Everett kneaded the muscles in her neck. "There's nothing wrong with Julie."

"I never said there was. That helps my headache."

"Get in bed," he said, still holding her shoulders.

She pulled back the sheet with one hand, slid the straps of her slip down with the other, and kicked off her straw sandals. Lying on the sheet, she watched Everett close the shutters again and take off his clothes. She had always liked the rangy way he looked

9

without his clothes. He was the only man she had ever seen whose bones looked right to her.

"Oh, Christ," she whispered as she reached for him. "Everett, baby, we're so tired."

Before he was finished she began to cry, a tearless weeping compounded in part of pleasure, in part of weariness, and long after it was over she still clung to him, her shoulders moving in faint convulsive sobs, her legs caught around him. (They could lie together now only in the afternoons or in the middle of the night, after both had been asleep; not since the first years of their marriage had they been able to turn out the lights and turn to each other. Some pride overcame them instead, some reticence or aversion. Each, over the years, had read a great deal.) Nerveless, Lily lay listening to the fan, to the mosquitoes, to Knight's car outside the house; listening without moving to the persistent ring of the telephone and finally to the knocking on the bedroom door.

"Your ma's sleeping, Knight," China Mary called up from the kitchen; "she don't want no telephone callers now. You tell him he can call back."

"Call back, hell," Everett murmured, half asleep. "Why'd they answer it at all. Why don't they turn it down so they don't hear it ring."

"Why don't you go to sleep," Lily whispered, kissing his cheek. Everett's aversion to answering the telephone had seemed, when they were first married, a great compliment: *we won't have it known, dear, that we own a tel-e-pho-own.* It had taken her almost two years to see that it had nothing to do with her, that Everett was about the telephone exactly the way he was about the mail, as wary as if he were investigating night noises at the basement door.

"You lie still a minute," she added, "and I'll get you a drink."

Although she would just as soon have sat on the
10

bed whispering with Everett and drinking bourbon
for another hour (the telephone rang twice again),
they did, eventually, go downstairs for dinner. Julie
was late, coming in some time after the artichokes
with her face flushed and her eyes bright, a cotton
shirt pulled over her swimming suit and a faded pink
grosgrain ribbon tied around her wet blond hair (she
had driven Mrs. Templeton's T-Bird and talk about
power on the *pull*out—*not* automatic, *a straight-
stick T-Bird* if you can imagine), and somewhere between the artichokes and Julie's arrival Lily took the
telephone call, told Ryder Channing that she could be
home, later on, which could have been easy enough
but *count on her.* Everett did not ask who had called
(he knew, he always knew) and as she saw the heat
and tension tightening the vein on his forehead she
knew that she had to say something. What she said,
elaborately casual in that rush of confused guilt and
love, was that she might go to the Templetons' after
all. *Count on her.* Never mind. Some of the tension
left Everett's face and it would be all right. She
could take her own car, leave early (she did, Everett
knew, have the headache), meet Ryder on the dock
but only for a few minutes; figure out, later, some
way to make it all right, make everyone happy. Dinner, at least, had been saved. Nonetheless, she began
to wish immediately that she had never answered the
telephone at all, began to wish that she and Everett
could have stayed in bed while the sun gradually
left the room and the crickets began and the night
wind came up off the river (they had done that sometimes the first year they were married, stayed in bed
in the falling dark, not talking, drinking a little now
and then from the bottle of bourbon Everett always
kept by the bed); began to regret that they could
not have lain inviolable on that walnut bed from
five o'clock until the following morning.

11

2

Everett sat on the dock fifteen minutes before Lily
came. He heard her long before he saw her, because
now at one o'clock the moon was entirely down. Although house lights flickered on the water downriver, the mile and a half of McClellan riverfront
showed only the even flash of the Coast Guard channel markers; the light on the dock was gone, burned
out he didn't know when. *Remind Liggett,* he thought,
abruptly alarmed about the dock light. (A dock light
first, a torn fence next, maybe the pump goes off and
loses its prime: before long the whole place would
come crumbling down, would vanish before his
eyes, revert to whatever it had been when his great-
great-grandfather first came to the Valley.) Through
the growth of oak and cottonwood Everett could see a
single light on the third floor of the house; the lower
stories were blocked out by the levee.

During those fifteen minutes Everett thought only
of the dock light (*Liggett should watch these things*)
and of the hops. Although he still held his father's
.38-caliber revolver in one hand, he did not think
about that, any more than he thought about Ryder
Channing's flashlight, still burning, its thin light
filtering through three inches of muddy water, caught
there in the tangle of roots that showed where the
current had undercut the bank. Next week they
would be taking the hops down, stripping the vines
from the strings. Each August, just before picking,
Everett was suffused with a single fear, an apprehension specific in exactly the sense that nightmares

12

are specific: the unshakable conviction that his kiln
would explode as the hops dried. He could never
sleep during the week the hops were drying. Sometimes he would go downstairs and sit all night in the
kitchen, because he could see the kiln from the
kitchen window. It was not, this or any year, that
the loss of the crop could ruin him: he had fewer
acres in hops this summer than any since his father's
death, fifteen years before. There was no longer any
money in hops: everyone on the river was getting
out of them. *"It's a combination of factors,"* he had
*tried to explain, repeating by rote what the buyers
told him, to his sister Sarah and her third husband
when they came through in June on their way from
Philadelphia to the Islands. ("Not Honolulu, Everett,"
Sarah had corrected him. "Maui. Oahu's been ruined
for years.")* *"Your shares aren't paying what they
used to pay because we aren't making what we used
to make. For one thing people aren't drinking as much
beer as they used to drink. For another the brewers
are making what they call a lighter beer, using fewer
hops."*

The loss of the hops would not matter to Sarah.
Nothing about the ranch had ever mattered to Sarah.
But Everett had seen little all week but that familiar
image: his drying kiln burning, the flames breaking
out against a night sky and still (impossibly, as in a
nightmare) throwing no light into the dark. *It would
happen this year for certain,* he thought now.

When he heard Lily he sat perfectly still, aware
suddenly of the .38 in his hand, the blood on the
sleeve of the Dacron suit Lily had bought for him at
Brooks Brothers in San Francisco. He heard her high
heels on the wooden steps down the river side of the
levee (*Jesus Christ,* he thought with abstract tender-
ness, *high-heeled shoes to get screwed on the beach*),
heard her pushing aside the oak branches, heard her
call his name.

13

Everett, she called, long before she could have seen him on the dock. She called him, not Channing, answering the question he had never asked: would she hear the shot and come to him or would she come as usual to meet Channing; would she come to him, knowing, or would she come to Channing, come clean and unaware from the shower where she had been maybe twenty minutes before, come intending to take the boat downriver half a mile, meaning to lie there with Channing on the stretch of sand where Knight and Julie gave beach parties. (He had heard the shower when he went into the house to get the gun. Standing in their bedroom after he had taken the gun from the drawer, he had watched the steam through the open bathroom door, had listened to her humming a song to which she could never remember the words, *we will thrive on keep alive on/just nothing but kisses.*) Well, she had heard the shot and come to him: she had called *Everett.*

Still holding the gun, he got to his feet. Lily stood in the clearing by the dock, looking first at him and then at Channing's body where it lay sprawled over a rotting log. In that moment before either of them spoke, it occurred to Everett that Lily was not as pretty as she had once been. No one had ever called her beautiful, but there had been about her a compelling fragility, the illusion not only of her bones but of her eyes. It was not that her eyes were any memorable color (hazel, her driver's license must say), any extraordinary shape. It was simply that they seemed larger than anything else about her, making her very presence, like that of someone on a hunger strike, a kind of emotional claim. It exhausted him to look at her now: her eyes were too large.

"I guess he came here to meet you," Everett said, swiping at a mosquito with his free hand. He did not look at Channing's body.

She did not speak.

Unable to think, Everett wished that they could go back to the house and to bed; he wanted to make her a drink, bourbon with crushed ice the way she liked it, sit with her in the dark calm beneath the mosquito netting.

"There was no need," she said finally, her voice barely audible. "No need."

She began crying then. Everett stood watching until her sobs took on the helpless, automatic quality which meant that she was losing control, crossing an invisible border into some unmapped private terror. Sudden or expected death, the sight of a stranger planting daffodil bulbs, or the recollection of some commonplace, forgotten afternoon (say when they had taken the children to look at the seahorses in Golden Gate Park and the seahorses had been gone) could tap Lily's reserve of hysteria. ("That's how people should live," she had said about the planter of daffodils; he had suggested that she set out some daffodils around the house.) He wondered without interest if Channing had ever seen Lily cry. He supposed he had. He supposed every son of a bitch on the river had.

He laid the gun on the dock and walked over to her. Her sweater had fallen from her shoulders, and he stooped to pick it up from the dirt. It was a pink cashmere sweater that belonged to Julie; one of the name tapes Lily had bought when they sent her down to school at Dominican was sewn in the neck. *Julia Knight McClellan.* Julie was as pretty now as Lily had once been. Although her fine, almost white blond hair had always reminded Everett of his sisters ("She may look like Sarah but she looks nothing *like* the way Martha looked," Lily had said this summer, nearly screaming. "I don't know how you can even *say* that"), Julie looked, on the whole, more and more like Lily: she moved the way Lily moved, had even the shy, hesitant smile which by now was only a mannerism for Lily. (Only about an hour ago, at the Templetons' party, had he not looked across the room to see Julie brush a strand of hair from her face with Lily's own rapid, tentative gesture? *Lily,* he had thought, his face suddenly cold with relief and shame, in that instant between seeing the gesture and realizing that it was not Lily at all, but Julie. Until that moment when he thought he knew he had refused to ask himself where Lily was. Only then did he realize that he had not moved from the room in half an hour, had stayed there deliberately so that he might believe Lily to be on the terrace, or downstairs in the room with the piano. *We will thrive on keep alive on/ just nothing but kisses.* Julie had been wearing a white dress cut low in back, and he had stared at her sunburned back as if he had never seen it. What he had never before noticed was that her back was exactly like Lily's. You could see the small bones. Both Lily and Julie stood very straight, holding their narrow shoulders back as if to hide the bones. He had been staring at Julie's back as if in trance, wondering with intense irritation why she had not worn a dress which covered her bones, when he felt someone's hand on his shoulder. In his irritation, he jerked away; it was Francie Templeton. "You need a drink, Everett," she had laughed; he smiled and put his arm around her bare shoulders. "Sure, Francie," he had said. "Sure I do.") *She was already gone then,* he thought now, trying for the first time to make chronology of it.

The wind was rising off the river, breaking both the quiet and the still heat, disturbing the dry leaves and splashing water against the dock, rocking the little cruiser in its mooring, knocking Channing's flashlight free from the tangled roots and into the drift of the water. *Willows whiten, aspen quiver.* It was the only line of verse Everett knew: he had learned it maybe thirty years before and he did not remember who had written it or what followed it, but often when the

16

wind came up on the river he found himself repeating it in his mind. Once in Colorado he had seen aspen trembling, miles of them, and had wanted them for the ranch.

He brushed the leaves and dust from Julie's sweater and wrapped it again around Lily's shoulders. *If a wind comes up when the kiln burns,* he thought distantly, *the house could go.* He stroked Lily's hair, imagining the flames flashing down through the windbreak of eucalyptus, catching the immense dusty growth of ivy on the north walls, smoldering, then flaring up irrevocably through the entire wooden frame of the house. He could not get it out of his mind that Lily would be trapped in the fire, and he shut his eyes in vain against the ugly image of her fragile bones outlined in the incandescent ruin.

"You knew," she said finally, her dry sobs mixed with coughs now. "You knew there wasn't any need."

He recognized her plea and could not answer it. He wished that he could comfort her (*there was no need, Lily, no need, you weren't involved, Lily, count yourself out*), because she had not, in fact, been involved. Now that it was done, now that Channing lay dead between the river and where they stood, it seemed to Everett that none of them, least of all Lily, could have been involved; that all of them, he, Lily, and Channing, had simply been spectators at something that happened a long time ago to several other people.

"You shot him," Lily whispered.

Everett nodded, abruptly exhausted. *Maybe she didn't realize,* he thought, inert with the new possibility that he would, after all, have to explain it to her. (He had thought they were at least done with that, had thought she realized that for once she had something worth crying about.) *Maybe she just now figured it.* Then he saw that she was looking beyond him at the dock where his gun now lay, and realized

17

that she was doing no more than framing a question: *what would he do now.*

He had not thought of there being alternatives, solutions, next steps. Although he could not now focus upon how it had happened or what would happen next, he seemed to have known all along, as surely as he knew about the kiln fire, not only that it would happen but that everything he knew would be obliterated by it. Lily meant something else: *you shot him,* she meant. *Now what.*

It occurred to him that Lily had always been keyed to picking up pieces, peculiarly tuned for emergency. What eluded her was the day-to-day action. She would not buy a dress without his approval, but she had driven into the hospital without waking him the night last Christmas when they called to say that Julie had been in an accident after a dance. She had gotten a respirator down on the dock in ten minutes the night his sister Martha drowned. And once, years and years before, she had literally saved Knight's life: he had been playing with Knight on the grass when Knight crawled away and tore his foot open on a broken Coca-Cola bottle. He had knelt there for whole minutes with Knight in his arms, helplessly watching the blood spurt clear red on the grass. Then as now, he could not think. (That time it had been Lily who had seen them from the house, had come running with a dishtowel and had known how to make the blood stop, and finally shoved Everett and the baby into the pickup and had driven twenty-five miles in to the emergency hospital in Sacramento, her foot down on the accelerator all the way in along that twisting river road. Knight nearly died and he might have died anyway, there in the waiting room of the hospital, if Lily had not slapped the attendant and screamed *I don't give a goddamn what the rules are you're going to help my baby whether he's a resident of the city of Sacramento or*

whether he's not and you'd better get to it or my fa-
ther's going to have every one of you on trial for man-
slaughter. On the way home, with Knight in her
lap, she had begun crying for the first time: she had
forgotten, she said, that her father was dead.)

Lily's hands were on his arm.

"Did Ryder have a gun?" she whispered.

"I can't hear you," Everett said harshly. Why did
she whisper, knowing full well that there was only one
person for miles around (Julie and Knight would still
be at the Templetons', and Liggett and the Mexicans
in town; it was Saturday night) and that this one person, this single listener, the topic at hand, was dead.

Lily had stepped back and was staring at him.

"I mean you don't have to whisper," he said, brushing a mosquito from his face.

"I said did he have a gun."

"What do you think? You think he had a gun? He
wasn't out here for the goddamn pheasant, was he?"

"He threatened you."

Everett looked down the river. "No," he said. "He
did not have a gun and he did not exactly threaten
me."

"He might have, you see." Lily spoke slowly and
clearly, as if to the children when they were small.
"He could have threatened you."

Running for her life, Everett thought. He did not
say anything.

"He'd been drinking and he might have come out
here and tried to—" She broke off and looked away.
"Tried to hurt me."

"Sure thing," Everett said. "That's a nice one. You
think the smartest Jew lawyer in California could find
twelve friends and neighbors between here and Stockton who'd believe you hadn't asked for it?"

"We could make the reasons."

"Listen," he said. "You listen to me now, this once,

19

and mind what I say. It's not as easy as that. There aren't any reasons. I don't want that."

"It's a little late for choosing."

"You don't see. I don't want that."

"What is it you want," she said without inflection.

He looked down the river. *What is it you want.* He had wanted to go away with her, for one thing. The idea of *going away* had been weaving itself into the fabric of his daily life for months. He had not in the beginning (say in April) thought of it as a trip, a possibility, something which might easily be arranged by travel agents, steamship pursers, airline clerks; even by July, his desire had acquired neither the brilliantly attainable colorings of travel posters and *Holiday* magazine nor the subtler, more exotic pastels of Rand-McNally cartography. The want would strike him briefly, and at odd moments: while he talked price to the hop broker, or waited for someone to answer the telephone. Even before the idea took real shape, he had begun to count on it: *when we're gone,* he would think without perceiving that he had thought it.

But a trip was not much to want. More than that, he had wanted this summer to do something with the children; he had not. In a few weeks Julie would be going back down to Dominican, and all he could remember of the summer was the heat. That was all he could make of it now: the heat, and Lily lying upstairs with the shutters closed against it, and Julie coming in jumpy from it, and how it had bothered Sarah when she came through in June, and how the coolest place was down in the dust among the hops. The house had seemed too small all summer. Three floors, seventeen large dark rooms, room enough for three generations of his family before him: the house had not seemed, this summer, big enough for the four of them. It had been the heat. ("*I didn't remember the heat this way,*" Sarah had apologized breathlessly to her husband. "*When you've lived where it's green*

20

you forget how it is out here. You realize it hasn't rained since April and it won't until September? You realize that?" As disturbed still as he had been when Sarah first went away, Everett had said that if she wanted to see green, she had only to look out into the hops. Counting the new system they were spending maybe ten thousand dollars this summer keeping those hops green. *"That's exactly my point,"* Sarah had said.)

It had been the heat, and Sarah, and the way the summer had begun. Everett had wanted to find some way to talk to Julie, to tell her that he would take care of her, that she need not be frightened of anything. He had not even found a way to tell her that she drove too fast. He had once seen her doing eighty in the Lincoln on the river road. And Knight would be going East, alone. It was not that Everett minded. Although Princeton had not been his idea he thought it a good idea; he even thought that he might have liked, himself, a year somewhere other than Stanford. But he knew that Knight considered the trip back East less an interlude than a beginning. No matter what Knight said, he was not thinking of coming home to the ranch. *What is it you want.* Whatever he had wanted, none of the rest of them did. Before his grandfather had died, he had told Everett's father that the riverfront and the other ranches, some seven thousand acres in all, were to be divided equally among his three grandchildren: Sarah, Everett, Martha. Although they had sold off some here and picked up some there, they still had the riverfront and they still had about seven thousand acres, all controlled by the corporation, the McClellan Company. (There was even a corporate seal, although Julie had broken the stamp years ago, trying to make an imprint on a leather suitcase.) Since Martha's death, Everett and Sarah had each owned half of the McClellan Company, and Everett had managed all of it. Knight

21

would hold even more land than that. All the old Knight orchards would come to him through Lily, and he would probably have everything up for sale before the ink was dry on the papers. (It had been Knight who had first pointed out to Sarah that the piece immediately upriver from the ranch was a tract called Rancho Del Rio No. 1 and the piece immediately downriver, developed a year later, a tract called Rancho Del Rio No. 3. "They're just biding their time," Knight had laughed, "waiting it out for Rancho Del Rio No. 2.")

What is it you want. He had said it to Martha (*what do you want, baby,* he had said, *what did you want*) the night she drowned off the dock where his gun now lay. He had wanted to say it to Sarah, every time she came home (only she did not now call it home). He had wanted to say it to Knight and he had wanted to say it to Julie. He looked at Lily again. She had the blank, frightened look that she had some nights when he woke her from bad dreams. She had always been afraid of the dark. *Sweet Jesus, what had she wanted?*

"I want to go up to the house," he said.

3

We could make the reasons. Everett's mind began to function now for the first time since he had left the Templeton house (it must have been about midnight, because someone had shouted "no dancing on Sundays," and then Francie Templeton had gone to get him a drink he did not need, Joe Templeton had asked him where Lily was, and he had walked out of the house, across the lawn and down the graveled drive to the car; he had seen Knight kissing Francie's niece from Santa Barbara down on the stone bench by the swimming pool, had discerned Francie's laugh among the voices and music from the house, and had seen then that Lily's car was gone); began to weigh the potentialities now as he stood on the levee waiting for the headlights to pass so that he and Lily could cross the road to the house. (Oh God remember how it was to drive the river road late on hot summer nights with Lily asleep, her head dropped on his shoulder, to hear the mosquitoes above the sound of the motor and to know that ahead was the cool white room, the walnut bed with the mosquito netting, Lily's room and his, his grandfather's before him. Lost in the night fields, his body, Lily's body, the house ahead: all one, some indivisible trinity. But maybe it had never been that way except late at night, never except when Lily was asleep. He knew this road so well that he could drive it with his eyes closed, could have plotted every curve in his sleep, knew exactly when to expect the jolt where the roadbed changed at the county line. Remember how it was. Asleep, Lily was any way he willed her.)

"Don't be afraid now," Lily said, her voice harsh. She put her hand on his arm as if to pull him along.

He realized then that the headlights were long past, that he still stood in the gravel with his head dropped forward. He had remembered, while they waited for the car to pass, what had happened between the time Joe Templeton asked him where Lily was and the time he walked out of the house. He had taken a swing at Joe, grazing his jaw and causing Francie, Everett's drink in her hand, to step between them, almost sober for a change. *What happened,* she kept saying. Everett had not known what had happened but it had something to do with Joe. *You've really got it made, haven't you, Templeton,* he had snarled. *Swimming pools. New Thunderbirds. For a lousy dirt farmer you really*

23

got the world by the tail. As he walked out Francie was laughing: *I don't notice you driving any Model T, Everett McClellan. I don't notice your kids swimming in the river. Between semesters at Princeton.*

Straightening his shoulders, Everett pulled his arm from Lily's touch.

"When's Julie coming home?" he said.

"I don't know." She dropped her hand. "I don't know about Knight or Julie. She was with one of the twins again."

He looked toward the house. "The lights are on downstairs."

"I left them."

"I just don't want to see Julie."

"Listen," she said. "We can make it all right."

"Not Julie," he said.

She put her fingers against his cheek and he caught them there with his hand. Her skin was soft and in the darkness she looked about twenty again, and vulnerable. Well, vulnerable she was. *Pity her simplicity and suffer her to come to Thee.* It could be easy enough. He could go back to the river now, lift Channing's body off that rotten log, weight it, and roll it into the river. It would lie there three, maybe four months, anyway until the river picked up a little water, began running fast enough to move the body downstream. Then it might be found: might catch on a piling or wash into a slough, be dragged up. How much could they discover by probing that disfigured, disintegrating mass of flesh? He tried to recall detective novels, but could think only of the kind in which the room blacks out an instant and the victim, when the lights go on again, is discovered slumped across the chemin de fer table. At any rate, he need deal here with neither the C.I.D. nor the Sureté, but only the incalculable expertise of the county coroner's office, an unknown quantity. This was less the stuff of detective novels than of newspaper murder accounts, which he had read throughout his life with a disinterest born of disbelief. They had never seemed probable. *Father Kills Daughter's Swain, Argument over Car Keys. Wife Kills Mate, Wounds Child, Did Not Mean to Fire. Carhop Slain, Assailant Unknown.* He could dredge from all those years of reading only the impression that dentists were frequently key witnesses when it came to identification; he had a further notion, even more dim, that no matter how advanced the decomposition an autopsy would show whether or not the cause of death had been drowning. The lungs either did or did not contain water, he could not remember which. Even if the body did not turn up for months, in that case, there would be inquiries, questions asked of all Channing's acquaintances and particularly of him, particularly of him and of Lily. Everyone knew, everyone must know, about Lily and Channing, about Martha and Channing. Fifteen years.

Anyway, it might be discovered tomorrow, next week. Nancy Channing would miss him, if nobody else did: she was suing for back alimony and had her father's lawyers after him all the time. For all Everett knew a hearing was scheduled for Monday. Were Channing reported missing, they might think—would certainly think, in a summer when there had been three or four drownings a month—to drag the river; might drag up the weighted body, leaving no question of accident, no possibility that the generally disorganized details of Ryder Channing's life had led him to drown himself. There were altogether too many variables.

"Where's his car?" Everett asked suddenly, and as he said it the variables began crowding in, the elements he could never calculate, the other factors overlooked. Channing's car still on the ranch; China Mary, not at her sister's as she usually was on Saturday night but maybe in her own cottage beyond the house, hearing the shot, knowing; the possible appointments set up for Monday. Not that suicides didn't set up appointments; not that Channing, in any case, had made much of a practice of keeping appointments the past few years. But still.

"Down the back road to the dock," Lily said, calm, and the old resentment flared briefly, obscuring everything. (Parked just off the levee road, hidden in the trees and darkness along the old dock road; the black Mercedes still unpaid for. "I was down on the dock, baby," she would have said in the same calm voice had none of it happened, had he simply come home from the party and found the house empty, simply waited upstairs as he had waited other evenings, listening for her high heels on the wooden verandah, listening for the screen door, for her humming. *We will thrive on keep alive on/just nothing but kisses.* "I was down watching the water. Didn't Francie tell you I'd gone on home? Didn't she tell you I had a headache?")

He could get rid of the Mercedes, all right, but it would be like sandbagging a levee already breached. Something else would keep turning up. There was still, however, Lily's way, the almost straight way, the way which would still give them something to talk about but the way which would be, in the end, the easy way: he could call the sheriff's office now—he could call Ed McGrath at home, they had gotten him at home the night Martha drowned—and tell him that he had shot Ryder Channing in self-defense. Or protection of property. Or whatever they wanted to call it. He had come home, heard Lily screaming on the dock, had picked up his gun and run down to investigate. When he found Lily struggling with Channing he had tried to break it up; Channing had gone for him and he had shot him. *Rancher Shoots Friend in Row over Wife, Did Not Mean to Kill.*

It was plausible only if you accepted as given

26

Lily's alleged resistance. Get some hotshot District
Attorney in there—who would it be? Everett no
longer knew—he could make something of that, make
it clear how many times Lily had heard the song before. Although they could probably prove nothing
about Lily and Channing (Nancy Channing, he
thought, would not have bothered to get whatever
evidence there had then been; she had divorced him
a long time ago and simply said mental cruelty but of
course she might have had the evidence anyway—
more variables, incalculable again), they could imply
plenty, maybe prove something else, possibly even
drag Martha's name into it once they talked to Nancy
Channing (he did not know how much if anything
Nancy Channing had known about Martha), sink the
knife in Lily, make it hard for a jury to believe she
would have drawn a line, started screaming after that
many times around.

But it was possible: Lily could probably make it
work. They would drag it all out in the newspapers
(give Francie Templeton two drinks, she'd probably
testify herself) but Lily could make it work. She
would say anything now, not particularly to save
him but to save them all, him, Knight, Julie, herself.
It would be a sweet trial, all right; a sweet trial for
Julie. Well, he wanted to save them too. (Never had
Julie seemed more precious to him than she had tonight: he would consider the world well lost to keep
her intact, her small bones, her sunburn, her white
dress, her hair so like Martha's, her longing for a
straight-stick Thunderbird. And his entire commitment to Lily had become an unbreakable promise
to protect her from the mortal frailties which were,
since they were hers, his own.) He wanted to save
them and he would. It was only that he was not sure
how. He could sort out no clear reason, no starting
point. It was the kind of letters he got from Sarah
and it was Martha buried there by the levee and it

was the way Knight had talked in June; it was the way he had always felt about the kiln burning, only that no longer mattered. It was as if the kiln had burned already. Everything seemed to have passed from his reach way back somewhere; he had been loading the gun to shoot the nameless fury which pursued him ten, twenty, a good many years before. All that had happened now was that the wraith had taken a name, and the name was Ryder Channing.

1938-1959

4

A little late for choosing, she had said to Everett, quite as if it hadn't always been. Was there ever in anyone's life span a point free in time, devoid of memory, a point when choice was any more than sum of all the choices gone before? A little late for choosing: her father had known it, even as he denied it. But deny it he had. *You say what you want and strike out for it,* he told Lily on the morning of her sixteenth birthday: it was one of their rare attempts to grope through a conversation with each other, deafened as always by the roar of the blood between them. (Neither Walter Knight nor his only child ever forgot that blood: dumbly, they exchanged deliberate commonplaces, phrases perhaps dry and hard enough to carry the weight of something for which there was no phrase at all. Take care of yourself. Do you need any money. Write.) *You say what you want and then go after it, and if you decide to be the prettiest and the smartest and the happiest, you can be.*

"Just you remember that everybody gets what he asks for in this world," Walter Knight repeated, making two stacks of the sixteen silver dollars he had dropped on her bed.

"Maybe that's not such a prize," she said. "Getting what you ask for."

She was aware that the attainment of her own most

inadmissable wish, to be asked to play Scarlett O'Hara in the movie version of *Gone With the Wind*, was not only outside the range of probability but not, over the long stretch, in her best interests. It would not, *per se*, build character. On the other hand her father was not talking about her character, which was one of the things that distinguished him from other people's fathers. Another was that he was good-looking enough, despite what was called in her mother's family "a weak mouth," to play Rhett Butler.

"I didn't say it was any prize." Walter Knight took a fruit knife from his pocket and began cutting up the apple he had brought for Lily's breakfast. "I didn't say that at all. I said it's nobody's fault but your own. My own. Anybody's own."

He paused, dropping the core of the apple in a wastebasket. "Eat this apple and we'll get some waffles. You're too thin. I said you play the game, you make the rules. I said if a lot of people a long time back hadn't said what they wanted and struck out for it you wouldn't have been born in California. You'd have been born in Missouri maybe. Or Kentucky. Or Virginia."

"Or abroad," Lily suggested.

Walter Knight paused. To have been born abroad was not, even within the range of his own rhetoric, quite conceivable.

"Or abroad," he conceded finally, seeing that the point was his own. "What I mean is you come from people who've wanted things and got them. Don't forget it."

"Maybe I don't know what I want. Sometimes I worry about it."

"I'll do the worrying," Walter Knight said. "You know that."

With a faith that troubled Walter Knight even as he encouraged it, Lily believed at sixteen, as firmly as

32

she believed that it was America's mission to make
manifest to the world the wishes of an Episcopal
God, that her father would one day be Governor of
California. It was only a matter of time before he
could be rightfully installed in Sacramento in the
white Victorian house he still called, in an excess of
nonchalance (it had been since 1903 the Governor's
Mansion), "the old Gallatin place." Any time Walter
Knight spent in town could be explained in view of
this end, and he spent, the year Lily was sixteen, a
great deal of time in town: more time than he would
ever spend again, for 1938 was to be, although they
did not then know it, his last year in the Legislature.

Gomez ran the ranch, even bargained with the
fruit buyers, while Walter Knight sat in the familiar
gloom of the Senator Hotel bar and called at the
white frame house on Thirty-eighth Street where Miss
Rita Blanchard lived. (Miss Rita Blanchard was, as
he so often said, his closest friend in town, a good
friend, a loyal friend, a friend whose name could
be mentioned in the Senator Hotel bar in the presence
of Walter Knight only by Walter Knight.) Gomez was
the most dolorous of men; one might have thought
him intent only upon disproving the notion that our
neighbors from south of the border were so *muy
simpatico*. Patiently, he illustrated Walter Knight's
contention that honesty could be expected only of
native northern Californians. "I pay that bastard
more than any Mexican in the Valley gets paid,"
Walter Knight would say periodically. "Yet he cheats
me, finds it necessary to steal me blind. Add that one
up if you will. Rationalize that one for me." The challenge, although rhetorical, was calculated to lend
everyone present a pleasant sense of *noblesse oblige;*
as Walter Knight was the first to say, he had never
hired a Mexican foreman expecting that they would
operate under the Stanford Honor Code. Once Edith
Knight had taken up the challenge, but the rationale

33

she offered had little to do with Gomez. "Maybe that wouldn't happen," she said one night at dinner, her hands flat on the heavy white linen cloth and her eyes focused at some point away from her husband and daughter, "just possibly that wouldn't happen if you were to spend, say, one-half the time on this ranch that you spend on Thirty-eighth Street."

Walter Knight demanded that Lily observe the delicacy of the asparagus, grown, despite an extraordinarily poor season for asparagus growers in the southern part of the state, not three miles away on the Pierson place.

"Walter," Edith Knight whispered finally, flushed and rigid with regret as if with fever. Without looking at her, Walter Knight reached across the table and touched her hand. "Sarcasm," he said, "has never been your *forté*." Edith Knight stiffened her shoulders and picked up her water goblet. "The word is *forte*, Walter," she said after a moment, entirely herself again. "Quite unaccented."

Such lapses were rare for Edith Knight: a change for the better was among the prime tenets of her faith. That was the year, Lily's sixteenth, when she tried parties. Through the holidays and late into spring, she entertained as no one on the river had entertained in years, confident that the next party would reveal to her the just-around-the-corner country where the green grass grew. *I thought of floating camellias in the silver bowls,* she would write to Lily at Dominican, *or do you think all violets, masses and masses of violets? p.s. bring someone home if you want but don't come if it's an Assembly weekend, you'll miss meeting a great many nice people if you keep on missing those dances.* Because Lily would have gone to extraordinary lengths to avoid an Assembly (the sight of the inexorable square envelopes in her mail slot at school turned her faint, chilled her with a vision of herself stranded on a gilt chair at the St. Francis Hotel, her organdy dress wilting and her hands wet in kid gloves), she always came home for her mother's parties.

She would arrive on the Saturday morning train, and Gomez would meet her in Sacramento. ("*Como esta usted, Señor Gomez?*" she called one morning as she stepped off the train. "I don't get you," he said, picking up her two bags and handing her the heavier one.) Although Gomez would sometimes agree to stop at a place in the West End where she could eat tacos with her fingers, he never spoke on those occasions unless Crystal was along. Crystal was his common-law wife by virtue of mutual endurance, and if Gomez brought her into town on Saturday morning it was only to confront her with the scenes of her Friday-night defections. In a moment of misdirected intimacy, Crystal once told Lily that she had worked the whole goddamn Valley in season before Gomez latched on to her in Fresno. "I don't mean picking, honey, you get that," she added, producing as evidence her white hands, each nail filed to a point and lacquered jade green. Ignoring Lily, Gomez would vent his monotonous fury in Spanish, which Crystal pretended not to understand. "You're a nutsy son of a bitch," she would drawl from time to time by way of reply, nudging Lily hilariously and inspecting the dark roots of her Jean Harlow hair in a pocket mirror. (Although Crystal had lived with Gomez three months before Walter Knight noticed her presence on the ranch, she had become, the moment he did notice her, one of his favorite figures, referred to alternately as "Iseult the Fair" and "that sweetheart.")

About seven o'clock, when the house was full of the faint sweet smell of wax and the almost palpable substance of Edith Knight's anticipation, Lily, dressed in the pale blue crêpe de Chine her mother thought most set off her hair, would take a glass of cham-

pagne up to the third floor and sit by a front window, watching the cars swing off the bridge and up
the road to the ranch. Everyone came to those parties:
river people, town people, and, when the Legislature was in session, people from Red Bluff, Stockton, Placerville, Sonora, Salinas, everywhere. Even
the people from down South came, proof to the doubt-
ful that Walter Knight was more interested in California than in water rights, than in small disagree-
ments, than in a bill he had once introduced pro-
posing the establishment of two distinct states, the
border to fall somewhere in the Tehachapi. "I'll tell
the world," a lobbyist from down South once said to
Lily, "L.A. is God's own little orchard." His wife
echoed him: God's own little orchard. Neither was
actually from California; he had met the little lady
in a band contest, an all-state high-school competition held in the Iowa State football stadium. His
band won first prize, her band won third; and the
three winning bands were awarded all-expenses-
paid trips to the Palmer House in Chicago, where he
and the little lady had decided, he said, to make it
legal. "Came to L.A. with a bride on my arm and a
dime in my pocket," he added, "but baby won't
you look at us now. God's own orchard." "I've got a
few of your compatriots in my orchard," Walter
Knight said; the Okies were still pitching tents at the
far end of the ranch, near the main highway south.
Although he said it pleasantly enough, Edith Knight
looked at him, reproof in her eyes. That wasn't the
way to the green grass.

No matter who else came, Rita Blanchard always
came. As if she had lain in a dark room for days,
conserving all of her animation for this one evening,
she smiled constantly, watching Edith and Walter
Knight even as she talked to someone else. Her
apologetic inattention was part of her face to the
world, vital to that air of being irrevocably miscast,

fatally unfitted, the kind of woman who appears for dinner a day before or a day after the day appointed, who inevitably arrives dressed for tennis when the game underway is bridge. Her mooring in the world seemed so tenuous that every spring when she went away (to Carmel for the month of April, abroad for the month of May), there were those who said that she had in truth been committed. In spite of what she knew, Lily felt a guilty love for Rita Blanchard: even at thirty-five, Rita seemed always to be sitting on those gilt chairs at the St. Francis. Although she must have known that she was considered something of a beauty in the Valley, the very way she walked into a room belied that knowledge, announced her certain faith in her inability to please. She dropped her head forward, brushing her long hair back from her face with nervous fingers; should someone startle her by speaking suddenly, she would begin to stutter. Each tale in the folklore of spinsterhood had at one time or another been suggested in explanation of her official celibacy: the secret demonic marriage and subsequent annulment; the dead lover, struck down on the eve of their public betrothal; the father who would allow no suitor close enough. Not even the fact that Rita's father, the gentlest of men when alive, had been dead since Rita's twelfth birthday could abate the popularity of the last theory. The truth was simply that Walter Knight had kept her company for twelve years, and if Rita had once expected something else, her diffidence and Walter Knight's lack of it had combined to dispel those shadows. Although it was rumored that there was not the money there had once been, enough remained of the Blanchard estate to enable Rita to give Lily expensive presents every Christmas ("You be sure now you *thank* poor Rita," Edith Knight always ordered— the adjective "poor" was for her a part of Rita's Christian name—"but French perfume is not what I would call a suitable gift for a *jeune fille*"), to bring home all her clothes from Jean Patou in Paris, and to ask favors of no one but Walter Knight.

So Rita came, along with everyone else, and if everyone had a good time at those parties, who enjoyed them more than the Knights? When the evenings grew warm that year they threw open the French doors and set up the bar in the garden, to catch the first cool wind off the river. "Edie says hot nights make better parties," Walter Knight would say, drawing her toward him, "and Edie's right about most things." There seemed a tacit promise between them, lasting the duration of each party: all they had ever seen or heard of affectionate behavior was brought to bear upon those evenings. One might have thought them victims to a twenty-year infatuation. As they said good night at the door, Edith Knight would stand in front of him and lean back on his chest, her face no longer determined but radiant, her manner not dry but almost languorous, her smallness, against Walter Knight's bulk, proof of her helplessness, her dependence, her very love. "Take care now," she would say softly, her eyes nearly closed, "we're so happy you came." All the world could see: there was bride's cake under her pillow upstairs, and upstairs was where she wanted to be.

After everyone had gone, she would hum dance music as she and Lily blew out the candles, closed the glass doors, picked up napkins here and there from the floor. *Of thee I sing, ba-by, da da da da da da-spring, ba-by.* "Do you know," she would break off suddenly and demand of Walter Knight, "how many times Harry Scott's sister saw *Of Thee I Sing* when she was married to that man who did business in New York City?"

"I can't imagine."

"*Fourteen.* She saw it fourteen times. With customers."

"I trust she knows the lyrics better than you do."
"Never mind about that."

Still mesmerized by her own performance, she would go then to sit on the edge of Walter Knight's chair. "You go on up, Edith," he said invariably, kissing her wrist. "I'll be along. I want to finish this drink." Embarrassed, Lily would find more ashtrays to empty, more glasses to pick up: she did not want to follow her mother upstairs, to pass her open door and see her sitting by the window in her violet robe, filing her nails or simply sitting with her hands folded, the room a blaze of light. *Of thee I sing, baby.*

Walter Knight would sit downstairs, looking at the pages of a book until it was time to go to the earliest Mass. He did not, however, go to Mass; only to bed. "I like to watch the sun come up," he explained. "Most people are satisfied to watch it go down," Edith Knight said one morning. "Ah," he answered. "Only in California."

Edith Knight spent the day after every party in her room, the shutters closed. Although the doctor had told her she had migraine headaches, she would not take the medicine he gave her: she did not believe in migraine headaches. What was wrong with her, she told Lily and Walter Knight every Sunday morning, was a touch of the flu complicated by overwork and she never should have taken two drinks; what was really wrong with her, she had decided by the end of May, was a touch of pernicious anemia complicated by the pollen and she needed a change of scene. She would take Lily abroad. She had always wanted to see Paris and London, and the way they were abroad, you could never tell. It was the ideal time to go.

A week later they left for Europe, and it occurred to Lily later that the highlight of the trip for her mother, who kept her watch all summer on Pacific

39

Standard Time, had been neither Paris nor London but the night in New York, before they boarded the *Normandie*, when they met Rita Blanchard for dinner at Luchow's. In New York for a week on her way home from Paris, Rita looked pale and tired; she dropped a napkin, knocked over a glass, apologized, stuttering, for having suggested Luchow's: possibly Lily did not like German food. Lily loved German food, Edith Knight declared firmly, and it had been an excellent choice on Rita's part. She for one did not hold with those who thought that patronizing German places meant you had pro-German sympathies, not at all; at any rate, anyone could see, from Rita's difficulty with the menu, that Rita's sympathies were simply *not* pro-German, and that was that. The night was warm and the air heavy with some exotic mildew—the weather was what Lily always remembered—and after dinner they walked down a street where the sidewalk was lined with fruit for sale. Rita noticed that some of the pears were from the Knight orchards; unwary in her delight, she drew both Lily and Edith Knight over to examine the boxes stamped "CAL-KNIGHT." "Do tell Walter," Edith Knight said to Rita in her dry voice. "Do make a point of ringing him up when you get home. He'll so enjoy hearing."

After Walter Knight left the Legislature that fall they did not have as many parties. Possibly due to his failure to comprehend that three speeches at dinners at the Sutter Club in Sacramento and a large picnic attended mainly by various branches of the candidate's family did not in 1938 constitute an aggressive political campaign, he was defeated in the November general election by the Democratic candidate, a one-time postal clerk named Henry ("Hank") Catlin. Henry Catlin made it clear that the "Gentleman Incumbent" was in the pay of Satan as well as of the

Pope, a natural enough *front populaire* since the Vatican was in fact the workshop of the Devil. In neighborhoods of heavy Mexican penetration, however, Henry Catlin would abandon this suggestion in favor of another: that Walter Knight had been excommunicated for marrying out of the Church and other sins, and he could send his Protestant daughter to Catholic schools until hell froze over and it wouldn't make a whit of difference. "I don't know how *you* folks think a family man ought to behave," he was frequently heard to remark at picnics and rallies. Quite aside from Walter Knight's not inconsiderable personal liabilities, he was, as well, the representative of "the robber land barons" and the "sworn foe of the little fellow." Henry Catlin, on the other hand, stood up for the little fellow and for his Human Right to a Place in the Sun, and if he failed to quote *Progress and Poverty*, it was only because he had not heard of Henry George.

On the night of the election, Lily and Edith Knight sat in the living room alone and listened to the returns on the radio. Although the shape of Walter Knight's political future was clear by ten o'clock, Edith Knight waited until the last votes had been reported before she folded her needlepoint and stood up.

"Don't cry," she said to Lily. "It's nothing for you to cry about."

"I'm not."

"I can see you are. It's your age. You're going through that mopey phase."

"He can't be Governor now. He couldn't lose this election and ever get nominated."

Edith Knight looked at Lily a long time.

"He never could have been," she said finally. "Never in this world."

From the stair landing, she added: "But don't you

41

dare pay any mind to what those Okies said about him. You hear?"

Lily nodded, staring intently at the red light on the radio dial.

She was still crying when Henry Catlin came on the radio to accept his sacred burden. He explained in his Midwestern accent how humbling it was to be the choice of the people—of all the people, you folks who really work the land, you folks who know the value of a dollar because you bleed for every one you get—to be the choice of the people to help lead them into California's great tomorrow, the new California, Culbert Olson's California, the California of jobs and benefits and milk and honey and 160 acres for everybody equably distributed, the California that was promised us yessir I mean in Scripture.

"Well," Walter Knight said, taking off his hat. "Lily."

She had meant to be upstairs before he came, and did not know what to say. "I'm sorry," she said finally.

"No call to be sorry, no call for that at all. We're in the era of the medicine men. We're going to have snake oil every Thursday. Dr. Townsend is going to administer it personally, with an unwilling assist from Sheridan Downey."

She could tell that he was a little drunk.

"Snake oil," he repeated with satisfaction. "Right in your Ham and Eggs. According to Mr. Catlin, we are starting up a golden ladder into California's great tomorrow."

"I heard him."

Humming "We Are Climbing Jacob's Ladder," Walter Knight opened the liquor cupboard, took out a bottle, and then, without opening it, lay down on the couch and closed his eyes.

"Different world, Lily. Different rules. But we'll

42

beat them at their own game. You know why?" He opened his eyes and looked at her. "Because you've got in your little finger more brains and more guts than all those Okies got put together."

She tried to smile.

"Now, Lily. Lily-of-the-valley. Don't do that. I'm going to have a lot more time to spend on the ranch. We're going to do things together, read things, go places, do things. I don't want to think you're crying about that."

"That'll be nice," she said finally, crushing the handkerchief he had given her and jamming it into the pocket of her jumper.

"You're still my princess."

She smiled.

"Princess of the whole goddamn world. Nobody can touch you."

He opened the liquor cupboard again, replaced the bottle he had taken out, and picked up instead the squared, corked bottle which held the last of his father's bourbon, clouded and darkened, no ordinary whiskey.

"This is to put you to sleep," he said, handing her a glass. "Now. What you may not have realized is that Henry Catlin happens to be an agent of Divine Will, placed on earth expressly to deliver California from her native sons. He was conceived in order to usher in the New California. An angel came to Mr. Catlin's mother. A Baptist angel, wearing a Mother Hubbard and a hair net." He paused. "Or maybe it was Aimee Semple McPherson. I am not too clear about Scripture on this point."

"He's not at all a nice man," Lily said firmly, encouraged by the bourbon.

"Everything changes, princess. Now you take that drink to bed."

Everything changes, everything changed: summer

evenings driving downriver to auctions, past the green hops in leaf, blackbirds flying up from the brush in the dry twilight air, red Christmas-tree balls glittering in the firelight, a rush of autumn Sundays, all gone, when you drove through the rain to visit the great-aunts. "Lily is to have the Spode, Edith, the Spode and the Canton platters Alec brought from the Orient, are you hearing me?" And although Aunt Laura dies neither that year nor the next, she does die one morning, fifteen years later: the call comes from the hospital while you sit at breakfast telling Julie that soft-boiled eggs will make her beautiful and good, and the Spode does pass to you, the Spode and the Canton platters Alec brought from the Orient. (You have seen only one yellowed snapshot of Alec, and that was much later, after he had lost his health and mind and all memory of the Orient. But imagine him a young man, a fine figure of a man or so they said, sailing out from San Francisco and Seattle in the waning days of the China trade, touching home once a year with Canton for his sisters and sailing out again.) Things change. Your father no longer tells you when to go to bed, no longer lulls you with his father's bourbon, brought out for comfort at Christmas and funerals. Nobody chooses it but nothing can halt it, once underway: you now share not only that blood but that loss. A long time later you know or anyway decide what your father had been after all: a nice man who never wanted anything quite enough, an uneven success on the public record and a final failure on his own, a man who liked to think that he had lost a brilliant future, a man with the normal ratio of nobility to venality and perhaps an exceptional talent only for deceiving himself (but you never know about that, never know who remains deceived at four o'clock in the morning), a good man but maybe not good

*enough, often enough, to count for much in the long
run. When you know that you know something about
yourself, but you did not know it then.*

5

"You might marry Everett," Martha McClellan had
suggested to Lily, once when they were both children,
"if I decide not to." "You aren't allowed to marry
your own brother," Lily had said, quite sure of her
ground until Martha smiled wisely and predicted, apparently interpreting the regulation as something else
initiated during the first hundred days, "Roosevelt
won't be president forever, you know."

It seemed in retrospect an amusing story, and Lily
wondered, the June afternoon in 1940 when Everett
and his father came to the house for a drink,
whether or not she should tell it. She decided that she
should not: his four years at Stanford and her one at
Berkeley had made Everett seem almost a stranger.
She could not remember even seeing him for a couple
of years, except once that winter when she had gone
down to Stanford for a party and had gotten sick on
Mission Bell wine at the Deke house. (Everett had
gotten her some cold coffee from the kitchen and had
made her date stay in another room until she felt better; she had thought herself humiliated, and neither
she nor Everett's girl, a blond tennis player from Ath-
erton, had much appreciated his gallantry.) He
looked, now, taller than she remembered, and older.
She wondered whether some small tragedy had be-
fallen him and hardened his face, whether perhaps he

had thought himself in love with and spurned by the tennis player. He would be, she thought, the type.

"I tell him he ought to go into the law," John Mc-Clellan said, taking off his rimless glasses and polishing them on a corner of his jacket. "Into politics. We could use some growers in Sacramento."

"Maybe I better get to be a grower first," Everett said politely. He had been, Lily remembered, a precociously polite child. Her clearest recollections were of him assuming full responsibility for Martha's social errors, gravely apologizing for the split strawberry punch, the uprooted azalea, the hysteria when someone other than Martha pinned the tail on the donkey.

"You tell him how they need us," Mr. McClellan said. "You're the one to tell him."

Walter Knight picked up a pair of garden shears from the tiled terrace floor and pruned a branch from a dwarf lemon.

"I'm not sure they do," he said finally, intent upon the lemon. "I'm not at all sure they need us. The San Joaquin still makes itself heard."

"Hah," Mr. McClellan said triumphantly. "The big boys. The corporation boys. There's your point."

Lily did not look at her father. When he spoke at last there was no inflection in his voice.

"This isn't the San Joaquin. They don't run ranches around here from offices in the Russ Building in San Francisco."

"There's your point," Mr. McClellan repeated.

"Here's my point," Walter Knight said. "We're expendable."

Everett smiled at Lily. The sun was setting behind his chair and his blond hair, cut close, looked white in the sunset blaze. Lily extended one bare foot and contemplated it, not smiling back. Neither she nor her mother ever mentioned politics to her father any more: it had been tactless to speak of the Legislature.

Although Everett called her at six-thirty the next morning he did not wake her, because the heat had stayed all night and she had gotten up at five-thirty to lie on the terrace in her nightgown. By six o'clock the sun had been high enough to make the heat shimmer in the air again. Looking to the east and squinting to block out the sun, she could make out the Sierra Nevada swimming clear on the horizon.

She wanted to go somewhere but did not know where. There was a glass of beer on the table, left from the night before, and she flicked a small colorless spider from the rim with her fingernail and let the warm flat beer trickle down her throat. That there was really nowhere to go (she did not like the mountains and had only a week before come home from the coast) made her no less restless, lying almost motionless in the still morning heat and chewing absently on the sash to her nightgown. She wanted to stay here and she wanted something else besides. Her grades had arrived from Berkeley yesterday, neatly and irrevocably recorded on the self-addressed postcards she had left in her bluebooks. One B-minus, in English 1B; a C in History 17A, a C in Psychology 1B, a C-minus in Geology 1 (commonly known as a football players' course in which it was impossible to get below a B), and a D in French 2. Because the single B was in a three-unit course and the D in a four-unit course, she supposed that she was down grade points and therefore on probation. Had the postcards arrived at school, she would have been embarrassed. Here, it did not seem to matter. As her mother had observed, she had read some interesting books and gone to some nice parties; once she was home, that was about the sum of Berkeley. She did not want to go back anyway. She could read books at home; she could have a better time at parties at home. It was not that she had not been asked, at least at first, to the parties which were the parties to go to; she had. On a cam-

pus where healthy color and easy smiles were commonplace, her fragile pallor, her uncertainty, had attracted a good deal of attention and speculation. Only
when the boys who asked her out discovered how real
the uncertainty was did they begin, bewildered and
bored, to lose interest. As one of them told Lily's roommate (who, reprovingly, told Lily), taking out Lily
Knight was like dating a deaf-mute. "You have to kid
around with them, be more fun," the roommate ad-
vised. "Be yourself." Although these admonitions
seemed to Lily in some sense contradictory, she tried,
the next weekend, to be more like the girls who were
considered fun. Out with a Sigma Chi who had just
been accepted at Princeton Theological Seminary, she
had attempted some banter about Reinhold Niebuhr;
when that failed, she admired the way he played the
ukelele. After several drinks, he told her a couple of
double entendre stories, and although she neither
understood them nor thought he should be telling
them to her, she laughed appreciatively. When he
asked if she would like to drive up in the Berkeley
hills, she smiled with delight and said it sounded like
fun; later, she reflected that it had not been entirely
his fault that he had misinterpreted her behavior that
evening, which had ended in front of an all-night
drugstore on Shattuck Avenue where, the prospective
theologian told Lily, he could get some rubbers.
("Rubbers?" she had said, and he had looked at her.
"Safes. Contraceptives." She had begun shaking her
head then, unable to think what to say, and he,
sobered, had driven her in silence up the hill to the
Pi Phi house.) After that, she had refused all invitations for three weeks. During the spring semester she
had gone out briefly with a graduate student who
read for her psychology class, a Jewish boy from New
York City named Leonard Sachs. He had graduated
from the University of Chicago and knew none of
the people Lily knew. They had taken long walks in

the hills above the stadium, back through Strawberry Canyon; had eaten dinner by candlelight in the
small apartment he shared with a friend who did not
like Lily and made a point of going to the library
whenever she was around; and had sat on Thursday
nights in the empty box at the San Francisco Sym-
phony for which the Pi Phis paid every year. He gave
her articles clipped from *The New Republic* outlining
the intrinsic immorality of an itinerant labor force,
hunted up for her an old pamphlet demanding repeal
of the California Criminal Syndicalism Law, took her
to San Francisco on the F train to hear a tribute to
Harry Bridges, and urged her, after he had observed
her knitting a sweater for her father, to utilize what
slender talents she had by teaching handicrafts in
a settlement house. Unable to locate "settlement
houses" in the Berkeley Yellow Pages, she finally
abandoned that project. He referred to the ranch as
"your father's farm," and regarded her with an uneasy
blend of the disapproval in which he held defective
mechanisms and the craven delight he secretly
took in luxury merchandise; she asked him if he
would not miss being home at Easter, and regarded
him in constant and only occasionally unwilling wonder. What both aggravated and enthralled him was
her total freedom from his personal and social
furies, and those Eumenides at his back were what
attracted and repelled Lily. "You're my haunted
lover," she would laugh, although he was, literally,
neither; a fact which, in his roommate's eyes, tended
to confirm Lily's social uselessness.

She had even invited him up the river for a day
during spring week. Once home, she regretted having
asked him. But he was delighted by the prospect of
observing her in her native decay, and so she drove to
Sacramento to meet him one morning. As soon as she
saw him standing on the lawn in front of the Southern
Pacific station, radiating the same intense concern

49

which had first charmed her in Berkeley, she knew that it would be a difficult day. He was as alien to the Valley as she might have been to the Bronx, and the alienation went deeper than his black turtle-necked sweater, went beyond the copy of *In Dubious Battle* with which he had been briefing himself on the train. By the time she drove him to the station that evening (he had tried throughout dinner to correct the errors in Walter Knight's impression of Upton Sinclair and EPIC), she was too exhausted even to speak. "You'll be glad to get away from all this," he said tentatively, taking a last drag on a cigarette and throwing it out the window. "Get away from all what?" she said, watching the sparks in the rearview mirror. "I meant you'll feel free in New York. You'll develop." Uncomfortably aware that she had at some point agreed to go to New York with him (although she had never had the slightest intention of doing so), she increased her pressure on the accelerator. "I'm not likely to get away from all this," she said, for once safe enough to say what she meant, her hands on the wheel of her father's car, driving the roads for which her father paid. "Any more than you're likely to get away from wherever it is you come from. And we don't throw cigarettes out the window here. It starts fires." She had meant to go to bed with him but because she had still to discover, at seventeen, the possibilities in someone she did not like, she had not.

Abruptly, Lily stood up and lifted the damp hair off her neck. With aimless violence, she threw the beer glass down the slope, then ran after it to where the lawn faded into dirt and dry yellow grass. Kicking a faucet open with her foot, she let the clear water (well water, not the river water they used for irrigation) splash over her arms and face. It was a waste of water early in a dry summer, and its extravagance relieved her. That helped some, that and swinging from an oak branch about to break from the tree, and by the time she reached the house in her wet nightgown the telephone was ringing.

"Sorry if I woke you," Everett McClellan said. "I'm about to take a truck into town for some extra help."

"You didn't wake me." This was more like it. Hoping, although it could not matter, that her mother had not picked up the extension in her bedroom, she tried to smooth her hair with her free hand.

"I mean I thought—" He spoke with some difficulty. "I thought you might like to ride in."

"Right now?"

"You're probably busy."

"Not really." She wondered what he thought she did between six-thirty and seven-thirty in the morning. "I'll get dressed."

As she shook out her wet hair with a towel she hummed softly, and looked in the mirror for the first time in months without regretting the waste of her perfectly good but constantly depreciating body.

"You look younger than Marth," Everett said when she climbed into the truck.

"I'm older. A year." She glanced down at her thin arms, brown against the white of her dress. Martha McClellan was not yet seventeen, a freshman come fall at the University of California at Davis. When Lily's mother, on the behalf of the Pi Beta Phi Alumnae Club, had urged Martha to enroll at Berkeley and participate in rushing, Martha had told her that it was necessary that she go to Davis, which was mainly an agricultural station, because her father wanted her to marry a rich rancher. And as a matter of fact so did she. Martha McClellan, Edith Knight had observed, was "a case."

"I know how old you are," Everett said without looking at her.

Lily pressed her forehead against the window, closed against the heat. Now in June the hops were starting up the strings, miles of them, ready to bear the thick green weight of the August vines. It was said to be a good year for the hops; because her father did not grow them she did not know why. She supposed that it had to do with when the rain had come. Everything else did.

"The hops are pretty," she said.

"You think so?"

"Yes, I do," she said, rather at a loss. When it came to conversation, Everett McClellan was not one to give much away. "I think they're very pretty and I'm glad I'm home."

They did not exchange another word until they reached the Labor Center in the West End, where Everett, getting out of the truck, ordered her to lock both doors from the inside and wait until he came back. As soon as he had entered the office, one of the Mexicans standing on the sidewalk outside made a face at Lily. She smiled, embarrassed, and then pretended to be reading a book in her lap. After Everett had recruited thirteen men, they started back out to the McClellan place; Everett looked once at her, when he had trouble starting the truck, and then neither looked at her nor spoke. Her eyes closed, she listened to the men in the back of the truck, singing Bing Crosby songs and passing around a bottle of dago red, and wondered why Everett had called her at all.

Mr. McClellan met them at the ranch, flagging wildly when he caught sight of the truck, an unnecessary exertion since he was standing where the trucks were habitually parked. Lily could not remember ever having seen him calm: even years before, when he had brought Everett and Martha and Sarah to call, he had given the appearance of a man beset by his own energy, scrawny with tension. He would leap to his feet when Edith Knight entered the room, accidentally knock over a chair, institute a prolonged search for a handkerchief, bound across the room to collar one of the children. He had always spoken to them as if they were puppies. *Down, Martha. Sit, Martha.*

"You should have got in there earlier," he muttered now, leaning over Everett's shoulder as Everett entered the names on the payroll ledger. "Nobody left come seven o'clock but high-school boys and drunken wetbacks. Here's one fact you won't learn in college, Miss Lily Knight: there's nobody in God's green world has less native intelligence than a goddamn wetback." Everett had once explained that his father referred to all Mexicans and to most South Americans—including the President of Brazil, who had once been entertained on the river—as goddamn wetbacks, and to all Orientals as goddamn Filipinos. There was no use telling him that somebody was Chinese, or Malayan, or Madame Chiang Kai-shek; they were goddamn Filipinos to him. Easterners fell into two camps: goddamn pansies and goddamn Jews. On the whole, both categories had to do with attitudes, not facts, and occasionally they overlapped. His daughter Sarah had for example married a goddamn pansy and gone East to live, where she picked up those goddamn Jew ideas.

Lily stood watching Everett, aware of the dust on his Levis and of her incongruously white dress. There was one thing about the McClellans not true of her father: they wouldn't run their ranches out of an office in the Russ Building even if they could afford to.

Everett looked up. "We could ride along the river when I'm finished."

"I don't ride very well."

"Hah," Mr. McClellan said. "I'll say you don't. She used to ride like she was sitting on a barbed-wire fence. I remember that much about Miss Lily Knight.

Don't be a fool, Everett. Take her swimming."

"I don't have my swimming suit." Lily remembered that Martha not only jumped horses at the State Fair every year but had twice beaten the Del Paso Country Club junior swimming champion in unofficial competition. "That child sees a bird, she tries to race it," Edith Knight had once observed of Martha. An admirer of competitiveness in all forms, Edith Knight had frequently urged Lily to "take a leaf from Martha McClellan's book"; that Martha was a notoriously poor loser did not bother her, since she did not believe that losing was the point.

"There's one thing Martha has plenty of, that's tank suits," Mr. McClellan declared. "We can suit you fine." Pleased with this play on words, he repeated it, and then bounded up to the house, screaming ahead for China Mary to get Martha on the stick and rustle up some tank suits.

The McClellan house had the peculiarly sentimental look of a house kept by men. There were pictures of Sarah and of Mildred McClellan, who had died at Martha's birth; above the piano ("How's that for a piano?" Mr. McClellan liked to demand affectionately. "Came 'round the Horn in 'forty-eight"), the California Republic Bear Flag hung at what appeared to be half-mast. One wall was covered with framed certificates from the Native Sons of the Golden West and river maps showing channel depths during the summer of 1932; China Mary's efforts toward brightening up ran to crocheted antimacassars on the chairs and orange zinnias crushed haphazardly into Limoges cream-soup bowls. In one corner of the living room, on a table covered with a mantilla, was an assortment of gold nuggets and ivory fans. Although the table had always been there, there had been, since Lily's last visit to the McClellans, certain additions: over the table hung an old *Vanity Fair* cover, a photograph of Katherine Cornell and her cocker spaniel as Elizabeth

Barrett and Flush, and a yellowed front page from the *Sacramento Bee* showing pictures of the Duke of Windsor and the English princesses. The headline read "KING EDWARD ABDICATES! DUKE OF YORK WILL RULE. 'My Mind Is Made Up,' Says King." The words *Sacramento Bee* had been partly obscured with adhesive tape, in deference, Lily assumed, to Mr. McClellan, who had little use for the English but even less for the *Bee*.

"I see you're admiring my memorabilia," Martha said from the stair landing.

Startled, Lily looked up: she had not seen Martha since the Christmas parties, at which Martha had, night after night, in some indefinable way made a spectacle of herself. Although she had not been drinking and had done nothing extraordinary, it had been impossible not to notice her, as it might have been impossible not to notice someone running a high fever, or wearing a cellophane dress. She had the same look about her now: her long straight blond hair hung loose around her thin face, so tanned that her eyebrows looked bleached, and she had on what appeared to be a leotard and a long green silk jersey skirt which trailed after her on the stairs.

"What in the name of sweet Christ is that get-up?" Mr. McClellan said. "You been practicing your ballet dancing?"

"I haven't taken ballet since I was twelve years old, thanks to the fact that nobody in this family except Sarah would ever drive me to my lessons. I've been reading."

"Nobody gives a goddamn what you've been doing. Get Lily Knight here a tank suit."

"Everett," Martha called imperiously. "Guess what I've been reading."

Everett looked up. Throughout this exchange he had seemed to withdraw: Lily had watched him fish in his pocket for a cigarette, inspect the cover of a

Reader's Digest which lay in a chair, whistle between his teeth.

"What?" he said now. "What have you been reading, baby?"

"*The Anatomy of Melancholy*. It's number twenty-two on the list."

"She asked me for a reading list," Everett said as Martha started back up the stairs. "I gave her one from Stanford. She's already read about half the books on it."

"Strange little creature," Mr. McClellan said.

"You upset her," Everett said with apparent effort.

Mr. McClellan ignored him. "Melancholia's one study you don't need any lessons in," he shouted up the stairs. "You strange little creature."

"Your brother thinks I upset you," he added as Martha came trailing downstairs again with a swimming suit in one hand.

"Poor old Everett," Martha said indulgently.

"Don't be a fool, Everett. Now let that girl get suited up."

They swam in the river, striking out for the far bank and swimming downstream with the current, still running cold with late melting snow from the mountains. When Everett reached the bank he waded back out to where the shallow ledge dropped off into the channel and pulled Lily, still struggling with the current, across the ledge and up onto the bank.

"You do all right," he said, pulling himself up after her.

"I always think I'll get dragged under." She did not let go his arm.

He moved as if to push her back into the water and then caught her, laughing, his arms low on her back.

"You better not," she laughed.

"Why not?"

"You just better not." She was pleased with their dialogue: it had about it the authentic ring of teasing, of inconsequentiality, that had eluded her at Berkeley. She had known all along that she could do it with someone she knew. Delighted, she lay back over Everett's arms and stretched her legs in the hot dry air. By contracting her stomach she could make it concave beneath the wet coolness of Martha's swimming suit. She lifted one leg and saw, besides the water still glistening on it, a long scratch on her left thigh, gradually turning bruised where Everett had pulled her across a submerged root into the shallow water.

"You look good." Everett touched the scratch.

"I feel good."

"You have the prettiest legs," Everett said slowly, "of any small girl I ever saw."

"I guess you like tall girls better." There: she was still doing it.

Everett looked at her, not smiling, and she was struck by anxiety: in her ignorance of how the game was played she had said the wrong thing, broken some rule.

"I like you all right," he said after a while, still looking at her. "I never thought about it until last night."

"Never thought about what?"

Everett said nothing, and she wondered if she had angered or disappointed him, wondered if it was possible that she could lose Everett McClellan, in the sense that you could lose people who were not your father or your brother.

"I wish you would kiss me," she whispered, feeling again that Everett was suddenly not Everett but a stranger, someone to be won.

He kissed her, and she clung to him a long time, watching the oak leaves swimming against the sun and feeling the ends of her hair floating just on the surface of the water and after a while opening her mouth and pulling down the straps of Martha's bathing suit, before his hand tightened over the scratch on her left thigh. *All right,* she whispered over and over, and after a while she began to think it could never happen because it hurt so much. When Everett finally said, again and again in a kind of triumph, *you feel it? baby feel it,* she assumed that it had happened. Later the scratch on her thigh became infected from the river water and left a drawn white scar noticeable whenever her legs got brown, but she did not think of it at the time.

6

Lily, he whispered every time as he lay spent in the rising morning heat, but she hesitated, equivocated, wondered if she was really obliged to marry him simply because he had wanted and taken her.

That was in June. In July, when she figured that she had been screwed (the word, which she had heard Everett use in reference to someone else, pleased her with its crisp efficiency, its lack of ambiguity) a total of twenty-seven times, they once had an entire morning to spend: coming back from the narrow strip of beach they waded in the irrigation ditches, knee-deep in the soft ditch grass and slow muddy water, the sun hot on their heads. All around them were her father's orchards: the pears hanging warm and heavy, dropping to rot on the ground beneath the trees, going brown and bruised and drawing flies, going to waste in that endless summer as she, *thank God and Everett,* was not. She let her dress trail in the water and ran splashing through the ditch with her eyes closed against the sun. Catching her,

Everett rubbed her face and bare sunburned arms with the cloudy river water that bubbled from a supply pipe; they laughed (*Everett you fool my sunglasses I like you for being so brown Everett baby so hard I love you*) and fell down again together, for the pickers were working the far orchards that week, and when she screamed beneath him, remembering that snakes infested the ditches, he neither told her that there was no snake nor told her that the snake (if there was one) was harmless, but picked her up and held her until she was quiet and until the snake (if there was a snake at all) had gone away. Shortly before noon she told Everett that she would marry him, and then she ran up to the house to change her dress for lunch. It seemed as inescapable as the ripening of the pears, as fated as the exile from Eden.

She mentioned it, however, to no one; scarcely thought of it away from Everett. Through day after summer day she moved as if sunstruck, dimly aware that any announcement would disturb the delicately achieved decision which had been, really, no decision at all: only an acquiescence. Was it, after all, so inevitable? The word *why*, once spoken out loud, could bring the pears all tumbling down. She would have to say that she loved him: it was the only incantation which would satisfy them, even as it would dispel her own illusions. Unspoken, it might still be true.

Everett remained the flaw in the grain. His constant and incontrovertible presence intruded upon her, prevented her from contemplating the idea of him, from polishing that idea into some acceptable fact. Sometimes when she came downstairs in the morning Everett would be sitting there, reading the *Chronicle;* he would call her several times during the day, and a suggestion, from Edith Knight, that she and Lily might go to San Francisco for the day could throw him into such despair that he would call every half-hour, all evening, to see when they were going, what they would do, when they would be home. Every scene Lily saw seemed to include Everett; all she heard was Everett's voice, asking when they would be married.

"I don't know," she said finally one morning on the river. "I mean I don't want to think about it right now."

"When do you want to think about it? Next year? The year after?"

"Everett. Stop talking that way. I'm nervous. All brides are nervous." She had read in a magazine that all brides were nervous, and had wondered whether that might not be her only problem: an apprehension which would turn out to be not unique but common to all women.

"If you could just leave me alone a little," she added, hopeful that she might be right.

"Leave you *alone*," Everett replied. "I want to marry you. I don't know how many times I have to say it."

"Wait until the hops are down," she said finally. "You're too busy now, you know that."

"I'm not too busy to tell people. Don't you want to tell people?"

"No," she said faintly. "I don't."

"You have to. You have to do it now."

"I told them I'm not going back down to Berkeley. So they might have guessed." She had told her parents that she wanted to take a semester off; as far as their guessing the other went, she had invested her faith in the extreme improbability of their guessing anything at all. Putting asunder the delicate balance of dependency among them seemed every day more unthinkable.

"You have to tell them. Your father likes me all
60

right. Although nobody'd know you did, the way you act when they're around."

"I'm not demonstrative." She picked up a white pebble and skimmed it across the surface of the water, angling it downstream to catch the drift. "I don't guess you learned to skip stones like that at Stanford."

"Lily," he pleaded, sitting up and grasping her shoulders. "Listen to me."

She traced an *L* and a *K* and half of *McC* on his chest with her fingernail, not looking at his face.

"There's no use talking to Daddy until he gets the fruit out of the way," she said at last.

But when all the pears had been shipped to the canneries and the hops on the McClellan place had been down six weeks, she still had told no one.

"I don't think you want to," Everett said finally. "I don't believe you want to marry me."

"Ah, sweet." She kissed the back of his neck, ran a finger down his backbone. "It's not you."

"What is it?"

"It's anyone. Sometimes I don't want to marry anyone. Some afternoons I lie on my bed and the light comes through the shutters on the floor and I think I never want to leave my own room."

"You'll have a whole house. Isn't that better?"

She patted his hand and looked away down the river. "It's your father's house," she said finally, grasping at the nearest point although not the one she had in mind.

"We'll build another house if you want. Would you like that?"

"I don't know." She was abruptly weary of trying to talk to Everett at all. "I don't think you understand what I mean."

He turned away from her. "No. I don't think I do."

She felt, as physically as she would a headache, the weight of Everett's vulnerability.

"Of course I want to," she said flatly. "You know I want to."

Although they agreed that she would have told Edith and Walter Knight by the time Everett came by for dessert that night, she had not. Telling them, she whispered to Everett when she opened the door, was impossible. Accepting this as fact, he got up from Walter Knight's table and drove Lily to Reno that October evening, the night the year's first snow settled over the Sierra Nevada, and had her declared his wife in the name of Washoe County and the State of Nevada. The ceremony was witnessed by the wife and son of the justice: the son pulled on blue jeans, the fly open, over his maroon-striped pajamas; the wife, roused unwillingly but dutiful, smiled drowsily and patted Lily's hair. Not quite eighteen, Lily had the distinct impression throughout the ceremony that her lie about her age would render the marriage invalid, nullify the entire affair, no tears, nothing irrevocable, only a polite misunderstanding among good acquaintances. Later, from their hotel room, she called down a telegram reading "MARRIED EVERETT NOW AT RIVERSIDE RENO HOME SOON LOVE LILY"; whatever her extravagances, long telegrams were not among them. Everett called the ranch to tell his father, but Martha answered the telephone.

Covering the receiver, Everett turned to Lily, who sat, still wearing the skirt and sweater she had worn at dinner, on the edge of the bed with *Hotel Riverside* embroidered on the sheets.

"Martha's crying. She says I'm leaving her alone."

"You'll be living right there."

"She says that's not the same thing and I must be a fool to think it is."

Lily lay down on the bed and buried her face in the pillow. She wanted nothing so much as to have her father there, to be downstairs watching him shoot craps, lulled by the action, the play of chips and silver on the green board, the ring of the silver dollars as he stacked them. *Make it the hard way.*

"Maybe she's right," she said, her voice muffled.

They stayed a week in Reno. Lily bought a toothbrush and a pair of stockings in a Rexall drugstore, located some white cotton underwear in a shop specializing in trick holsters and mesh briefs embroidered with the days of the week, and ran into a Sacramento girl, Janie Powers, in the Riverside lobby. Apprehended by Janie as she stood, that first morning, wondering whether Everett would think himself slighted if she ate breakfast without waking him, Lily could not at first think how to explain her presence in Reno; as it turned out, she did not have to. "I'm getting a div*orce,*" Janie caroled across twentysome feet of lobby. "What are you doing?" Although Lily could not remember knowing that Janie had even been married, she supposed she must have heard and forgotten; she could never keep straight the social details which so absorbed her mother. "I'm going out to buy a sweater," Lily said guiltily. "I'm just up for a few days and I forgot an extra sweater." "Never mind that," Janie said. "I've got dozens. Have breakfast with me." Once they were seated, Janie launched into a monologue about her husband, who was being *très impossible* ("I can't even spend one night on the California side of the *lake* or he'll contest my residency, he's got somebody watching me night and *day*"), and it was not until they had finished a second cup of coffee that she again asked what Lily was doing in Reno. "Nothing special," Lily

63

said, pretending to look for a clock. "Listen. I promised to wake up my mother."

Two days later, Everett saw Janie Powers sitting at a blackjack table in Harold's Club and asked her to have dinner with him and Lily. ("You darlings," Janie kept saying at dinner. "Up here on a honeymoon and this sweet little thing keeping it a secret from Janie." After two whiskey sours and a bottle of wine, Janie was struck by "the irony of it: Lily getting married, me getting—anyway. *Très symbolique.*")

Other than Janie, they saw no one. Everett slept late in the mornings (Lily seemed to have known, always, the way he would look and feel beside her in bed, a comfortable if not particularly electrifying thing) and shot craps a little in the afternoons; Lily got up early, careful not to wake him, and walked by herself up one side of Virginia Street and down the other, stopping always on the bridge to watch the ducks on the Truckee River. She had asked Everett, thinking it might be wifely, if she could get him some toothpaste or shorts or something; he had looked at her a long time, laughed, and said that he could take care of himself. One morning she thought she saw the son of the justice who had performed their marriage, and she turned immediately into a coffee shop and began dropping nickels into a slot machine. Although she did not want him to see her, it seemed important that she see him (had it, after all, happened?), and after he had passed by she ran out and watched until he turned the corner, but could not be certain that he had been the one. All she could remember clearly was his voice, an Okie voice: *Ain't she the prettiest little bride we had all week, now.* One evening they had dinner on the California side of Lake Tahoe; another they drove at twilight over the Geiger grade to Virginia City and found, there in the cemetery on the hill, the grave of someone in Everett's family. *Francis Scott Currier:*

B. 1830, D. 1859. R.I.P. 2000 miles from home, 1½ miles from the Ophir. They played tennis twice, and Lily ate lobster, in the dining room at the Riverside, for the first time in her life. It seemed then that the lobster alone lent those few days in Reno a distinct air of celebration, the flavor of a wedding trip.

When Everett took Lily home a week after their marriage, Edith Knight presented him with a kiss on each cheek and Lily with a list of two hundred people who had been invited to the reception. A practiced saver of situations, she had already begun a scrapbook pasted with clippings from the Sacramento and San Francisco papers. Each showed Lily in a white middy blouse, her Dominican graduation picture. There was even one clipping from the *Los Angeles Times,* headlined "Former Solon's Daughter Wed in Nevada."

Everett seemed bemused not only by the clippings but by the prospect of the reception: he took the list from Lily and studied it, asked about a few of the names on it, seemed to forget, and asked again. "This is quite a large party," he said finally.

"You were the one so crazy to get it institutionalized," Lily whispered absently, touching the back of his neck with her fingers. It had just occurred to her that in all the years she had known the McClellans, they had never, except for Sarah's wedding, four years before, given a party. Even Sarah's wedding, or as much of it as Lily could remember, had seemed oddly improvised, an affair which included all the accouterments of other weddings but remained, in some vital way, not entirely a party.

"I just wanted to marry you," Everett whispered.

"Well, you did." Lily raised her voice. "Where's Daddy?"

"It's such an off season," Edith Knight fretted. "It

can't be a garden party and it can't be a holiday party. If you'd waited six weeks we could have used Christmas trees. Something festive."

"The bride," Lily said, "is generally considered attraction enough. I said where's Daddy."

Edith Knight shrugged. "In his office, I suppose. I don't believe he's left the house in five days. He's been no help with the arrangements. No help whatsoever."

Lily stood outside her father's office, then opened the door without knocking. He was sitting behind his desk, looking out the window toward the island bridge. Everett's Ford was clearly visible in the driveway; her father had known she was home.

"Well Lily," he said, turning away from the window. "The child bride."

"I see we got a good press."

"Lily McClellan." He gave the dry laugh Lily recognized as forced. "How does that sound?"

The words seemed to hang unnaturally between them. Lily averted her eyes.

Laughing again, Walter Knight walked around the desk and put his hand out, tentatively. "Well," he said.

Although it did not seem likely that he had intended shaking hands with her, his hand was there, and so Lily shook it. He did not seem to know what to do then, and patted her shoulder gingerly.

"Good to have you back," he said finally, as if she had been a long time in a far place, and then, apparently relieved to have hit upon the phrase, he repeated it.

"It's nice to be back," she whispered, able neither to look directly at him nor to speak normally.

"You'll be closer to home than you would have been in Berkeley, actually."

Encouraged by this view of the situation, Lily nodded.

66

Her father smiled and patted her shoulder again. "The McClellans are old friends."

She said nothing. In view of a fact she had just remembered—that Everett was a second cousin to Rita Blanchard, whose grandmother had been a McClellan—her father's remark seemed obscurely pointed. The issue seemed confused beyond repair, and Lily, blushing, took a silver dollar from the pocket of her polo coat and began to throw it up and catch it.

"It's snowing on the Pass," she said rapidly. "We had a nice time in Reno. I won two twenty-five-dollar jackpots and ate a lobster."

Her father nodded gravely.

She dropped the dollar, which Everett had given her one night when he was winning, and watched it roll across the floor.

"Well, princess, there's no place like Reno." Walter Knight picked up the dollar and dropped it into her pocket. "For all the mortal delights. Now let's see if we can't get a drink before lunch. You could probably use one. Or two."

She tried to smile. Although she had hoped, all week and even this morning, that her father would tell her not to worry and somehow take things in hand, she saw now that it would be more or less up to her.

Whenever she thought later of that week in Reno —and she thought of it quite often that first year, thought of it while she sat at dinner, listening to the clock in the hall and to Everett's father chewing; thought of it in bed, and reached to touch Everett's face in the dark so that she would know she was not alone; thought of it sometimes before Knight was born, when she had been so frightened and Everett so reasonable, bringing her, every morning, the flowers she did not know how to arrange,

the words she did not know how to accept—it was
with a longing she could never quite place, a
nostalgia neither entirely truthful nor entirely imagined. It was as if the week had existed out of time,
as if they might happen upon it again one day by
accident and find the same limpid air, forever suspended there between autumn and winter; the same
faces in the Riverside bar; the same wild ducks
lighting down on the same rocks along the Truckee,
although even that week they had been on their way
south: everything untouched, impervious to erosion,
not exactly shining and not exactly innocent but
preserved exactly as it had been, absolute proof
against further corruption. She had said to her father that morning everything she could have said:
We had a nice time in Reno.

7

Young married, river matron, mother of two: on the
February morning in 1942 when she learned she was
pregnant the second time she knew the rôles she
should be playing. It had not seemed as urgent
when she had only Knight. Knight's birth had pleased
Everett; Knight's birth had pleased her, once it had
happened. In the six months since Knight's birth,
however, nothing had changed. China Mary took care
of him, just as she took care of everything else that
needed doing in the house; Martha worried about
him, just as she worried about everyone else. She
would call up from Davis in the middle of the
week. "That fever," she would begin. "What fever?"
Lily would ask. "That 104° fever he had a week

ago Sunday. What fever. Anyway. You don't think it could have damaged his heart?" "We had Dr. Dubois," Lily would say. "Dr. Dubois. Dr. Dubois has been senile since shortly before he delivered *you*. Let me speak to Everett." As far as Mr. Mc-Clellan was concerned, Knight was a small animal still too inert to be entertaining; he largely ignored his presence, pausing by the crib upstairs only when he suspected Everett or Lily to be watching. Nothing about Knight's arrival, in short, had changed the mood of the house: Lily continued to stay upstairs as much as possible, nervous whenever she was downstairs that she was intruding upon the family she continued to think of as the McClellans, a house guest who had stayed on too long; Everett became every day more abstracted, the way, she saw, he had always been around his father. "If you don't stop whistling through your teeth," she had whispered one night after dinner, "I'm going to start screaming." "Everett has always whistled through his teeth," Martha had interrupted; it was impossible to say anything, when Martha was home from school, that Martha did not hear and work into an issue. "Whistling is simply Everett's way," Martha had added, looking directly at the book in Lily's lap, "of pretending to be reading." Everett seemed to Lily to act himself only when they were alone, and Knight did not change that. They could lie in bed in the mornings with Knight between them and laugh, but that did not quite make, Lily thought, a family.

With two children, however, she would have to make more of an effort. Nothing about her *modus vivendi* was appropriate to a young wife and mother of two: the doctor, quite inadvertently, made that much clear. Examining her, he asked whether any of her friends had told her about Dr. Grantly Dick-Read. "I suppose you mean natural childbirth," she said quickly, uncomfortably convinced, as she lay in ignominy on the table, that both the doctor and his even more disapproving cohort, the nurse, had divined the shameful fact she had only then realized: she had no friends. She had her family, she had the McClellans; she had a neat leather address book respectably if not completely full of names, mostly those of girls with whom she had gone to school, to which she could address Christmas cards. But she had no one with whom she might have sat around over coffee and compared obstetrical notes. It was a failure she had never before fathomed: she did not much enjoy the company of women.

"Natural childbirth," she repeated, stalling. "I'm not sure I'd like that. I was in labor thirty-four hours with Knight."

"That's because you were afraid," the doctor said genially. He was a young obstetrician recommended by Martha; Dr. Dubois had retired.

"I don't know." Lily wondered with some irritation how she had happened to think Martha an authority on obstetricians.

The doctor patted her thigh, affably. "You talk it over with your husband."

The notion that she might talk over natural childbirth with Everett seemed only slightly less ludicrous than the notion that she might have already talked it over with friends, and when Lily left the doctor's office she walked through Capitol Park, distracted by the vistas of social failure opened up by the doctor; sat down on the wet steps of the Capitol Building, and tried to think exactly what it was that young wives and mothers did. For a starter, they did not sit around by themselves on the Capitol steps smoking cigarettes in the rain; she was sure of that. If they found themselves downtown after an appointment in the Medico-Dental Building they would have swatches to match, War Bonds to purchase, friends to meet for lunch. They would have an entire circle of friends with whom they lunched regularly, played bridge, talked about natural childbirth and saddle-block anaesthesia and twilight sleep and the last time the Lunts played Memorial Auditorium.

Deciding as she drove out to the ranch that the first step toward social regularity might well be the proper equipment (she could not think what else it might be), she wrote immediately to Shreve's in San Francisco and ordered six hundred sheets of pale blue letter paper monogrammed L.K.McC., four hundred lined envelopes engraved *McClellan's Landing, California* (an address acceptable to both Everett and the Post Office and one which she thought had a good deal more innate style than the Star Route number Mr. McClellan persisted in using), six hundred folded notes (with matching envelopes) engraved *Mrs. Everett Currier McClellan,* and something she had seen described in *Vogue* as a "hostess-saver," a small book similar to one used by Mrs. Roosevelt's social secretary to record the preferences, disinclinations, and favorite menus of all one's guests.

On the day the package arrived from Shreve's, she set up a card table on the sun porch, filled Everett's fountain pen, arranged a tray with a glass of iced tea and a fresh package of cigarettes, and set about writing some notes. Unable at first to think where to begin, she located the neat leather address book and turned the pages methodically from A (Alice Adamson, an unattractive but popular girl with whom Lily had once shared a room at a Stanford house party and had never seen again), through the heavy concentration of relatives under K, right on to Z (Zenith Jewelry in Berkeley, where she had once left a bracelet to be repaired): there was no one to whom she could reasonably write a letter.

By the end of the afternoon, nonetheless, using rather larger than normal handwriting and in one case asking for a recipe she did not want (Baked Alaska made with cottage cheese would be beyond, she could not help feeling, even her expanding horizons), she had managed to write three: one to her roommate at Dominican, a girl she had not felt one way or another about; one to the rather sententious widow who had been housemother in the Pi Phi house the year she was at Berkeley; and one to Martha, who had not been home from Davis in eight days and had twice called Everett and urged him to write. Although the box of folded notes remained untouched, she had a definite purpose in mind for them: invitations. Starting with luncheons and afternoon desserts, she would progress to mixed entertainments —cocktail parties, Sunday-night suppers, little dinners so well planned that even Mr. McClellan could not turn them awry; simple but perfectly done, suitable wartime entertaining. "My mother is a *great* hostess," she explained to Everett as they drove to the post office to mail her three letters. "When Daddy was in the Legislature she was possibly *the most noted* hostess on the river. Now. There's no reason why I can't give a simple little party. Is there." Everett, his eyes on the road, could see none. "Let's stop for a drink before we go back," Lily said happily. "Let's have a drink by ourselves in a roadhouse or something. There's time before dinner." All right, Everett agreed drily, kissing her hair at a stop sign, they would have a drink in a roadhouse or something. "To celebrate," she added. To celebrate, he repeated after her, smiling, although she could see that he was not entirely sure what they were celebrating, or why.

Fifteen days later, after drawing up several lists and then abandoning them in periods of retrogression, she opened the box of folded notes and wrote out eighteen invitations for a luncheon one afternoon in

May. Everett put up card tables on the verandah for her, Martha called from Davis to encourage her (as well as to suggest that the unprecedented number of people might upset Knight), and for a few hours that afternoon the McClellan place had about it the illusion that someone other than Lily lived there, someone used to casual friendships, at home with the sound of women's voices, luncheon forks, bridge being dealt. But although Edith Knight declared after everyone else had left that it had been the loveliest afternoon possible, Lily knew that it had not quite worked. It was nothing she had done or not done. It was simply that there existed between her and other women a vacuum in which overtures faded out, voices became inaudible, connections broke. With increased apprehension but unalloyed determination, she set about correcting it: if she was incapable of having a circle, she would then direct her efforts toward cementing Everett's circle. But when she discovered that Everett's disinterest in her friends or her lack of them was equaled only by his disinterest in seeing his own friends with any regularity (did he have any friends? she sometimes wondered), she was at a loss as to what to do next, and when her father died in June she had every reason not to do anything. The single luncheon, the handful of letters and telephone calls, the Sunday-night supper to which Everett had finally agreed and at which no one, not even Martha, could think of any conversation that quite caught on: she could repeat none of it. She would become a wife and mother later, for as she said to Everett in the terror of the day she found out, *I'm not myself if my father's dead.*

8

A man and woman from Chicago discovered the accident: they had been told at the Texaco station downtown in Sacramento that they might get a breeze that
hot June night by taking the river road instead of
staying on U.S. 40. They slowed down (the man told
the Highway Patrol) because of the curious light rising off the river. Tired and bored and sticky from sitting all day in the car, his wife said at first it was
another California trick, and wanted to go on. Five
would get you ten there was another Giant Orange
drink stand involved in it somewhere, and for her
nickel you could take every Giant Orange drink stand
between here and San Berdoo and sink them five feet
under. He parked the car, however, and got out to
stand on the levee. When reconnaissance of the ter-
rain turned up no evidence of a Giant Orange drink
stand, his wife became apprehensive (it was eerie,
she said, it was so creeping eerie), and would not get
out of the car. It took him three or four minutes to
comprehend what anyone from the river would
have known immediately, for this was a bad curve,
frequently miscalculated, or at any rate frequently as
that kind of miscalculation goes; to realize that the
glow on the water was rising through twenty-five feet
of muddy water from the headlights of a car. The
light filtered up through layer upon layer of current
and cross-current, and flickered all about the channel
as the wind disturbed the surface water. *If I told her
once I told her twenty times, there was something
funny going on here and it was up to us to see what*

was what, the man said again and again to the state
patrolmen, his curiosity already transmuted into the
sense of civic responsibility which would become, in
future tellings, the leitmotif of the story about the
night they were someplace in California and saw this
light Melba claimed was a Giant Orange, which is a
kind of drink stand they have out there shaped like a
giant orange. It was well after midnight before the
river salvage people could get there from Yolo County with a hoist, and nearly five o'clock before they
knew enough to call Edith Knight.

She drove into town alone, a silk robe pulled over
her nightgown, to identify the bodies. Because the accident had been discovered so quickly, identification
was only a formality. Walter Knight's face, unmarked,
bore only the featureless look of the recently drowned.
Rita had been cut, across her left cheek and down that
long Blanchard throat; she had been thrown, they
said, against the dashboard before the car hit the
water. Her long hair was still wet, and Edith Knight
wondered, irrelevantly but obsessively, if it would dry
before they buried her. She did not see how it could
dry in the grave. Although she asked the coroner's
emergency attendant if it could, he did not seem to
know. A small man possessed of a large curiosity
about people under stress (an interest which relieved
the general tedium of his work), the attendant took
advantage, however, of this opening: he wondered,
probing delicately, if the lady with the beautiful hair
had been visiting Mrs. Knight and the late Senator.
The late State Senator.

"Miss Rita Blanchard has lived all her life on
Thirty-eighth Street," Edith Knight said sharply. "She
is from an old, old family in the Valley. A family," she
added magnanimously, "which crossed the Great
Plains a year before my own."

"A great tragedy, Mrs. Knight," the coroner's as-
sistant said, abandoning the opportunity to pursue

Sacramento Valley genealogy further and reaching instead for her hand. "A tragic loss."

"The Lord gives it and takes it, Mr. Paley," she said, turning away from his outstretched hand.

By the time she left the morgue the sun was completely up, and the heat rising. She drove directly to the McClellan place and found Lily in the kitchen. "Oh Christ," Lily whispered. "He'll never have the marmalade." She had gotten up at dawn to make pear marmalade for her father before the heat came up. The marmalade was a kind he especially liked, from a recipe of his mother's, and she had planned it as a surprise. She had gone to the ranch the day before to get the pears from Gomez. "The marmalade would have shown him," she whispered. "Shown him what?" Edith Knight asked, but Lily did not answer because she had put her knuckles against her teeth to keep from screaming and had slipped down beside the sink to the linoleum floor. Shaking but not moving in any other way, she stayed there until Edith Knight pulled her to her feet, untied the apron she was wearing over her nightgown, and led her upstairs to Everett, who was shaving. Later the doctor gave Everett enough pills to keep her quiet for two days and Edith Knight said she had never, never in her entire life, seen anybody react the way that child reacted to a death in the family, she had always been morbidly sensitive and frankly it would have been better if they had gotten the pills before they told her, they might have known it would happen and she of all people should have known Lily was not strong enough to cope with the things other people had to cope with, but when do you think at a time like that.

On the morning of the funeral, Edith Knight and Martha, together, managed to get Lily dressed. She sat on the edge of the bed, staring at the floor while Martha went through her closet. She had nothing which approximated mourning except a black silk

suit she had bought in Berkeley; now, six months pregnant, she could not fasten the skirt. "Everett said it
didn't matter what I wore," she said again and again,
and finally, after her mother and Martha had conceded that it did not, she put on a maternity skirt, a
pink and white flowered blouse that her father had
once admired, and, an afterthought, a black lace
mantilla. She looked, Martha whispered to Everett,
like a stray from *The Grapes of Wrath*.

It was another bad day, close to 108° at eleven
o'clock. Lily sat between her mother and Everett in
the car, her composure so precarious that she could
look at neither of them.

"I feel stronger every minute," Edith Knight announced, trying to work her long gloves onto her fingers. "Here," she added, pulling off one of the gloves
and twisting a large ring from her finger. "I meant
for you to have this some day anyway."

Lily slipped the ring over her wedding ring and
closed her eyes again. It was a diamond her father
had given her mother the day she was born.

"Thank you," she said.

"I don't know." Edith Knight lifted Lily's left hand
and appraised the effect. "You're really too young."

"She's really too skinny," Everett said. "She'll lose
it."

"I *want* it," Lily said, opening her eyes; it was the
first unequivocal statement she had made in two days.

They did not have a Catholic funeral. Because only
a handful of the Knights were Catholics in the first
place and because even their Catholicism was more
an accident of birth or marriage than an act of faith,
the family was not troubled by the Episcopal service,
the unconsecrated ground: the family graveyard, near
the ranch, where no one had been buried since 1892.
"I don't care if he was brought up Catholic or

brought up Hindu," Edith Knight had declared. "I guess I know where he'd want to lie. I guess I know that much."

From all over the Valley and from the Sierra foothills the family came; everyone from the river came and everyone from town came. Gomez and Crystal came, the Governor came, and the bartender from the Senator Hotel came. As if she were immune to grief, love, all the transient passions, Edith Knight stood throughout the funeral without moving. Lily stood behind her, looking away from the grave toward the distant line of cottonwoods which marked the river. She had thrown the mantilla back from her hair because it seemed to draw the heat; now it lay, fallen from her shoulders, on the ground behind her. She could not stoop to pick it up.

There was a certain comfort in the unkempt graveyard. Dried grass obscured the markers, and the wings had been broken years before from the stone angels guarding the rusted wire gate; there was about the place none of the respect for death implicit in a well-tended plot. Once, a long time before, Walter Knight had brought Lily to see this graveyard. He had made her trace out with her finger the letters on the stones, the names and their dates, until she found the small, rough stone which marked the oldest grave. *Matthew Broderick Knight, January 2, 1847, until December 6, 1848.* The baby had been the first of them to die in California. It was a favorite story, passed on from Knight to Knight and documented periodically in the historical supplements to the *Sacramento Union.* Born in Kentucky, the child had begun to burn with infant fever on the way west. Another child in the party had died of it, and that mother had carried the dead child in her arms for three days, telling no one, afraid they would bury her baby before they came to a station. But Matthew Knight had lived out the crossing; he died instead in a room in Sacramento that first winter, while his father, Lily's great-great-grandfather, was building the first house on the ranch. His mother, twenty years old that winter, was deranged for months, believing herself at home in Bourbon County even as she hauled buckets of Sacramento River silt to cover the hardpan around her raw house. She wanted to grow a garden of forget-me-nots and love-lies-bleeding and the dogwood she remembered from her mother's kitchen stoop, but as summer broke and she began to feel herself again she planted those same alien poppies and lupine that grew on the child's grave. *By the rivers of Babylon, there we sat down,* she had ordered cut into the gravestone, but that had been when she was ill. The symbolic nature of Amanda Broderick Knight's first garden on the ranch was, for the Knights, this story's *raison-d'être.* "I think nobody owns land until their dead are in it," Walter Knight had said to Lily, playing a familiar variation on a familiar motif. Even as she recognized that all he was giving her was the official family line, Lily could not help but be disarmed. She answered in the same rich vein: "Sometimes I think this whole valley belongs to me." "It does, you hear me?" Walter Knight said sharply. "We made it." She had never doubted that.

The grave was covered by noon. Her arm through Everett's, Lily sat in the car, twisting the diamond on her finger and watching her mother. Edith Knight stood in the dry grass by the wire gate and received: accepted as her due the certified recollections, the ritual testimonials which serve as visas into that comfortable territory where no dead man is less than noble. *You remember when Walter came up that summer, 'thirty-three, we were in the middle of a crop and there was all the trouble and Walter sent in his own men and cleaned up the crop. You remember how Walter held the note on the Hawkes place all those years after it was due until the son could pay it*

off. Remember now. Remember. The litany of Walter
Knight's shining hours continued until one o'clock,
long after most of the mourners, including Mr. Mc-
Clellan and Martha, had left for Rita Blanchard's funeral in town; Edith Knight stood impassive and triumphant throughout. Were they not attesting, after
all, that he now belonged to God alone and that she,
Edith, had sole rights to his relics in this world?

Two weeks later, the lawyers notarized her victory.
In 1933, Rita Blanchard, needing cash, had sold to
Walter Knight 120 frontage feet of a downtown block
which had been in her family for eighty years. Although his will provided that this parcel be returned
to Rita, their simultaneous deaths meant that it now
belonged to Edith. To the lawyers, the family, and
to the reporter who was writing up the disposition of
the estate, she announced that she wanted the sizable
income from that property placed annually in a
University of California scholarship fund to be ad-
ministered by the Department of English and to bear
Rita's name. "If there is one thing I will remember
about poor Rita to my dying day," Edith Knight explained, "it's that Rita was a *reader*." Because the entire estate went to Edith (passing to Lily at her death
and held throughout both their lifetimes in a loose
trust which would vest in Knight at some point after
his twenty-first birthday), she could now afford, in
every sense, to dispose of Rita with that grand gesture.
(The impact of the Rita Blanchard Scholarships was
somewhat weakened, however, when it became apparent a month later that Rita had left half the Blanchard estate to Lily, the other half to be divided among
sixteen cousins, including Everett, Martha, and Sarah
McClellan. As Martha said to Everett in the Blanchard
lawyer's office, you really had to grant that round to
Rita.)

9

There were roses (so many for September) and late poppies: the room was full of them. Everett must have brought them in from the ranch. No matter what way Lily turned her head on the pillow she saw roses, dropping their petals in the closed gray room which looked exactly like the room they had given her when Knight was born. Somewhere among the roses were jasmine gardenias, sweet and heavy as the drugs. The nuns would not open the windows in the storm. The rain had begun the night before she started labor and was still falling; she watched it washing down the narrow windows all that morning. When she closed her eyes she saw rain beating the leaves from the camellias around the house. It must be raining in every part of the world, flooding all the valleys: she was certain that her baby had died in the night, that the nuns were concealing the death from her, and she knew as well that before long she would begin to hemorrhage and die herself. She had recently read *A Farewell to Arms* and now she cried to think of Everett walking out of the hospital into the rain like Lieutenant Henry.

Everett had come yesterday. When she woke from the drugs he had been sitting by the window, and she had watched him for several minutes without speaking. The San Francisco papers were spread on the floor around his chair. He had been reading three or four papers all that year, since before Pearl Harbor. Although she tried every few days to read a paper through, she seemed always to have come in too late

on any given action to understand that day's plays.
After a while she had tried concentrating only on the
war in the Pacific, which as far as she could gather
America seemed to be losing. Although this did not
seem entirely credible, it seemed, winning or losing,
more credible than anything about the war in Europe; what the war in Europe so notably lacked, for
Lily, was a Pearl Harbor. As Mr. McClellan had said
the morning of Pearl Harbor, when Martha ran downstairs wrapped in a towel to tell them, "That tears it."
(That was all he said, and he did not say that until he
had shouted at Martha "You keep on listening to the
radio in the bathtub, Missy, you're going to fry yourself," but he spent the rest of the day pacing up and
down in front of the house, scanning the sky and
muttering to himself.) Until Everett had explained to
her that the Germans and the Japanese were pledged
to defend one another, a point which had eluded her
for the first two weeks of the war, Lily had been at a
loss to understand what the United States was doing in
Europe at all. The Pacific, of course, was another case.
It did not please her to think, as she had thought,
that this baby might have been conceived the morning of Pearl Harbor. It was not propitious.

Everett, yesterday, had been looking out the hospital window into the rain. The lights seemed to be
just coming on outside. It would be about five o'clock,
she supposed, and there would be lights in all the
windows down Thirty-eighth Street. Only Rita
Blanchard's house would be dark; the house had been
empty since the accident. She could never remember
that the house now belonged to her, to her and Everett and Martha and Sarah and thirteen other people,
but mostly to her. Everett had talked a few weeks ago
to a man who wanted to buy the place and have it re-
zoned for a day nursery. That would be the day.
Painted wooden rabbits on Rita Blanchard's lawn.

"Tell me what's in the newspaper," she said finally.

Everett was always trying to tell his father what was in the newspaper. Because Mr. McClellan neither read the papers (none of them, he said, carried anything but pictures of that crew in Washington) nor listened to the radio, his many ideas about how the war should be conducted were based almost entirely upon information given him by Everett. Once he had absorbed two or three facts, usually tangential, he would cut Everett off by saying that it was no news to him, he knew those yellowbellies and all their tricks like the back of his hand.

Everett folded the newspaper and smiled. "How long you been awake?"

She laughed and put her hands to her stomach. It was still swollen. "You needn't whisper. Where's the baby?"

He came back in a few minutes with one of the nuns, who held the baby wrapped in pink flannel.

"A girl," she said. "That would have pleased Daddy."

"It pleases me."

Lily turned her head on the pillow so that she could see Everett's face.

"Listen," she said. "I was all right this time, wasn't I."

"You were fine."

She lay back. "I can't feed it, you know."

"They'll feed her."

"It's funny to hear you say *her*. I don't even know what we'll call it."

"You said Julia. Julia Knight McClellan. I thought we decided that."

"I just said that because of my grandmother. I never really thought it would be a girl. I was thinking of Walter." She laughed. "It's entirely too small to call something like Julia Knight McClellan. It sounds like a suffragette."

"She's big for a baby." Everett turned to the nun. "Didn't you say she was big for a baby?"

"Everett, I *know*. She's a regular King Kong of a baby."

"Listen," she added after the nun had left the room. "We'll have more. We'll have about six. And Martha can have about six. And they'll have these terrible fights because there won't be enough land to go around."

"And Sarah. Don't forget Sarah."

"That's right, and Sarah." She had in fact forgotten Sarah. "Anyway. There'll be this one runt. Likable but you know, a loser. He'll be conned out of everything but some little back piece with no water. Then one day while the rest of them are playing golf—they'll be forever hanging around the country club, that type—and he's scratching around his place, you know what happens then?"

"Gold."

"Everett, baby. You live so in the past. It turns out his piece is the only exit for one hundred miles on a proposed transcontinental freeway."

"A freeway?"

"An *exit*, Everett. Standard Stations. Motels. Piggly Wiggly Markets. Long-term leases."

Everett smiled.

"Listen," she said. "I behaved this time, didn't I."

Everett sat down by the bed and took her hand. "Yes."

"I didn't get scared and make a lot of trouble. I mean all the way through it was all right this time."

"You didn't make a lot of trouble before."

"I did. Your father told Martha he hoped I never got pregnant again because I was impossible."

"Who told you that?"

"Never mind. I was, that's the point."

"Martha didn't mean it if she told you that."

"Never mind. It was better this time, you saw."

"It was fine."

"You have to take care of me," she whispered.

He held her hand and looked out the window a long while. "I will," he said. "I do. Don't I."

Although she had thought for a moment that she had never been so happy, Everett had left when her mother came ("I meant to come earlier but I was downtown," Edith Knight said, remotely bewildered, the way she had been since a few weeks after the funeral; despite a new vicuña coat and an absolute lack of any visible defect in her grooming, she presented a curious impression of disarray, twisting her rings, smoothing her hair; straightening the sheet as she kissed Lily goodbye), and after her mother left Lily was alone. The nuns had begun their evening visits, walking the corridor in pairs. When one paused outside the door, the light blinking off her thick glasses, Lily turned away from the door, pretending to be asleep, and as she watched the street lights blur through the blown branches outside the window she wondered how the nuns had known, and if they had once been as she was now. She thought of her mother, who by now would be sitting alone with a tray in the living room at home, picking at her inevitable lamb chop and watching the same rain. Rain seldom fell so long so early; if it kept up there could be floods before Christmas. Once when she was a child a levee had broken on Christmas Eve, and the churches were filled with tired women in raincoats and children in blue bathrobes. At Edith Knight's insistence she had given all but one of her unopened Christmas presents to the evacuated children, whose own, Edith Knight had explained, were floating over to the poor Chinese children. Put that way, it had seemed an ideal situation, one in which only Lily came out behind.

Although Everett should have eaten with her mother tonight, eaten with her or taken her down to the ranch, he would not have thought of it. And her mother was so lonely that she seemed to have lost even the idea of communication. "Some nights when the wind comes up I think I'm the only person alive on the river," she had said a few weeks ago. "Why don't you call me?" Lily said. "Why don't you call me or one of the Randalls?" "I could, of course," her mother said without interest, as if Lily had introduced a quite irrelevant topic. In a sense she had: there was little that Lily or the Randalls or anyone else could do to mend the web of concern which Walter Knight and Rita Blanchard had woven around Edith Knight for a dozen years and had torn apart in June. It had once occurred to Lily that her mother missed Rita more than she missed Walter Knight; it had been Rita, after all, who provided her with her rôle, who might well have gone on providing it, walking proof not only of Walter Knight's failure (dead or alive) but of Edith Knight's strength in the face of it.

Well, her mother had chosen her rôle, the nuns theirs. But how did they know. How had Mary Knight known. Mary Knight Randall had entered the Sisters of Mercy the summer she was eighteen. She had gone to Europe with her father, Walter Knight's cousin, and when they got off the boat in New York that August she told him that she did not intend to go to Berkeley in September. Although he tried to reason with her all the way across the country on the train, even promised that she could have a new robin's-egg blue Ford convertible and spend the entire month of January skiing at Aspen, Mary Knight entered the convent the same week Lily went down to Berkeley. It was the week of rushing, and because Mary Knight had planned to be with her, Lily had a double room alone at the Durant Hotel. She lay awake every night,

listening to the Campanile strike in the coastal fog
and feeling intensely sorry for herself, partly because
she did not know how to talk to the golden girls
from San Francisco and Pasadena but mostly because
she had been deprived of Mary Knight, who was older
than she was but had never known anything at all,
had moved through adolescence in an untroubled in-
nocence which had obscurely reassured Lily, made
her want to have Mary Knight with her always, a
talisman. (Once at a beach party, Joe Templeton's
younger brother, Pete, had tried to get Mary Knight
up on the bluff in a car with him. "Why do they
want to do that?" she whispered later to Lily. "Never
you mind," Lily said, throwing sand on the fire. She
had disliked Pete Templeton for trying and loved
Mary Knight for not knowing.) Even the Catholics
mourned Mary Knight; Helen Randall, who had refused to go to Europe with them because she wanted
to go to Banff, still put the blame on Mary Knight's
father. Mary Knight was an impressionable girl and
if he had not exposed her day after day to those
morbid European cathedrals it simply would not
have happened. He should have taken her, as she,
Helen, had suggested in the first place, to the Calgary
Stampede. Now there was a portrait in the dining
room of the Randalls' house, hung as prominently as
if it were of someone dead, Mary Knight at sixteen,
absurd but oddly indomitable in a pink tulle dress.

Mary Knight, her mother, the nuns in the corridor:
they all seemed to know something she did not. Well,
she had at least given Everett what he wanted. Even
Martha could scarcely have given him two children.
But she could not escape the uneasy certainty that
she had done so herself only by way of some intricate
deception, that her entire life with Everett was an
improvisation dependent upon cues she might one
day fail to hear, characterizations she might at any
time forget. Except when she was in trouble (when

her father died, or when she was pregnant with
Knight), she could think of little to say to Everett:
she was not, nor was he, a teller of anecdotes or gos-
sip, and sometimes whole weeks passed without their
having what could be called, in even the crudest
sense, a conversation. Usually in bed she pretended
that she was someone else, a stranger, and she supposed that Everett did too; when she did not pretend
that she was someone else, she pretended that Everett
was. The only times she did not pretend that either
or both of them were someone else, she pretended
that it had never happened before, that it was again
that first time on the river. There had been about
that first time a sharpness, a finality absent since. For
a long time, even after she had done it hundreds of
times, the fact that it had happened at all would
come to her with a shock; it had seemed improbable
that anyone else could do it, and the hearsay knowledge that not just anyone but almost everyone had
done it remained a persistent flaw in her satisfaction
with her own performance. It was as if she had
stumbled alone across the plains and found that
everyone else had already arrived, by TWA. Even
now, two years later, those few minutes were more
vivid than any since: she had lost neither the sense
of wonder nor the sense of deprivation that the ex-
perience had not been uniquely hers. The summer
smell of that morning, river water and sweat and
the acrid sting of weeds breaking under them (and
that would always be summer's smell), was stronger
still than all the roses and jasmine gardenias in the
whole of Mercy Hospital.

I should have taken the Holy Ghost not Everett,
she had thought when she woke this morning, and
she had snapped at the nun who was trying to take
her temperature. A pillow over her head, she had
lain still all morning, lifting the pillow only to watch

the rain outside. She should sit up and comb her hair, wash her face, put on the silk bedjacket her mother had brought. Everett would come again this morning, and she did not want to see him. She was not sure that it would be all right even if they could go back to that morning on the river and start over again; because she could not put her finger on what was wrong it would only go wrong a second time. She wanted now only to see her father, to go back to that country in time where no one made mistakes. *For a thousand years in thy sight are but as yesterday when it is past, and as a watch in the night.* She had memorized those words at the time of her father's death, had repeated them as she walked down streets and brushed her hair, as she lay in bed and as she drove the river road, and she repeated them now against Everett's arrival.

10

"You'll get along fine," Everett said, the morning he left for Fort Lewis. "You're a big girl now. You wait. You'll be all right here. Wait and see."

He spoke very low; both Knight and Julie were asleep in the next room.

"You didn't have to go," Lily repeated. She could not view Everett's enlistment as anything other than personal and possibly deserved retribution. Bataan might fall, Corregidor might fall, and the Japanese might occupy Attu and Kiska, but Everett could not have gone had she not failed him somewhere. "You have a son. You have a two-month-old daughter. Your father needs you."

Everett sat up on the edge of the bed and lit a cigarette. Although light now filtered through the shutters, they had not slept. After Mr. McClellan went to bed they had, between them, drunk most of a bottle of bourbon, and then Lily had cried (partly the bourbon) and they had lain in the dark awake, oppressed less by the parting than by some uneasy apprehension of how the parting should be affecting them.

"Lily," he said. "You keep saying the same things. I want to go."

"I don't see why."

"I waited a year. Almost a year. Now I have to go."

"You don't have to. You want to. You said you wanted to."

"All right. I want to. I don't see any difference."

Lily lay without moving, her head aching dully.

"I believe you want to die," she said after a while.

"All right. I want to die. Now I have to get up."

While Everett shaved she finished packing his bag, trying dutifully to memorize the way his shorts felt to the touch, the particular color and translucency of his toothbrush. They seemed things that she might want, at some future point, to remember. Although she considered putting on the same plaid skirt and paint-stained sweater she wore most mornings, she thought then of ships going out under the Golden Gate in fog, of Wake Island, of that hot golden summer before they were married, and pulled on instead the white cashmere sweater that Everett had given her on her nineteenth birthday.

He was to take the Shasta Daylight from Davis station at seven o'clock. It would take them close to an hour to drive there. Although Lily wished now that someone would drive over with them, all the goodbyes had been said already: Martha had come over from Davis for dinner, and had driven back before midnight to study for a midterm. ("Daddy is of the opinion I'm meeting all kinds of rich citrus growers from down South," she had said at dinner. "When all I'm doing is taking midterms and lending my clothes to rich citrus growers' daughters so they can go out with rich citrus growers' sons." Everett had seemed puzzled. "What do you want to run around with people from down South for?" he had wanted to know. "Oh you know me, Everett," Martha had said. "An old One-Worlder.")

The house was perfectly still, and cold from the November night. Chilled through, Lily stood in the hallway and ran her fingers along the grain of the stair railing. When she heard Everett on the stairs she began, nervously, straightening some letters left on the hall table.

"Now listen," he said. "I'll write you tomorrow. Then will you please write me and tell me how you're getting along?"

"Yes," she said, her eyes fixed on the fireplace in the living room. The house downstairs had the same curious appearance it always had in the early morning, the look of a house abandoned in an emergency years before. It was hard to believe there were not really dusty sheets thrown over the faded slipcovers, impossible to think that the magazines thrown on the tables were actually dated 1942. "I'll write you," she added. "Every day."

"And try to get my father to slow down."

"Yes."

"And see people and get some sleep. Gain some weight."

"Yes," she said. "I'll knit you some khaki socks."

"Well." He held out her coat. "The home front."

"That's right," she said. "The home front."

She drove to Davis; they scarcely spoke. She watched the road and he stared out the window. A light fog hung low on the river and the knotted, broken strings fluttered among the fields of bare hop poles. There had been frost in the night; it would warm toward noon.

Although the train was due in fifteen minutes, there were only a few other cars at the station. They sat in the station wagon, the heater on and the windows steamed, and Everett put his arm around her shoulders. She said that the sweater made her feel pretty; he said that she was pretty, pretty hair, pretty eyes, pretty arms. Be quiet, she said, pressing his arm. There was little now that she wanted to say, and in the end she did not say anything, because Martha came to the station. They saw her running down the platform, clutching a book and a bunch of yellow chrysanthemums, a dirty poplin raincoat over her nightgown.

"You look like a goddamn refugee," Everett said, opening the door of the station wagon.

"I was afraid I'd miss you if I stopped to get dressed. So I just came."

"Lucky you didn't run across any rich citrus growers," Everett said.

Martha pushed the book and the chrysanthemums into Everett's arms. Embarrassed then, she stood outside the car, looking off toward the station, her hands shoved down into the pockets of her raincoat.

Everett opened the book and looked up at Martha.

"It's my copy," she said. "I knew you didn't have one."

"What is it?" Lily asked.

Martha did not look at her. "A family book."

"*The McClellan Journal*," Everett read. "*An Account of An Overland Journey to California in the Year 1848.*"

"Privately printed," Martha added.

"Imagine," Lily said.

Everett and Martha, she thought. *Forward into bat-*

92

tle with the Cross before. She remembered her surprise at finding on the walls of Martha's room, when they had been children and she had been sent to play at the McClellan place, neither Degas ballet dancers nor scenes from *Alice in Wonderland* but a framed deed signed by John Sutter in 1847, a matted list of the provisions carried on an obscure crossing in 1852, a detailed relief map of the Humboldt Sink, and a large lithograph of Donner Pass on which Martha had printed, in two neat columns, the names of the casualties and the survivors of the Donner-Reed crossing. Martha's favorite game as a child had in fact been "Donner Party," a ritual drama in which she, as its originator, always played Tamsen Donner and was left, day after day, to perish by the side of the husband whose foolish miscalculations had brought them all to grief. (In Martha's re-enactments, the Winning of the West invariably took on this unobtrusively feminist slant; in another game, "Central Pacific," the power behind the transcontinental railroad turned out to be not Collis Potter Huntington at all, but Leland Stanford's wife Jane, and Lily grew up with the distinct impression, planted by Martha and uncorrected for years, that the *éminence grise* behind the California Republic had been Jessie Benton Frémont.) It seemed to have been an ineradicable mote in Martha's eye that everyone from whom she was descended had, unlike Tamsen Donner, gotten through, and when Lily told her that someone in her father's family had traveled with the Donner-Reed Party as far as the Applegate Cut-off, Martha had been despondent for several days. As a matter of fact she had mentioned it querulously only a few weeks before.

"You could lend it to people," Martha suggested, her hands still in her pockets. "I mean it might be very inspiring."

"It's the nicest present you've ever given me,"

Everett said, getting out of the car and putting his arms around her shoulders. "The nicest anybody's ever given me."

After they had put Everett on the train ("The *train*," Martha screamed, and the three of them ran, Everett trying to take his other bag from Martha and Martha wrenching it away, to the platform, where Everett kissed first Lily, then Martha, and then a small girl who had wandered, carrying an American flag on a stick, from a family at the far end of the platform), Lily and Martha sat in the car, not speaking, until the train began to roll. Tapping an unlighted cigarette on the dashboard and humming "The Battle Hymn of the Republic," Martha had seemed, until then, in trance. When the train whistled, however, she jumped out of the car and ran again to the platform, calling Everett's name, looking in all the windows as the cars gathered speed, and then she walked slowly back to the station wagon, her raincoat fallen open and her pale blue nightgown trailing through the leaves that blew across the concrete parking lot.

"Get in," Lily said. "We'll get some breakfast."

"He left the flowers."

"He's got *The McClellan Journal*. That's what counts."

Martha looked away. Lily saw that she was crying.

"They'd only have died on the train," Lily said. "You put them in your room."

Martha slammed the door closed. "I think I'll go over home with you."

"I thought you had a midterm."

"I do."

"We'll get some breakfast," Lily repeated, turning the ignition key.

They stopped at a drive-in near the Davis campus. Martha talked animatedly for a few minutes about the rôle played by Alice Lee Grosjean in the Long

Administration in Louisiana (it seemed she was writing a paper about the Longs) and about someone at Berkeley who had invited her down for the Miami Triad dance. (It was to be at the Fairmont and she really wanted to go, except this boy had an unfortunate predilection for saying things like you're the most terrific girl I've ever known, and she really wasn't up to that kind of thing, not these days, not any more.) Then, abruptly, she stopped talking and began examining her fingernails, three of which were enameled a brilliant American Beauty red.

"Everett said last night I shouldn't wear fingernail polish," she said after a while. "So I started to take it off this morning but I was in a hurry and spilled the whole bottle of remover. All over Betty Jean's V-Mail." Martha giggled. Betty Jean, who was engaged to a Marine, was her roommate and current *bête noire*. According to Martha, Betty Jean saved on board money by eating cheese and crackers in their room instead of lunch downstairs; the further economy was that she then saved the cheese glasses for her hope chest. Martha claimed that Betty Jean had twenty-seven cheese glasses, fifteen with red tulips and twelve with blue cornflowers.

"It's a pretty color," Lily said.

"Everett doesn't like it. I told you." Martha began drumming her fingernails on the metal tray.

Lily did not say anything.

"You'll miss Everett," Martha said finally.

"Yes."

"A whole lot?"

"Of course."

Martha looked out the window. "How much?"

"A whole lot," Lily said, faintly irritated. "What did you mean about the boy who asked you to the Miami Triad? Why don't you go?"

"Daddy thinks I should get married."

"What's that got to do with the Miami Triad?"

Martha did not answer.

"Who do you want to marry?" Lily said.

"I don't know. Somebody." Elaborately, Martha lit a cigarette. "It doesn't much matter who, does it?"

Lily shrugged, and after a while Martha reached in front of her and flicked on the lights to call the carhop.

"I better take my midterm."

When Lily stopped in front of the dormitory, Martha opened the door but did not get out. "Listen," she said. "Do you think I should?"

"Not unless you want to. Not unless you love someone."

"Come off it, Lily. I didn't expect you to talk like such a fool. Whoever loved anybody for more than two weeks. Except your own family. Or maybe somebody you've lived with for years and years. I don't know about that."

"There's a lot of time."

" 'There's a lot of time,' " Martha mimicked. "There's no time at all. That's exactly the point. Everybody's going away, and half of everybody's going to die, and the war may go on twenty years, and Everett's gone away—"

"Anyway," she added. "I'm sure I don't know who I'd marry. I'm sure I don't know anyone who could take care of me."

"Maybe," Lily said after a while, "you could marry someone you could take care of. Maybe that's the same thing in the end." As she said it, it occurred to her that she might well have happened, while fumbling through platitudes for Martha's benefit, upon an actual fact, a profound truth: someone could take care of you or you could take care of someone; you could be told or you could tell the comfortable loving fictions (*If you loved me you would steal for me, and tell me fairy tales of a happy land*, it was, she thought, a German song), and in either case what

96

was involved—all that was involved—was a commitment. Perhaps it did not matter much who made it, or how or why: it might very well be the same thing in the end. *It doesn't much matter who does it.*

Martha picked up one of the chrysanthemums and began rolling and shredding the petals into small balls.

"Maybe it would be the same for you," she said finally. "You're so strong."

"I am not," Lily said, jarred by Martha's moodiness and by the note in her voice. "I'm not a bit strong."

Martha shrugged and got out of the car. "All right, you're not a bit strong. It's your act, Lily baby, you play it any way you want. Anyway," she added, "you're strong enough to make people take care of you."

Even if Lily had been able to think what to say it would have been too late: Martha was already running up the walk, her hands over her face, running and stumbling on the lace hem of the pale blue nightgown, last year's Christmas present from Everett, picked out by Lily, extravagantly expensive, handmade at Maison Mendessolle in the St. Francis Hotel.

"We saw Martha this morning," Lily said to Mr. McClellan at dinner. Although she had intended to stop by her mother's on the way back from Davis, she had driven instead directly to the ranch, and had spent the rest of the day upstairs, aimlessly taking things from drawers and putting them in other drawers, sleeplessly lying on her back in their bed, still unmade, the sprigged lawn spread her great-grandmother had quilted thrown down on the floor along with Everett's worn sneakers, the November *Fortune*, and the bottle of bourbon they had almost finished the night before. Not until five o'clock did

she go downstairs to see China Mary and the babies;
then she kissed Knight absently and carried Julie upstairs in order to feed her in the bedroom. Finishing
the bottle of bourbon as she spooned Julie's puréed
carrots, she avoided Mr. McClellan for as long as she
could and then felt guilty about even that: there
she was, pointlessly depriving him of a small pleasure, the opportunity to watch Julie eating, one of
the few activities on her schedule animated enough
to interest him.

"I said we saw Martha," she repeated. "She came
to the station."

Mr. McClellan did not answer.

They were alone in the dining room, absurdly
cavernous, oppressively lined with glassed cabinets
of crystal and china; the shelves held two complete
services of Limoges, each for forty-eight, although
in two generations the McClellans had not, to the
best of Lily's knowledge, entertained more than
three guests at dinner on any given evening.

Mr. McClellan had not spoken since the fruit cup,
during which Lily had said that she did not agree
that the International Workers of the World were the
principal threat facing the United States in 1942. Apparently because he had seen mention of Tom
Mooney's name in an unprecedentedly thorough
reading of the *San Francisco Chronicle*, Mr. McClellan had been brooding all day upon causes and ef-
fects. He guessed Miss Lily Knight, since she was so
smart, knew every detail behind the 1916 Prepared-
ness Day Parade bombing in San Francisco. No, of
course not. Well here it was: ten people in their
graves, thanks to anarchists and Wobblies. He guessed
Miss Lily Knight knew all about the 1913 Wheat-
land Riot, three thousand hop pickers running amok,
a tragedy so close to home it might as well have
taken place on the kitchen stoop. No, of course not.
Possibly Miss Lily Knight still had a few things to

learn about Wobblies. He, on the other hand, knew the details behind such events, and was therefore in a position to know that wherever you found trouble in California today you had those boys to thank for it. *Cherchez le Wobbly*, Lily had suggested, and Mr. McClellan had withdrawn into injured silence, broken only when he was moved to place his knife and fork side by side on his plate, wipe his mouth with his napkin, slap both hands palms down on the table and demand loudly: *"What are laws for?"*

Lily raised her voice now. "I said Martha came to the station. She's upset about Everett."

Mr. McClellan cocked his head to one side, apparently to get a different light on the picture which hung on the wall opposite him, a large oil painting of a cornucopia.

"What about Everett?" he said finally.

"His going away."

"She's not a gold-star sister yet," Mr. McClellan said, his voice flat.

11

Their communication did not improve noticeably during evenings to come, that winter when the rain fell for what seemed weeks on end. Quite often Mr. McClellan would not speak at all, not out of any hostility but simply because the capacity for random conversation seemed to him less a grace than the certain expression of a weak mind; other nights he would become quite voluble, usually on the subject of the county supervisor (who was, he had come to believe, a paid agent of Franklin Delano Roose-

velt), and then he would settle down after dinner
with a copy of the California Penal Code, pouncing
with intense delight upon certain loopholes and in-
consistencies. He had first hit upon this diversion
some years before, not long after Mildred McClellan's death, and had regretted ever since, he told
Lily, that he had not read for the law. Aside from
the evenings when he read aloud from the Penal
Code, their liveliest times together were spent playing hearts, for small amounts of money which Mr.
McClellan almost inflexibly won. If, after querying
China Mary and checking the pockets of all the coats
in all the closets, they could still find no change in
the house, they played for toothpicks, redeemable
no later than the next evening in cash.

Nonetheless, they had between them a curious com-
panionableness, a real, if not exactly infectious, rap-
port, most apparent to Lily on the occasional
evenings when Martha came over from school and
upset it. It did not seem to matter if Martha were
calm or nervous, buoyant or depressed (although
in practice she seemed to come home only in states
of aimless crisis): she invariably shattered the
balance of reserve and aggressiveness which existed
in the house when Mr. McClellan and Lily were alone
with the children. Lily did not know what it was
about Martha. She thought probably it was that
neither she nor Mr. McClellan were what her father
would have called "good company," and that possibly Martha was.

But in spite of the unexpected comfort Lily took
in Everett's father, it was still the sad season: Everett
gone from the McClellan house, her father gone
from her own house. All that month before Christmas the house was cold and dark, and Knight could
not play outside. In the afternoons Lily wrapped the
children up and drove through the rain, past the
eroded gullies where muddy run-off swirled along

the ranch road, to see her mother; in the evenings, no matter if dinner had been silent or combative or comparatively festive with the promise of hearts or the Penal Code, Mr. McClellan went to his room at ten-thirty, and Lily sat on downstairs alone, listening to the rain and night noises. At first she had tried turning on the radio, and had learned the lyrics to a great many songs including one called "I Spoke to Jefferson at Guadalcanal," but after a while the radio seemed only to intensify, with its impenetrable cheerfulness, whatever was ominous in the noises outside.

Again during those first few weeks after Everett went away, she began to think of little but her father's death. During the five months since it had happened, she had been distracted first by Julie's birth, then by Everett's desertion; now, it was with her every night. Sitting downstairs alone after Mr. McClellan had gone to bed she would take first her father's point of view, then her mother's; then, more and more often, once Rita had been revealed to her in the rôle of victim, Rita Blanchard's. It was not that there had not been something about Rita Blanchard from the beginning, some inability, some failure in her eyes, that marked her for Walter Knight. It was only that if he had wanted to love all of them and been capable of loving none of them, only Rita had really been deceived. Only Rita had put all her chips on that board.

Although Lily wrote to Everett at Fort Lewis every night, there was little to say. She could not write to him about Rita Blanchard; she had never even talked to him about Rita Blanchard. *The babies and I miss you:* that was what she could write to Everett. *China Mary sings Knight a song about how you're off to get a rabbit skin to wrap your baby bunny in, which delights him no end. Julie has a cold from the rain. You must please write your fa-*

101

ther to do something about the furnace. I do not mind eating breakfast in two sweaters but it is the last straw when he declares the cold is good for the children because look what it does for a collie dog's coat. Last night we played hearts and I won for the first time, although as it turned out I was sorry. The thing is we played with toothpicks again, and because I won thirty-three cents I ended up with thirty-three toothpicks. Well. Tonight before dinner he appeared with a quarter and eight pennies and demanded the toothpicks. I couldn't think what I'd done with them and he said in that case he could hardly be expected to turn over the thirty-three cents. I said all right, don't, we'd forget it, but he held up dinner an hour and fifteen minutes while we enlisted China Mary in a search for the toothpicks. Finally she found them in my apron pocket, but unfortunately there only seemed to be twenty-eight left. He finally gave me the full thirty-three cents in exchange for the twenty-eight toothpicks, but said he was setting a bad example and lectured me all through dinner on the importance of property rights and keeping one's accounts in order. It was, he said, the American way and we could not begin too soon setting an example for Knight and Julie. It seems funny now that I tell you about it but it was nerve-racking at the time. I love you and miss you especially at night.

The first week in January, there was at least some news: *Joe Templeton came by after dinner and spoke to your father about buying the Braden place at Auburn. He'll write you but your father hopes you won't sell.*

"Joe Templeton wants the Braden place," she said to her mother the next afternoon. Their afternoons together had taken on an unvaried pattern: after Lily had put the children down, she and her mother would knit; Lily for Everett, her mother for the Episcopal Guild bazaar. While they knitted, Edith Knight would resume a monologue about things which had happened some years before; the details, for example, of how the Blanchards lost their river place on a note to a man named C.T. Godey in 1927, or an analysis of a rumor, current in 1931, that one of Lily's second cousins (once removed) had been carrying on with a clarinet player in the orchestra at the St. Francis Hotel. (It was an untruth, according to Edith Knight, although it was no surprise it got started because Elizabeth was practically mental about jazz musicians and had once stood up in a speakeasy on Sutter Street with everybody on the river looking on and sung "Big Noise Blew in from Winnetka" with her arm around a colored drummer.) Once she had become familiar with the names and the chronology, Lily found these accounts generally interesting; she had never felt so close to her mother.

Edith Knight put down the Peruvian face mask she was knitting for the bazaar. "You saw poor Joe?"

"He came by last night. He didn't realize the piece was in Everett's name."

"If the McClellans have the sense God gave them they'll hang on to the Braden place. I used to go on picnics there." Edith Knight paused. "Francie wasn't with Joe?"

"No. He came alone."

"Alone," Edith Knight repeated with satisfaction. "Of course he would have."

Lily did not say anything. Her mother began to hum tunelessly, tapping one knitting needle against the arm of her chair. Her eyes were closed.

"Francie may have been outside in the car," Lily said. "Actually he only stayed a few minutes."

"Oh no." Edith Knight opened her eyes and started to work with fresh vigor on the face mask,

103

intended for use whenever there was danger of frostbite. "I wouldn't think so. He was no doubt quite alone."

Lily did not know what she could say that might not in some way corroborate her mother's fairly opaque conclusions. She rather wished that she had never mentioned Joe Templeton, and tried to think of some way to turn the conversation back a decade or two.

"Didn't Francie Templeton have a sister who wasn't quite bright?" she asked finally.

"That's right," Edith Knight said without interest. "She's been dead seventeen years next month." She continued knitting in silence.

"It's Francie again," she added at last, abandoning the hope of being prodded. "Helen Randall went up there one afternoon—Francie had invited her up, specifically *invit*ed her for that afternoon—and Francie didn't even come downstairs. Joe made excuses for her. She starts in the morning with vermouth."

"Vermouth, is it." Lily laughed. So often had she heard her mother say of someone who drank that he or she started in the morning with vermouth that she could not drink vermouth without a pleasant sense of discreet raciness; thanks to Edith Knight, vermouth was for Lily one of the small adventures that frequently made her day. Lily's day could also be made by ordering stockings by the dozen rather than by the pair; wearing expensive perfume around the ranch in the mornings; and, among other things, focusing for a fraction of a minute on some stranger's eyes and making him look back just until, say, the traffic light changed.

"I don't know what's going to become of those twins," Edith Knight said, ignoring Lily. "They will no doubt grow up to be zoot-suiters. Look and see if there's any sherry left."

Lily picked up the decanter and filled her mother's glass.

"On the other hand," Edith Knight added, "there's no need to pity Joe. He's been quick enough to find comfort in the past."

Lily sat down again without saying anything.

"If you understand what I mean. About Joe."

"Yes." Lily picked up her knitting again. "I understand you all right."

"Not that she hasn't been a cross. Lord no. But Joe doesn't exactly wear himself out carrying it, either. If you see."

"I understand," Lily repeated.

She had understood well enough. As had Joe. That had required no *roman de la rose*. Once the speculative glances and the accidental meetings were out of the way (the procedure, she saw, was a *way* of doing rather than anything done; first the miraculous awareness of the possibility, then the almost inaudible overture, the response so subtle as to be uncertain), they met in the late afternoons of that winter and in the long spring twilights, met in cars parked off the levee, bars frequented by Mexicans, and in an empty shack on the piece downriver which belonged to Francie Templeton's mother. They did not talk much, and she was never certain that either derived from the other much pleasure, as that word is commonly defined. She knew only that they continued to interest each other. A tacit complicity between them cut that interest away from everything going on in other places and at other times; Lily discovered that she could see Joe later any evening, or perhaps the next day in town, and not only behave as she would have behaved before but think of him as she had thought of him before. She had always thought him rather a likable fool; she still did. She did not for the time being find it necessary to make frequent connections between Joe and Everett, whose letters came from Georgia now, and Francie lived in Everett's country. It concerned, she thought, neither Everett nor Francie; it did not even seem, in any real way, to concern her.

When the nights grew warm, come May of that year, they occasionally met late at night. The wind blew off the river through the shack, its windows broken long ago by children or transients, and they lay on a torn mattress and listened to the current. Once in a while she asked him something about the war, and he explained to her about Tunisia; once in a while she told him about something which had happened a long time before, a dance she had gone to or a slight she had imagined, but mostly they simply lay there in the dark in the bare room littered with dead wisteria, blown through the windows during a wind in April, and listened to the water. *I love you,* Joe said once, *Lily Knight,* and she turned away from him.

"I mean now," he said. "I meant I love you now."

"I know." She twisted her shoulder free from his hand. "I knew what you meant. That's all right."

"Lily Knight," he repeated, drawing the sheet she had brought up over her shoulders.

She sat up, pulling the sheet around her. "My name's not Lily Knight. If you recall. I'm married to Everett McClellan and he loves me *very very much* and nothing I do can change it."

Joe did not answer, and when he pulled her down again she said *I'm sorry, baby it's all right,* and it was all right, possibly sharper and better and more interesting than it had ever been before.

In the beginning the afternoon was no more than
a question of sugar, or the lack of it. China Mary
had baked four cakes and given them as prizes in
a parish raffle; when Lily asked her what they were
going to use for sugar during the rest of October
—during the entire rest of 1944, for that matter,
since China Mary had traded some of their November
stamps to her sister for extra sugar—China Mary
shrugged and continued whistling "Coming in on a
Wing and a Prayer." Good works, Lily wanted her
to know, would cut no ice down at the OPA. It
was one thing for China Mary to go around in-
gratiating herself with Father Ford; it was quite
another to do it with the whole family's sugar
stamps.

There were some women in this world, announced
China Mary, untying her apron and throwing it at
Lily's feet, a great many women in this world—
for example that saint (God rest her) who had been
Everett's and Martha's and Sarah's mother—who
would count God more important than a little bitty
sugar. Thirty years she had worked on this ranch
and no McClellan, not one, had ever tried to tell her
how to run her kitchen, and there were some
spoiled young ladies who were going to be punished
by God if they didn't start thinking about their
Church once in a while. "It's not my Church," Lily
had snapped, aware that she was beaten: her error,
as Martha observed immediately, had been the mention of Father Ford, who had personally brought

about China Mary's conversion and secured a place high on her personal hagiology by assuring her that Dennis Kearney, who with several hundred exclusionist followers had set fire to a San Francisco laundry operated by China Mary's grandfather in 1877, had probably been a bad Catholic if indeed he had been a Catholic at all. As Martha pointed out, Lily would never learn how to get around China Mary if she couldn't get it through her head not to mention Father Ford.

That was at two o'clock. At three Joe Templeton called, and at five-thirty he arrived with twenty pounds of sugar. Although Martha had been sick for two days, she came downstairs in a new pale pink robe for which she had paid sixty dollars a few weeks after she had met Ryder Channing at the Mather Field Officers' Club that summer; she had torn the white silk roses from the sash, and Lily knew, from that, from the grateful satisfaction Martha was taking in a low-grade fever, and from the way she talked to Joe about Channing ("*Cap*-tain Channing," she kept saying, and referring to his slight limp as "something he allegedly got over Normandy"), that the affair must be running cool. Martha talked animatedly, laughed extravagantly at Joe's mild jokes ("Joe, you're too *funny*, you ought to be on radio, don't you think Joe should be on radio, Lily? Giving imitations of canaries and people? I mean he couldn't have sounded *more* like Harry Hopkins"), and urged him to stay for dinner. It would be, she explained, a kind of cook-it-yourself operation, catch-as-catch-can, because China Mary was off brooding, but it would be scads of fun, she promised, and one thing they would have plenty of was sugar, one thing they definitely would not run short on, thanks to Lily's foresight and Joe's mysterious resources, was sugar. As a matter of fact it was providential that China

Mary had used up all their sugar and inspired Lily to call upon Joe, because they had nowhere *near* twenty pounds to begin with. That was the old silver lining for you, all right. With interest. Joe must stay.

Joe could not. Joe was taking Francie and her mother out to dinner.

Which was, Martha said, very shrewd of Joe. Taking Francie's mother out to dinner. Making sure the bread stayed buttered, and all that.

Anyway, she added, picking up a bowl of camellias and starting for the kitchen, it was no wonder Joe didn't want to stay for dinner, the way this house was kept. Nothing but dead flowers in tasteless bowls, anywhere.

"It was a bowl of my mother's," Lily explained as she walked Joe out to his car, but the incident seemed to have eluded him. "What was?" he asked without interest, and then added immediately: "I met this Channing character." "He's quite a good friend of Martha's," Lily interrupted, annoyed at Joe's denseness about the bowl of camellias.

When she came back to the house Martha was lying on the couch, her face buried in a pillow. Lily pulled a comforter over Martha's back, and sat down to finish the letter to Everett she had begun before Joe came.

"You writing Everett?" Martha sat up, throwing the comforter off.

Lily nodded without looking up. "I want to see if he can't come home for a few days. You keep warm." She had asked Everett, in almost every letter since his transfer to Fort Bliss in July, if he could not come home for a few days. In the back of her mind she was uneasily convinced that he could have gotten home, had he wanted to, between the time he had left Georgia and the time he had been due in Texas.

109

Martha lay down again. "Some days I certainly can't abide Joe Templeton."

"Some days you certainly are rude."

"I mean sometimes I wonder where old Joe would be today if Francie didn't drink. I mean he absolutely *trades* on it, he's made an absolute *career* of it."

She paused, watching Lily's reflection in the mirror above the couch. "When really it's just the other way around," she added finally. "I mean I guess everybody on the river knows who puts up with who in that house. Who needs who. And it's more than just her money. Her money's only the half of it. Don't you think?"

"I don't know," Lily said.

"Well think about it a minute."

"All right."

"Now. Think about it right now."

"I want to finish this letter before dinner."

Martha pulled the comforter back up to her neck and resettled the pillow. "Tell Everett we're eating Joe Templeton's sugar, why don't you. Tell him you're sleeping around to keep us in black-market sugar. That should bring him. Write Everett-baby that."

Lily put the letter down. China Mary had been impossible about the sugar coupons. Knight had been running a fever; Julie cutting a tooth. Martha and her father had fought at dinner every night for a week, and Joe had been worried about Francie, who had sprained her wrist in a fall from a horse while she was drunk. Even that sure and quiet comfort had evolved into the garrulous ambiguity of friendship, a change that was probably irreversible; when Joe had tried, a few minutes ago, to draw her into a prolonged and clumsy kiss in the darkness by the car, she had turned her face away in irritation that he should try to so deceive both her and himself.

110

Once they had admitted sugar coupons and sprained wrists, it no longer worked. She was too tired even to be shocked by Martha, let alone angry at her.

"Martha," she said. "Please."

Martha had begun to cry, tears welling in her fevered eyes and splashing down her flushed cheeks.

"Martha, baby."

"You've got no right to my brother," Martha whispered, standing up unsteadily. "No right."

Lily was, then, less angry than frightened: harsh words between women seemed to her unthinkable, an irreparable rent in the social fabric. On those few occasions when she had quarreled with her mother, they had ended, both terrified of the consequences, weeping together. She thought now of the picture of Everett above Martha's bed, the roses torn from the sash of the new robe, of Martha's delight when she graduated *summa cum laude* in June ("Wait until Everett hears," she had said. "He'll be appalled"); thought of Martha at Julie's christening, Sunday before last, whispering out loud *please help her to choose right every day she lives.* Martha had held Julie, and none of the omens were good: the sky was overcast with the peculiar yellow haze Edith Knight called earthquake weather, Everett's father jammed on his Stetson and walked out of the church before the christening because the minister had a favorable word for Harold Ickes, and Martha cried. (She cried because Ryder Channing had not come to the christening; she would have cried had he come. "That girl will have shed enough tears by the end of the year 1944," Mr. McClellan said before he left the church, "to drown the entire Jap army. She is what you call an untapped resource.") Lily had worn the silly John Frederics hat with the black veiling that had cost her mother seventy-five dollars, and had known even as she smiled at Martha that Julie was already beyond choice. The tellers of fairy tales knew

111

about choosing what Martha did not know. An un-invited guest brings a gold ring or a spray of rue to the christening party.

"Martha," she called now, wanting to make it all right, but Martha had run upstairs.

Later, she arranged a tray for Martha with a roast-beef sandwich and an artichoke, soaked in olive oil as Martha liked artichokes best. ("Why can't she come down?" Mr. McClellan demanded, ripping the leaves from his own artichoke and clearly regretting the lost opportunity for another few rounds at din-ner. "Why doesn't she just check into a hospital and stay there?")

She found Martha lying in bed in the dark, the blanket littered with damp shreds of Kleenex.

"I didn't mean what I said." Martha's eyes were closed. "I didn't mean anything like that. You're fine for Everett. Everett loves you."

"Don't talk about it now." Lily sat on the edge of the bed and turned on the light. The reconciliation made her quite as uncomfortable as the scene down-stairs had; things said out loud had for her an aura of danger so volatile that it could be controlled only in that dark province inhabited by those who share beds. Although she could sometimes say things out loud to Everett, she did not know how to talk to Martha.

"My eyes are red." Martha turned off the light again. "Everett thinks the sun rises and sets with you. You should realize that."

"I realize it."

"I mean you should realize how really simple Ever-ett is."

Martha sat up in bed and fumbled on the table for a package of cigarettes.

"You better eat," Lily said. "Everything's getting cold."

"You mean that cold artichoke and that cold roast-beef sandwich and that cold glass of milk." Martha lit a cigarette. "Just a minute. How really straight he is. I mean maybe Everett gets scared and has bad dreams like anybody else, I don't know, but the difference is Everett wouldn't ever explore it. All Everett wants is a little *order*."

"I guess that's what everybody wants."

Martha lay down again. "Maybe everybody wants it. But most people don't want it more than anything else in the world. The way Everett does. You might want it, I might want it. But when the opportunity to *have* it practically hits us over the head, we just about knock ourselves out getting out of the way." She paused. "Take you for example."

Lily said nothing.

"All right, don't. Take me. What do I want? A nice ordered life right here on the river just like we've always had."

"Joe says the war is going to change everything." Snatching at what had seemed for a moment a chance to steer the conversation away from the particular and into the realm of topics so impersonal and so unweighted that they could be safely talked about, Lily had forgotten that Joe was for the time being a name loaded with peril.

"Never *mind* about Joe. He read it in *U.S. News & World Report*. Anyway. That's what I want. But what do I do about getting it. I get messed up with Ryder, who not only doesn't want to marry me, doesn't understand any of the things I need, but is so unfitted to everything I want that I get so nervous I practically break into tears every time he's in the same room with Daddy. That's what I do about it."

Lily looked away. "I don't know," she said. She did not want Martha to tell her anything more about

Ryder Channing. She had written Everett about how impossible Martha had been since she met him, had told him he had better come talk to Martha, and she did not know what else she could do.

"I don't even *like* Ryder," Martha added, wadding up her baby pillow and holding it against her face with one hand, groping with the other for the shreds of Kleenex on the blanket.

Lily took a tissue from her pocket and handed it to Martha. "I'll get you some Luminal," she said with relief. She did not like to see Martha cry but the conversation was at any rate closed.

At twenty minutes to eleven, after Mr. McClellan had gone upstairs and left Lily to finish her letter to Everett (*I wish you would please reconsider about coming for a few days because neither your father nor I can talk to her and I don't believe she has passed one day without crying since she came home in June, and this man, although he is quite nice, does not seem good for her, Everett, baby, please*), Ryder Channing arrived to see Martha.

"Actually she's asleep," Lily said, straightening her skirt as she took his raincoat. "I guess you know she's been sick."

"I thought she might feel better."

He did not sit down, and she noticed for the first time that he was about Everett's height, about six feet. He would not have looked unlike Everett had there not been about his face both a hardness and a softness absent in Everett's, the look of someone who has been in some sense spoiled. She supposed he must be older than Everett by four or five years, must be twenty-nine or thirty.

"I thought she might feel up to driving into town for a drink. I'm sorry." He picked up a book from

114

the hall table and opened it, pausing to read the inscription. "Maybe you'd like to go."

"I shouldn't go out. Won't you have a drink here?"

"Sure. Sure I will." He smiled. She had thought before that he must calculate the effect of his smile; its peculiar intimacy was a study in timing. It was something like the way John Wayne said "Hell-o there" when he first met the girl, on a train or in a construction camp or riding past on a horse. There was no mistaking John Wayne and there was, in a limited way, no mistaking Ryder Channing.

"That's real nice of you," he added, smiling again, sitting down, and examining the envelope she had just addressed to Everett. Seeing that it was empty, he yawned, closed his eyes and asked: "Where's that drink?"

It occurred to her, as she got the ice, that John Wayne had the jump on Ryder when it came to follow-through.

They had, in all, three drinks. At first Lily sat very straight on the wooden rocker by the desk; after he had made a second drink she sat across from the couch, where he lay sprawled with one leg propped on the arm. He told her about Memphis, where his mother and sisters lived, and about Charlottesville, where he had gone to school. ("You'd like that, Lily. You'd really like that, Charlottesville, springtime, you'd eat it up," he assured her in the Tennessee drawl that made everything he said seem a mild flirtation, made her feel that he had, in uncovering her previously unsuspected and more or less unprovable predilection for Charlottesville in the springtime, penetrated the very essence of her.) He praised Martha extravagantly (she had, he declared, one of the quickest minds he had ever encountered in a woman); asked to see a crayon drawing Knight had done; and announced that the three of them—he, Martha, and Lily—must have dinner at the Officers' Club at Mather Field the following Sunday. Or some Sunday. They would keep it loose. Under his gentle prodding, Lily found herself telling him about the parties her mother used to give, about the time her grandfather had challenged a neighbor to a gunfight over a right of way which (it turned out) belonged to neither of them; even about her father. It was the first time she had spoken about her father except in passing since his death. Ryder seemed fascinated by the most minute details of life on the river: he wanted to know why she had been sent to Dominican rather than to the union high school as Martha had been; why they did not belong to the country club and whether anyone else on the river did; why Walter Knight would not have been likely to belong to a San Francisco club, say the Pacific Union or the Bohemian. "He just wouldn't, that's all," Lily said, and it seemed to satisfy Ryder; he appeared to index it under *Growers, Social Eccentricities of*, and went on to explore whether Walter Knight had known anyone who voted for Culbert Olson for Governor in 1938.

As they were finishing their third drink and Lily was trying to explain why she had not liked going to the San Francisco dances when she was at Dominican, Martha appeared on the stair landing, tying the roseless sash and smiling wanly.

"I heard you all." Whatever Martha's malaise, it seemed to have so developed within the past few hours that she could not negotiate four steps without clutching the railing. "I'm sorry I didn't wake up before."

Channing swung his long legs off the couch and stood up, holding out his arms to Martha.

"You poor sick baby." He bent to kiss her neck. "You shouldn't be out of bed."

"I only wanted to say hello."

116

She stood there, neither sitting down nor taking Ryder's hand.

"Lily was telling me about the San Francisco Assembly," Ryder said. "Did you go to those dances?"

"No. I didn't go to those dances."

"Martha went to school up here," Lily said. "As you know."

"Listen," Martha said. "I meant to tell you. Daddy said something real funny the other night at dinner."

"What?"

"Well, see, he wanted to ask me something about you. But naturally he pretended not to remember your name. 'That fellow from Mississippi,' he said. 'Ryder's not from Mississippi,' I said. 'He's from Tennessee.' 'Mississippi, Tennessee, what's the difference,' Daddy said. 'It's all Del Paso Heights to me.'"

Lily laughed. Del Paso Heights was a district north of Sacramento noted for its large Negro population and its high incidence of minor social disorders.

"That's very funny," Channing said. He seemed obscurely pleased by the story, another entry under *Growers, Eccentricities of.*

"He really said it, didn't he, Lily."

"He really did. I have to go up," she added, kissing Martha on the cheek and taking Ryder's hand. He smiled at her.

As she walked upstairs she felt that Ryder was watching her, and kept her back straight. When she turned at the landing she saw that he was not watching her at all, but kissing Martha, pulling her very close, his hand at the small of her back. She wondered how Martha felt when Ryder smiled, and how much of the smile was calculated. Not that it mattered. Everyone had his own shell game, and if Ryder Channing had known tonight how to make her feel open and happy for an hour or so, they had, in the end, conned each other. He would probably understand that.

It occurred to her later, after she had undressed and turned down the sheets on Everett's and her bed, that Ryder Channing might have been someone to whom, under different circumstances, she could have said things out loud.

13

Everett was playing poker in the Officers' Club at Fort Bliss when they telephoned him on that Saturday after Thanksgiving, 1944. Lily had already called twice that week, asking if he could please come home for Christmas because everything was falling apart without him. First the baby had been down with measles, then Knight had caught whooping cough; there had been nothing but sickness since summer. *I need you,* she said. He could simply *not understand* unless he came; he must come. In the first place there was Martha. If he wanted to help Martha he had better come. She was still intimating that she was about to run off with that Air Corps captain from Tennessee; the week before Thanksgiving she did not come home for two days. She told her father she was in San Francisco. Which for all Lily knew she might have been but there was *one vital detail* missing in the version she told her father. (Not that it wasn't Martha's own business, but she managed to make it everyone's by making issues of everyone else's faults. If she heard once more from Martha that Ryder Channing said she had "no conversation" she was going to start screaming, and if any of them heard once more from Martha that Ryder Channing thought the house looked like something out of Charles Addams, Lily simply could not be responsible for what Everett's father might do. He objected to the way Ryder Channing wore his hat, without any stiffening, and referred to him always as "the fly-boy" or "the ninety-day wonder," phrases he had picked up Lily didn't know where since everything else about the war was more or less escaping him.) Anyway. Martha and her father fought every night at dinner until no one could eat, and then Martha would push her chair back and run upstairs. They could hear her crying at night and it upset everyone. She had in fact been behaving that way ever since she came home from school, so it did not in all fairness seem to have been brought on by Channing, but he was around all the time and when he was not around Martha was crying and it upset Everett's father especially. Not that it took much to upset him these days. Everett could not realize. Someone had approached him about subdividing the ranch after the war, and the man may have been rather unattractive and may even have been as Everett's father said an operator and a draft-dodger, but Everett's father still had no call to say the things he said to that man. There you had it. The children were sick and Martha was crying and Everett's father was losing his mind. If only Everett could come. *You don't know how I need you.*

Lily's letters and telephone calls had been the only disturbance in Everett's life that summer and fall; she seemed to have read none of the inspirational literature about building service morale, keeping the home fires burning, I'll be home for Christmas but only in my dreams. He missed her and the babies, but not as much as he told her he did, and then only in an abstract way. They were safe, and his absence from them was more than blameless; it was blessed by all the Allied Powers. More than he could remember being since his first few weeks at Stanford, he was peculiarly contented within the ordered limitations of his life at Bliss. Desultorily, he played poker and struck up guarded friendships at the bar; later, every night, he lay in bed and made new plans for the ranch: exquisitely rational arrangements, unmarred by the sloppy actualities of plans in operation. Once, when he had a pass, he went up to Dallas with another lieutenant, one of the group with whom he sometimes played poker; the lieutenant called some girls he had known in college at Austin, and they all went dancing at the Adolphus Hotel. Although he could not later remember how, Everett ended up alone with a girl who had pale strawberry-blond hair and access to her father's Cadillac. In the Cadillac they had driven out by a creek where they sat on the running board and drank bourbon out of paper cups and watched the sun come up, and the girl had made Everett feel her necklace (it liked to be touched, she told him, because it was made of real pearls from Neiman-Marcus) and had held his hand against her throat, but he had only kissed her gravely and driven her home. Later that morning, waiting for a transport he could hop back to El Paso, he tried to believe that it had been because she was a nice girl or at any rate because he was faithful to Lily, but he knew that he had left the girl alone for neither reason. He had left her alone because it was too much trouble; on a small scale she might have disturbed the even flow of his days at Bliss even as Lily did.

It was not that he did not like the idea of having Lily on the ranch, waiting: he did. Lily completed the picture, gave him the sense of having settled things, the sense he had missed before they were married. It was necessary, however, that things stay settled. During the past few weeks he had begun to regard Lily's messages as definite intrusions, to look upon life on the ranch as a bacchanalia of disorganization, peculiarly female disorder. No one, so far as Everett knew, cried all night in the Officers' Club at Bliss.

He had explained repeatedly that Christmas was out of the question; he had only a seventy-two-hour pass and transportation was at best uncertain. He would go instead to Mexico, although he did not tell her that. *You don't know how I need you,* she had repeated over the telephone two nights ago, and he had answered in a blaze of righteousness: *You don't seem to realize there's a war going on.* Immediately he had laughed, trying to cover not only his pomposity but his deception. It must be clear even to Lily that El Paso was not exactly Leyte Gulf, and that getting to the ranch for Christmas would not be impossible.

Now when the orderly told him that he had a call from California he felt the resentment return: they were forcing the issue, making him feel guilty. Annoyed with them all and with himself, he picked up the telephone ready to tell Lily once again that there was a war going on.

"Is that Everett?"

He was abruptly charmed by her small voice. For a moment it was as if he had never gone away from her, never discovered the siren lure of celibacy.

"Who does it sound like?"

There was a silence. "This is Lily."

"Not Lily McClellan, surely."

"Yes," she said, and paused again. "Now listen to me."

"What is it?"

She did not answer. He had stiffened, preparing himself for the last-ditch appeal, and now she did not make it, did not answer, said nothing.

"What is it?" he repeated, remembering suddenly what she had said about Martha.

She said nothing.

"*Operator*," he said. Then, with some relief, he heard Martha's voice, controlled and distant.

"We're at the hospital," she said rapidly. "Sutter Hospital. Daddy had a stroke and you'd better come home."

"Is he all right?" He realized the idiocy of the question as he asked it.

"Of course he isn't all right. He's dead. Or we wouldn't have bothered you."

All that night he sat in the washroom of a Pullman car, smoking cigarettes and watching the green-shaded lights flicker on and off as the train crawled across the desert to Los Angeles. He probably could have gotten a seat on a plane, but had not, even though Martha's sharp, precarious voice had finally broken: *I said he's dead, Everett, come home now oh Christ Daddy's dead and let's not have any more of that crap about how the lights are going out all over the world, Everett, please, come home fast.* The train would be at least two days, longer should he miss the Los Angeles connection. He had wired his father's lawyer to make arrangements for the funeral. He knew with certainty that although he might see Bliss again, he was as good as discharged now; although he had in 1942 given up his farm deferment in order to enlist, there was no one now to run the ranch. He would ask for and certainly get a hardship discharge.

That he would not see his father again did not really occur to him until he reached the ranch, six hours too late for the funeral (he had missed the connection in Los Angeles, and by then could not get a flight at all), and found that Sarah had flown home from Philadelphia. "It was sudden," she kept repeating to Everett, "it was terribly sudden." "Yes," he agreed each time, dimly reassuring her as he re-assured himself; they seemed to share some burden, the guilt of the children out playing when the trou-ble happened.

It was all they shared. He had not seen Sarah since the day of her wedding, in August of 1936. She had been married in the garden, in their mother's wed-ding dress, to a boy named Peter. Although she had met Peter at Stanford he turned out to be from Phila-delphia, a circumstance which seemed insurmounta-ble to all the McClellans except Sarah. Seventeen years old, Everett had been an usher. He had gotten a little drunk on champagne (Peter had not approved of the champagne, which was California; it had been Peter's conviction, expressed in company which in-cluded two Napa Valley grape growers, that if you could not afford a decent French champagne you did better by sticking to Scotch) and toward the end of the afternoon, when Sarah was cutting the bride's cake, he had told her and Peter a not very funny but very dirty joke. Peter had looked faintly annoyed. He never looked more than faintly anything. "I guess we've had enough of the local *vino*," he said, slapping Everett's shoulder in what he seemed to consider an appropriately fraternal manner. "You ass," Everett had said, and Sarah had thrown her arms around Everett, laughing and kissing him with white frosting on her mouth. She had been home twice since then, once before and once after the six weeks on the Nevada side of Lake Tahoe which legalized the end of Peter, but Everett had been away that summer, working in a lumber camp out of Tacoma.

Her presence now, even the trace of her perfume that was all through the house (the same perfume: it smelled again like the summer she was married, when the house was full of silver and tissue paper and girls), indicated that this was indeed an event, a

123

crisis, a death in the family. Sad and nervous, she walked aimlessly through the house straightening pictures, picking up plates and putting them back, opening and closing the shutters; through her alien's eyes Everett saw that what Lily had said was true: everything was falling apart.

It would be a difficult spring. Lily had not exaggerated; he had simply not wanted to believe her. Apparently his father had not been well for months before his stroke, and had lost interest in growing anything on the land he held so tenaciously. Everett could understand that; he never blamed his father. When it came down to it, beyond making enough to live on, he had little interest himself in using the land. Like his father, he wanted only to have it. The Braden place was a case in point. It was two hundred acres, near Auburn, virtually untillable, deserted for years. It had been in Everett's mother's estate. Although Joe Templeton had wanted to buy it, Everett had refused to sell, ostensibly because he planned to develop it himself. He knew now why he had not sold the Braden place. He had thought about it in that Pullman washroom crossing the desert. He wanted, all of his life, to be able to go up to the Braden place and stand on the hill and look up the Valley to the Marysville buttes, and he wanted to be standing on his own land. It had nothing to do with crops, development, profit. He understood, all right, how his father, sick, could have let the river ranch run down. He had just dropped his guard temporarily, and there it went.

Moved by this example, Everett was on guard, now, armed with the brisk decision, the semblance of efficient appraisal. Their Japanese foreman had been evacuated in 1942, and his replacement, to whom Everett's father had increasingly left the day-to-day operation, had proved incompetent. Everett had said, when they hired him, that the man was not responsible; "never mind," his father had muttered, dis-

turbed more than he saw fit to admit by the reloca-
tion of the Japanese. "Those bastards asked for it."
It was typical of him to have thought that the loss
incurred by an irresponsible foreman would be the
government's; he had apparently never at any point
seen that it was his own. On acre after acre, the redwood poles and wire trellises had been knocked down
and left to rot with dead vines, unpicked the summer
before. Part of last summer's crop, the foreman told
Everett, had mildewed; in the shed Everett found, unopened, the copper sulfate which would have prevented it. Machinery, unreplaceable until after the
war, had been left out to rust in the autumn rains; the
kiln was in no condition to use, the main road rutted.
Even the levee was eroded, neglected all one year.
The Army Engineers, as far as that went, were supposed to watch the levees, but Everett did not suppose that the Engineers had been deeply concerned
during 1943 and 1944 with the levee at McClellan's
Landing.

"I kept writing you," Lily reminded him, never
looking up from her knitting. It seemed to him that
she had been knitting steadily since his arrival. Whenever she caught him looking at her she would bite
her lip, ostentatiously readjust her needles, and knit
faster.

He turned, wordless, to Martha.

"I never noticed anybody letting me run this
ranch," she said. "I can't even write a check around
here."

"We did everything we could," Lily said. "Your
father wasn't asking for any advice from us."

"If only someone had let Everett know." Sarah
closed the box of old dance programs and pressed or-
chids which had claimed her attention since dinner.
"If only someone had let *me* know."

"If only someone had *thought*." Martha leaned to
touch Lily's arm. "Sarah could have forwarded us

125

some pamphlets from the United States Department of Agriculture. Or maybe she could have talked it over with *Peter*."

"I haven't seen Peter since 1939."

"This new one then," Martha said. "I can't ever think of his name."

"It's on all my note paper," Sarah said with an attempt at serenity. "Robert Carr Warfield, Jr." She paused. "Bud," she added doubtfully.

"Bud. That's it. Maybe you and Bud could have put your heads together and gotten this place in shape by air mail."

Lily put down her knitting and looked up at Everett.

He understood: he had never meant to cast doubts upon their intentions. Nonetheless, he would be away another few months until his discharge was processed, and someone would have to take hold. Could they do that, could they get the poles up and the fields cleared and above all could they get the Engineers to do something about the levee before they found themselves floating around the Delta?

"You tell the men I'm running it and I will," Martha said.

"Joe Templeton will help us," Lily said.

"Joe Templeton will help us," Martha repeated. "Oh my yes. Old Joe Templeton will absolutely leap at the opportunity to help us. Yes indeed. Joe Templeton can be depended upon, Everett, count on that." She had been playing nervously with one of Lily's knitting needles; now she jammed it into a ball of yarn and walked to the window.

Three days after the funeral Everett put Sarah on a plane back to Philadelphia ("back home," she said, apparently oblivious to the pain she could cause her brother simply by shifting the locus of her belonging), carrying a paper bag full of dried hops to show to her children and to the stranger who was now her husband. The hops had been Martha's idea. "They'll think I'm bringing candy," Sarah laughed, nervous as they stood in the rain at the gate. "I should have bought something, they won't realize I came for a funeral." Her voice trailed off as she watched the propellers catching. Tentatively, Everett put his arm around her shoulders, thick in her black fleece coat, too heavy for California. She turned, smiling brilliantly and blowing him a kiss. "You come visit us," she called as she ran to the plane, "come visit whenever you can."

After the plane had left the runway Everett sat in the empty parking lot, bent over the steering wheel of the station wagon with the rain blowing in through the open window and the strings of Christmas tinsel stars clinking in the wind between the low buildings, and cried for the first time that he could remember, not so much for his father as for Sarah's defection, because she had lost all memory of the family they had been on that day when he got a little drunk on champagne.

14

"Everett," she said. "Everett."

He turned toward her, fumbling blindly through the wrinkled sheets for her body, meaning to draw her to him in the hot bed and drop back into sleep, wanting only to quiet her.

"Everett. Please. Everett."

He opened his eyes. Lily lay on her back smoking a cigarette. He had been home from Bliss six months now, ever since his discharge in February, and through those two seasons of 1945 he had not slept one night without the dim troubled sense that Lily was awake, shifting in bed, walking around the room or sitting by the window in the dark. (She could not remember, she told him, a summer so hot: she had not been able to breathe for months.) Not until he woke in the morning would she be asleep, sometimes in the chair by the window, her legs stretched out across the low sill and her nightgown fallen from her shoulders; sometimes on the far edge of the bed, one hand flat on the floor, the other flung toward him but not touching him. She would lie for hours then without waking; one morning he had sat on the bed and held her hand for twenty minutes while she lay as if drugged, neither clenching nor withdrawing her fingers.

"Go to sleep," he said now. "Go to sleep, baby."

"I have to talk to you."

He ran his fingers over the moist ends of her hair and across her face. Her eyes were wet. *Jesus Christ.* How many nights had he heard Lily crying. As some parents sleep through fire, thunderstorms, and voices at the back door only to wake at a child's whisper, so Everett heard Lily crying at night. Her muffled sobs seemed to have broken his dreams for years. He had heard her even at Fort Lewis, even in Georgia, finally at Bliss. That was Lily crying in the wings whenever the priests came to tear up his mother's grave. Lily cried in the twilight field where he picked wild poppies with Martha; Lily's was the cry he heard those nights the kiln burned, the levee broke, the ranch went to nothing.

"What is it, Lily?"

She crushed out her cigarette. "I have to tell you."

He brushed the damp hair back from her forehead

and kissed her closed eyelids, tasting the salt on his tongue.

"I didn't want to tell you but I have to."

"What is it?" he said. "What do you have to tell me, baby?"

He did not want her to say it. He had known for maybe three weeks, since that morning (it was the morning the pump broke, the Monday after they had gone to Lake Tahoe with Marth and Channing) when he had gotten up and found Lily sitting on the edge of the bathtub, her head down, her arms crossed as if she were having a chill. Her nightgown was down around her waist and a glass of orange juice was spilled on the pink tile floor. Her hands were shaking, her eyes glazed; he knew she had been sick. As he helped her back to bed it occurred to him that she was overdue that month. He was not sure. She had not taken her eyes from his face as he pulled the sheet over her, and while he tried to clean up the orange juice with toilet paper (for some reason he had not wanted to leave it for China Mary to see) he recalled that she had been sick on orange juice the first few months both times before. He had hoped (so fiercely that it was a constant prayer, now after three weeks as automatic as breathing) that he was mistaken, about the one thing if not the other, hoped that she would not say the words. But he had known she would. He had known all along she would wake him some night. *I didn't want to tell you but I have to.*

He moved his arm beneath her shoulders. Her body was rigid. He would have to let her say it. He was the goddamn priest who would have to hear it.

"I'm pregnant." Her eyes were shut tight, as if she expected him to hit her. "I'm pregnant and I don't think by you."

Her voice was as smooth and anonymous as a recording. She must have rehearsed the words so often that all inflection had been erased. He threw off the

129

sheet and sat up on the edge of the bed, reaching toward the table for a cigarette, stalling less from shock than from a sense of anticlimax. Spoken, the words had lost their power.

Lily had not moved. *Well let her sweat it out.*

"You don't think by me," he repeated finally.

She was sobbing convulsively now.

"Any Mexican would know better." He could hear the flatness in his voice. "Any West End whore."

"Leave me alone." She was choking. "Just leave me be."

"Crystal on your mother's place would know better. Crystal Gomez. Or whatever her name is."

He persisted only because he did not know what else to do, and thought she expected it of him.

"What do you want?" she whispered, her head turned away from him. "What do you want me to say?"

"Nothing." His voice was gentler now. "I don't want you to say anything at all."

She sat up suddenly, as if anticipating a trick, suspecting some incipient violence.

"You want to know who it *was*," she sobbed, almost screaming.

You want to know who it was. He did not know whether she meant it as question or accusation. Without looking at her, he reached for the shirt and the pair of khaki pants thrown on the chair the night before. He supposed he knew who it was, if it mattered. He would rather it had been a stranger, someone who came and left. For it to have been someone he knew made the fault more subtly Lily's: she had at once violated several contracts. That kind of thinking, however, did not apply. No kind of thinking that led to the word "contract" could possibly apply to whatever it was between him and Lily. He would prefer that it had been a stranger but it did not matter that it had not been. It might as well have been.

130

"No," he said. "I don't want to hear it. I don't want to hear anything more about it."

He pulled on the khaki pants and left the room, carrying the shirt and a pair of sneakers. When he dropped one of the sneakers on the stairs he did not bother to pick it up.

Mostly because a light had been left burning on the sun porch, he sat down there on the edge of the rattan couch, one sneaker still in his hand, and wondered how long he had been asleep and how long it would be until dawn.

He sat there the rest of the night, occasionally taking a swallow of bourbon from a bottle left on the table, staring blankly at an album of snapshots Martha had left out. She had been showing their pictures to Channing the night before. (Channing, of course, had missed the point about Martha's showing him the pictures, had studied a snapshot of Martha on a horse at eleven years old and remarked only upon the resemblance in pose to Elizabeth Taylor in *National Velvet*; had examined the pictures of Martha on the beach at Carmel and been struck not by Martha but by the cypress formations. "They just blow that way, Ryder," Martha explained again and again with more patience than Everett thought either characteristic or necessary. "They just get blown that way and stick." It had so irritated and saddened Everett to see Martha spreading out their vacations at Carmel before Channing's disregard that he had gone upstairs at ten o'clock. "Now, Everett, baby," Lily had said, that deceptive mildness in her voice, "Martha's baby pictures do not exactly constitute Mount Rushmore.")

He saw a snapshot taken on the verandah of the Knight place when they were all children: Lily, he and Marth, and Sarah, holding Marth by the hand. It looked like a birthday party but he could not think whose. He remembered one party, perhaps this one, when Martha had become sick from excitement. They had

131

found her huddled in the corner of Edith Knight's bathtub, the daisy wreath Sarah had made for her wilted and down over one eye. Everett smiled now, seeing that on that day they had all worn navy-blue reefer coats in different sizes. Knight had an identical reefer now; Lily's mother had bought it.

He wished that he could go upstairs to Lily, tell her it would be all right, brush away the physical fact by making her laugh over the snapshot with the reefer coats. *Red Rover, Red Rover, let Lily Knight come over.* He could remember how Martha had sometimes kept herself hidden for hours when they played hide-and-go-seek; how Lily, who had never liked being It, had never even liked games much, had sat down under the lilac once and cried because no one would come from hiding and it was getting dark. "I thought you'd all gone and drowned," she sobbed, hiccuping, when they finally ran in from the dry place under the dock where Martha had insisted on hiding. "I thought you'd fallen in and been caught in a whirlpool." (The prospect of falling in and being caught in a whirlpool had always loomed impressively in Lily's imagination; he knew that she believed remotely to this day that whirlpools the size and power of the Maelstrom were commonplace in the Sacramento River.) Somehow that day, he could not recall how, he had made Lily stop crying and laugh. He had intended always to take care of her, to make her laugh. But somewhere they had stopped listening to each other, and so he remained downstairs in a paralysis not of anger but of lassitude and pride.

He had stopped being angry months before, if he had ever been angry at all: had passed through shock, hurt, and compromise already, and alone. Even then he had been hurt not so much by Lily as by his own failure to see. *Have a drink with me, Everett,*

Francie Templeton had said the night he finally saw; he had gone up to see Joe about buying a used Ford pickup, but Joe was in town.

"We'll have a drink together this fine June evening because Everett darling," Francie said firmly, "it's about to be one dry summer."

She emptied an ice tray into a pitcher and picked up a bottle of bourbon. Reluctantly, he followed her upstairs to the terrace of the second-floor landing; women who drank made him uncomfortable under any circumstances, and Francie fell besides into the category of women old enough to know better.

"I so enjoyed *talk*ing to you the other night," Francie said, dropping ice into two glasses. With an accuracy which surprised him, she threw one cube into the branches of an orange tree which brushed the terrace wall, tearing apart a spider's web.

"I enjoyed it too, Francie."

Everett was acutely uncomfortable; in the moonlight flooding the terrace Francie looked even more haggard than she had looked downstairs in the lamplight, and the other night had not been the other night at all, but a month before, on V-E Day, when he had drunk too much at a party down the river. "Walk me down to the water, Everett darling," Francie had said about midnight that evening, and he had walked with Francie across the lawn and over the levee to the dock, had half-carried her down under the cottonwoods and big oaks and had sat with her there maybe half an hour, singing. Perhaps because he had been drinking as much as she had, Francie's clear, slight voice did not seem in the least blurred to Everett, and she remembered all the lyrics to "The Battle Hymn of the Republic" and "The Yellow Rose of Texas" and even "There'll Always Be an England," a song which had always infuriated his father. On that warm May night with the lights on down the river and occasional strains of the *Oklahoma!* score drifting

133

down from the house and Francie's head on his shoulder, Francie whom he had known all his life, the world had seemed to Everett fine and noble and sweet and brave, a place of infinite possibilities for faith and honor and the grace of commonplace pleasures, and he was moved beyond any expressing of it by the worn words *Oh beautiful for spacious skies, for amber waves of grain.* Her shoes off, one foot trailing in the water, Francie had gradually dropped her head into his lap and stopped singing, fading out halfway through "There'll Be Bluebirds over the White Cliffs of Dover." Thinking her asleep, Everett sat stroking her hair for a few minutes before she sat up abruptly and began to untie the knotted silk halter strap of her dress. "Let's go in swimming, Everett darling."

"It's too early, Francie," he kept repeating softly, sober enough to see that neither of them was in condition to swim in the river, "it's still running cold." As he extricated the halter strap from her fingers and began to tie it again at the back of her neck, she at first dropped her head docilely, then, without saying anything, reached between his legs. "Don't, Francie," he said, getting to his feet and lifting her up; she had begun crying then, her hands over her face and the big diamond she had inherited from her grandmother blazing suddenly in the spotlight from a passing cruiser. When he tried to take her hands and hold her she wrenched away. "Go screw yourself," she had whispered, "that's probably the only way you like it anyway." He had hoped she would not remember it later, and had not really thought she would. (The next morning he told Lily that while she was inside dancing he had been singing songs with Francie Templeton, and she had laughed: "Everett baby. That's not much your style.")

"We had quite a sing for ourselves, didn't we," Francie said now, handing him a glass and touching it with her own. "To the old songs."

"That's right, Francie. The old songs."

"Quite a sing," she repeated reflectively. "On the Occasion of the Victory in Europe. A regular narrative by Norman Corwin." She paused. "You think Francie's changed since you went away."

"You always look the same, Francie," he said quickly, embarrassed that she had caught him out. She was wearing an old denim skirt and a wrinkled shirt which probably belonged to Joe; he knew that she must have been drinking most of the day.

"Well, yes and no." She poured more bourbon into her glass and waved him toward a wicker bench. "Yes and no. I'm thirty-seven years old today."

"Happy birthday." He wondered if she had a celebration in mind.

"Ha. It's not my birthday at all. I've been thirty-seven years old for months. Now old *Joe*," she added thoughtfully, "is forty."

Everett smiled gamely. He knew that Joe was thirty-six. Joe was ten years older than he was almost to the day. He happened to know that much with certainty because once Joe had come down drunk for a game at Stanford and collared Everett after lunch at the Deke house and explained all through the first quarter how much they had in common, give or take ten years. One of the things they still had in common, Everett recalled, was fifty dollars Joe had borrowed that day because Francie had temporarily left him and transferred all the money in their joint checking account into her private account, where she said it belonged in the first place.

"Forty—years—old," Francie said. "Or anyway he is almost. *Sic transit* old Joe, and all that."

"That's right, Francie." She was sitting on the low brick wall that edged the terrace, her body in profile to him, and he was nervous that she would fall from the wall and down one story onto the lawn.

"Tell me about the war," she said, swaying gently, almost crooning. "Tell me about how you were out defending democracy in El Paso and other foreign fields while old Joe here kept the home fires burning."

"I appreciate Joe's helping out after my father died." He was uncomfortably aware that Francie had at some point passed beyond neighborly conversation.

"Oh yes," she said. "Oh my yes. Joe was helping out down there right along."

"Martha and Lily appreciated it."

Francie sat holding her knees with her arms, her eyes closed.

"I'll bet Lily did," she said pleasantly. "He's pretty good."

Everett said nothing. It did not seem possible that he had heard Francie correctly, but the words seemed to hang on in the warm air, as continually and unmistakably audible as a prolonged high note on a piano. Although he had never been good at extracting subtleties from conversations, he tried, now, to imagine something else Francie could mean, to remember a word he had missed that would, once inserted into its proper place in the conversation, clear the entire thing up. But all he could remember was Lily, how she had been this spring (had sat reading night after night until he had asked her to come to bed, had turned away afterwards every time all spring—*what do you care*, she had whispered once, *what did you care when you were in Texas*—had gotten up and brushed her hair and returned to one or another of a series of books on sacred architecture she brought home from the county library); he remembered Lily and he considered Francie.

"Or anyway he used to be," Francie said in the same pleasant voice, unmarred by any trace of alcohol. "I wouldn't know any more. These days I'm just old Joe's cross, or you might say I'm the curse that Joe was born to, his albatross, his middle of the night. His checkbook. You might put it that way."

Francie paused, chewing a piece of ice. "Because frankly, Everett," she added finally, "I like to drink."

Everett said nothing. Beginning immediately to preserve what could be preserved, extending his carefulness of heart, he remembered stories he had heard about wives in wartime, and how it meant nothing. It would mean nothing to him if he could stop thinking about Lily, and think instead of a generalized Wife.

"You might even say I'd *rather* drink. So you *see*."

Everett stood up.

"I have to go, Francie," he said gently.

He had not seen, but he could not much blame Joe.

He had not seen: there was the crux of it. He sat on the sun porch holding the picture of Lily and Martha and Sarah and himself in the reefer coats until the first light came through the east windows, as if by tracing his finger down the crack in that yellowed snapshot he could recoup all their mortal losses, as if by merely looking long enough and hard enough he could walk back into that afternoon, walk back into Lily Knight's house, holding Martha by the hand, and begin again; could run with Martha up from the dock to where Lily cried beneath the lilac in the twilight and be home free.

15

He did not want to see Lily that morning, did not want to face her reddened eyes, her exhausted voice. *You want to know who it was.* She had placed the burden on him; all that had happened was in some way his responsibility. When China Mary came to the house he asked her to take Lily a tray, no orange juice, and to see that she stayed in bed awhile. "She's tired," he said. "The heat gets her. Try to keep Knight and Julie out."

He left the house then for the south fields to watch the last hops come down. Although he normally came to the house for lunch, at noon he instead drove one of the trucks down to a bar on the highway and had two bottles of Lucky Lager and a bologna sandwich wrapped in cellophane. While he drank the second bottle of beer he listened on the bartender's radio to the Yankees beating the Red Sox in the seventh at Fenway Park and did not think about Lily. By seven o'clock, when he started back to the house, the entire ranch was stripped bare of the vines. They had been picking all week, and this was the day he had liked least all of his life: the day the last hops came down, the day summer ended. All he could see as he walked back to the house were the bare poles, the broken strings hanging motionless in the heat, the dust stirred up by the picking machines. Tomorrow they would start the kiln, and during the next four or five days while the hops dried the whole year could go to waste. The kiln and the crop with it could go up in a flash of dry flame, and beyond taking the most elementary precautions there was nothing he could do about it. During the next week the agents from the insurance companies would be dropping by the ranches where the hops were drying, watching their risks; almost every August a kiln burned somewhere in the Valley. Last year it had been on the Messner place, up the Cosumnes River, the night they were to have finished.

Everett walked up to the house alone. Although it had been a custom of his father's to invite the foreman and his wife to the house the night they finished picking, the new foreman (Henry Sears was his name, he had come from down the San Joaquin, near Bakersfield, had arrived on the ranch a few days after Everett came home from Bliss) had driven a truck full of Mexicans into town, leaving before Everett could have spoken to him, even if Everett had intended speaking to him. At any rate Henry Sears would not know the custom since he had not known Everett's father, and anyway he had no wife. Everett did not know what he could have said to him if he had invited him. Everyone had always responded to his father: had liked him, disliked him, talked to him, talked about him; had become in one way or another involved with him. Five hundred and forty-seven people had sent flowers when he died, and every one of them had thought himself involved with John McClellan. He would have known, as Everett did not know, how to talk to Henry Sears. Even Martha would probably know, but Everett did not.

Everett did not even know how to talk to Lily. Although he had no idea now what he could say to her when he got to the house, he would have to make it all right, at least for this week. At some point during the afternoon he had worked out an inarticulate pact, and had invested in it all his un-

139

thinkable prayers: should the hops come through the drying, the child she was carrying was his. It differed from the game Lily had taught Knight to play with the evening star only that in Everett's game the odds were pretty much with him. *Make sure it's the first star you see at night, baby, and don't stop looking until you've finished the wish.* ("That's Venus," he had explained to Knight. "That's a planet, not a star at all. A planet named Venus." "I don't think so," Knight said politely, not looking away from the window; one twilight he waited at his bedroom window fifteen minutes so as not to risk seeing another star first.)

Even before Everett reached the steps to the verandah he heard Martha's laughter through the screened door and windows, and he heard in the particular pitch of that laughter the fact that Ryder Channing was with her. It was not that he disliked Channing. Channing in fact reminded him of Clark McCormack, his roommate at Stanford, and he admired their apparent easiness in the world even as he was vaguely troubled by it. Clark Mc-Cormack had seemed to Everett the center of a vast social network, the pivot for dozens of acquaintances, all of whom were constantly calling or dropping by the Deke house: one to bring Clark the stolen stencil for a mimeographed midterm; another to drop off a box of Glenn Miller records in anticipation of a party; others, usually extraordinarily pretty girls, to leave their convertibles for Clark to use. Like Clark McCormack, Channing conveyed the distinct impression that he could live by his wits alone. They were both free agents, adventurers who turned whatever came their way to some advantage; both pleasant, knowledgeable, and in some final way incomprehensible to Everett. Channing had once told Everett that wherever he was he made a point of getting a guest card to the best country club. It was that kind of thing, something Everett could not put his finger on. Channing had no business around Martha. He might even be married: you never knew about people like Channing. He would have to talk to Martha; he had meant to talk to her ever since he came home in February.

"Everett?" Martha called now from the living room.

He had wanted to see Lily before facing Martha and Channing, and he hesitated, playing for time by looking through the mail on the hall table. There were two pediatricians' bills, a notice of a sale on Germaine Monteil Superglow Solid Powder at the Bon Marché in Sacramento, and a report from the Pi Beta Phi Arrow Shop in Gatlinburg, Tennessee: all addressed to Lily.

"Everett," Martha called again. "Come here."

He walked into the living room, oddly conscious of the muscles moving in his legs. He was struck by the thought, although it did not sound scientific, that if he forgot where the muscles were he would be unable to walk.

"Ryder brought us some good gin for a change and I'm making martinis."

Everett did not look at Channing. "Where's Lily?" he asked with an effort.

Martha was sitting with her back to him, her rather too long hair hanging forward over her bare shoulders. She had on some kind of sun dress which made her look pale and thin, and the hair did not help. Although he had always liked it long she looked healthier when she kept it cut.

"She's in San Francisco," Martha said finally, measuring gin into a pitcher. "I drove her in this morning to get the train. *The City of San Francisco* was two hours late coming in over the mountains and that's why I wasn't here for lunch. I told China Mary to slice the ham," she added. "Was it all right?"

"I wasn't up for lunch." He paused. "You say Lily's gone to the City?"

"She just decided to go as long as it was so hot —you wouldn't *believe* how hot it was in town today, we saw Francie cashing a check in the Wells Fargo and she looked like *wrath*—and you're so busy. Anyway she had to shop. She claimed she didn't have anything to wear to the Horse Show in case you took her to the Fair."

"The Fair," Everett repeated.

Martha looked up. "The Fair starts Thursday. Anyway. She said to tell you she was going to spend all your money at Magnin's."

Sweet Christ. He could hear her saying it. *Tell your brother I'm going to spend all his money at Magnin's.*

"She staying at the St. Francis?"

"I wouldn't think so." Martha handed Channing a glass. "I don't know that she's ever stayed at the St. Francis in her life. I mean has she?"

He did not know. He had thought of the St. Francis only because it was her favorite hotel in San Francisco: *It makes me feel like violets, baby, violets and silver dollars from the Comstock Lode. All that tacky marble.*

"I mean I assumed she was staying with Mrs. Ives," Martha added. "I didn't really think. She said she might call tonight or tomorrow."

Charlotte Ives was Lily's great-aunt, a widow who lived out in the Marina. Lily might be at the St. Francis and she might not, but she would almost certainly not be with Mrs. Ives. *She said she might call tonight or tomorrow.* Wherever she was, he would not be able to reach her. That was all that meant. He knew now that he should have expected her to do this, knew that he would pay all of his life for letting her spend this one hour in some nameless doctor's office. If that was what she was doing, and he did not know what else she could be doing.

She must have been ready to do it before she told him. She had tried him at last and found no help. It occurred to him suddenly that something could go wrong, that everything could go all wrong and they would never let him know.

"What's going to happen to Knight and Julie?" He heard too late the uneven rise in his voice.

Martha looked at Channing, who shrugged, stood up, and walked over to the window.

"Now, Everett," Martha said finally. "Knight and Julie are at this moment asleep. China Mary has fed them and I have twice recounted for them the story of the little engine that could. Ryder has obtained at Knight's request three glasses of water, and perhaps you might—when you feel up to it—make certain that Julie has not misplaced her stuffed raccoon, which seems to do for Julie what Luminal does for Julie's Mommy. Now I would assume that we could carry on in this vein until Mommy's *return*."

Everett saw that Channing was watching him, and forced himself to smile. He was irritated, as he frequently was now, by Martha's tone: he was sure that if she could hear herself she would stop it, but did not know how to tell her that.

"We got the last of the hops down today," he said finally.

"Ah," Martha said to Channing. "We celebrate the harvest, chez McClellan."

"Some harvest festival." Channing smiled. "When the harvester won't have a drink."

"We call him the grim reaper." Martha blew Everett a kiss.

"You're wearing too much lipstick." He could at least tell her that. But as he watched her turn away, trying to bite the color off her lips, he was sorry that he had said anything.

He picked up his drink. There was nothing to do now but wait for Lily to call or come home, get

143

through the next day or so without letting Martha see that something was wrong, that everything had gone all wrong. She should have waited. He would have helped her. He swore to himself that he would have helped her had she waited. It might even have been his, and it would not have mattered much finally if it had not been. What real difference would it have made: it would have been Lily's, and Lily was his, and as far as that went Joe Templeton was a distant cousin of his, distant enough for Everett to seldom remember it but close enough to think about now. They went to the same weddings and funerals, which was what mattered.

"You should have gone down with Lily," Channing said now to Marth, filling his glass from the pitcher. "You look like hell."

"The heat bothers Martha." Everett wondered how much longer Channing would be at Mather Field now that the war was over.

"It sure doesn't bother that Lily-maid," Channing said. "She hasn't looked so good all year."

"She's tired," Everett said. "I don't care how she looks to you, she's tired and she needs a rest."

"She's your bride, Coop."

It was a great little thing with Channing, the Gary Cooper routine with Everett and especially the "that Lily-maid" business with Lily. When they had gone, the four of them, to Lake Tahoe three weeks before, he had kept it up all weekend, needling Lily unobtrusively at first but at last so constantly that it had begun not only to set Everett on edge but to humiliate Martha: Everett had watched her trying to divert Channing's attention from Lily, the strain on her face more and more visible as she began talking, too loudly, about things neither Channing nor Lily could know about, deliberately excluding them from recollections of how Sarah had behaved before her first dance, how China

Mary had feared a Great Dane they had kept for three weeks a long time ago. But *aren't we happy,* Lily had said, and despite Channing and despite Martha they had been: he had not been away with Lily since before he left for Fort Lewis, and they drove to all the places they had gone so often during the first year of their marriage: Reno, Carson, down into Glenwood. In the shining clarity of that afternoon in the mountains, the air so clear and sharp and the horizons clean and distant, it had seemed to Everett for a while that they could have again what he had wanted them to have, could lie in bed and laugh, neither accusing the other of anything. Their betrayal of each other (for had he not betrayed her in his mind, wished to stay away, wanted no trouble, *you don't seem to realize there's a war going on*) seemed for a few hours that Saturday afternoon and evening a simple dislocation of war, a disturbance no more lasting than the wash from a stone thrown in the river. They had stayed Saturday night in a house which belonged to one of Lily's cousins, a brown-shingled place on the north shore of the lake, and they had gambled on the Nevada line until about two o'clock in the morning. Although Lily would not play ("Women don't ever win, Everett, can't you see. Because winners have to believe they can affect the dice"), she stayed close to the table, watching over his shoulder, reaching now and then into his pocket for a cigarette or change for a drink, playing idly with a stack of silver dollars he had given her but never taking her eyes from the play on the table. He had tried once again to explain the odds to her, but she claimed to understand nothing at all about the game: she liked only to watch the movement on the table, the chips and the silver and the dice and the rakes the dealers used. *Let the little lady roll,* the dealer said gallantly (it was a slow table), and Everett

remembered now how she had leaned over the table
and closed her eyes and thrown with one hand,
come seven baby, while she clutched his arm with
the other, delighted to be playing with the grown-
ups; she put two dollars on the line and her yellow
sweater fell to the floor and she had been his
child bride all over again. All that evening he had
pretended with her, had played her game because
that was the way he wanted it too, and later they
swam in the lake, the water so clear that with only
the moonlight and the handful of lights strung out
on the dock he could make out rocks thirty feet
below the surface, so cold that swimming was
like grappling with dry ice. Lily had turned white
with cold, her pale tan fading at the first burning
touch of water; long after they came up from the
lake she sat shivering on the stone hearth, wrapped
in a towel. He had found it absurdly endearing that
she should warm her nightgown in front of the fire
before she put it on. *Keep me warm, baby,* she had
cried out later in bed, and he had forced her head
sideways and her mouth into the pillow as she moved
in his arms because he did not want Channing, in
the next room, to hear her. *Keep me baby please
keep me.* Well, he had not. He had lost her, and
now she was in some San Francisco hotel room by
herself and maybe it had happened already and
maybe it had gone all wrong and she was dying
there by herself (women died from abortions, you
saw it in the paper every so often, you heard about
it, and whether the odds were with her or not
she would be afraid of it) and he was here drinking with Martha and Ryder Channing as if it did
not matter what happened to Lily. It was all right
for Martha to sit here. Martha could not know; had
she known, she would have kept Lily from going.
But he had known all along, and he sat here now
with Ryder Channing, and it was all mixed up in

some way with the war, and Sarah's not being home, and people like Ryder Channing. Not that it was Channing's fault.

The future was being made, he heard Channing say at some point that evening, right here in California. Starting now. Channing had the hunch they were in on the ground floor of the biggest boom this country had ever seen. Talk about your gold rush. And he wasn't the only one who believed in Northern California. Just one example, the Keller Brothers believed in Northern California to the tune of five million berries.

"The Keller Brothers," Everett said. "I don't believe I know them."

The Keller Brothers, Channing explained patiently, were developers. Los Angeles developers who believed in Northern California, in the Valley specifically, to the tune of five million smackeroos. Which they were putting into the Natomas District.

"I never heard of any Kellers in the Natomas," Everett said.

With what appeared to be infinite restraint, Channing inspected and crumpled three empty cigarette packages before answering. "They aren't *in* the Natomas right now. They want to de*velo*p the Natomas."

"Who's putting up the money? How can they raise five million dollars on land they haven't got?"

"Those sweethearts could raise five million dollars with a plot plan on the back of a goddamn napkin. Anyway," Channing added, apparently abandoning his effort to justify the Kellers' ways to Everett, "that's just one example. The point is we're sitting right here on the ground floor with the button pushed go."

"Cut yourself in, Channing, it's a free country, plenty of room for everybody."

Everett realized that he must be drunk; he did not know what Channing had on his mind, but resented the "we." Martha was asleep on the couch, her head on Channing's lap. Lily had not called; he had known she would not. A few hours ago he had tried seven San Francisco hotels, the only seven he could think of, as well as the Claremont and the Durant in Berkeley. No one was registered as McClellan at any one of the nine. There had been a Miss Knight at the Mark Hopkins but when Everett got her on the line it had not been Lily at all. It had been some woman who wanted to know if she had met him with the National Cash Register boys and hung up immediately when he said she had not.

Channing seemed not to have heard him. "The point is we need everything out here. Absolutely *tabula rasa*. Christ, within the next ten, fifteen years somebody could make a fortune in the *agency* business."

"You mean real estate? Insurance?" Everett made a determined effort to follow Channing. "Or automobiles?"

"I mean *ad*vertising. Advertising agencies. You think branch offices are going to be enough for long, you don't realize what we're sitting on out here."

Everett had never known anyone who worked for an advertising agency, and although he had from time to time read articles in *Fortune* about Bruce Barton and Albert Lasker, he had no clear idea of what people who worked for advertising agencies actually did. When he thought of an advertising agency at all, which was not very often, he thought about Albert Lasker sitting around an office looking out into the falling snow and thinking about toothpaste, maybe even squeezing toothpaste onto a toothbrush. The next panel in his mind showed an electric light bulb over Albert Lasker's head and the single word "Irium." The falling snow was for some reason an integral part of the picture, and Everett had never considered it happening in California. Albert Lasker and Irium belonged to another world, a world teeming with immigrants and women who spent the day in art galleries and elevator operators who called you by name if you were a crack *Life* photographer. There was a kind of movie that always began that way, an elevator operator saying good morning to a crack *Life* photographer. They never called it *Life* but it was all part of the same goddamn world and it was always the same goddamn elevator operator.

The elevator operator brought him back to Channing, who had claimed to be sitting on the ground floor with the button pushed go. Speaking of go, he began to wonder why Channing did not go home to Mather Field or wherever it was he slept and he began to wonder why Martha was asleep with her head in Channing's lap. Picking up her sweater from the floor, he moved to spread it across her bare legs.

She shifted in her sleep, flinging one arm back across Channing's knee. "Ry-der?" she whispered.

"Go back to sleep," Channing ordered.

Apparently reassured, she withdrew her arm. Everett dropped her sweater and poured what was left of a bottle of bourbon into his glass. They did not seem to be drinking martinis any more and there was only a puddle of warm water in the ice bucket.

"You're like a goddamn radio announcer," he said suddenly to Channing. "You'd make one hell of a radio announcer."

"Maybe so," Channing said amiably. "Maybe I'll look into it."

"Charm. That's what you got, Channing, is charm. C-H-A-R-M."

He could not now think why he had turned on Channing, but because he was now, whatever the reason, more or less committed to it, he stood up, rocking a little on the balls of his feet while he watched Channing.

Channing stood up, waking Martha, who lay rubbing her eyes with one hand and trying to smooth her hair with the other.

"What is it?" she said, her eyes still closed.

"Your brother," Channing said, "could use a sandwich."

"Screw a sandwich. I've just been telling your gentleman friend, in words of one syllable, that he's not in your class."

"*Everett.*" Martha stood up, tucking her dress into her belt without taking her eyes from his face. "You shut your mouth, you hear me?"

"All right," he said. "I'm sorry."

She meant it, all right: he recognized that the tremor in her voice was not for Channing's ears alone. *She's in thrall,* Lily had laughed at the beginning of the summer. "Haven't you ever read in books about women in thrall? Martha's in thrall." "What does that mean out of books?" he had asked. "It means he's the first man she ever slept with," Lily said, not laughing then, and he had slapped her, had hit her across the face with all the revulsion he had felt that night on the terrace toward Francie Templeton. *He's pretty good. Or anyway he used to be, I wouldn't know.*

When he started upstairs Martha was still standing there with Channing. She did not move her eyes from Everett, and she shook her head, almost imperceptibly, as if she wanted Channing to stop stroking her hair but was not really aware he was doing it. For an instant Everett wanted to go back down and get her, tell her to pick up her sweater and a fresh bottle of bourbon and get in the car, tell her that they were going to San Francisco to bring Lily home. But he did not know where to find Lily, and he was afraid that Martha would begin screaming if he even paused on the stairs. He had not heard her scream since they were children, but it was a scream he had never forgotten, all panic and blind hatred, so piercing it was almost sweet, and as he looked down at Martha standing rigid in Channing's casual embrace it seemed to him that he could almost see the scream beginning in her eyes.

The bed was littered with things Lily had dropped when she was packing: her hairbrush, a satin case with stockings spilling from it, her book of telephone numbers, an alligator handbag he had given her on her last birthday. He looked in the bag and found nothing but pennies, tobacco crumbs, a couple of the silver dollars she always carried ("for luck, Everett baby"), and an old shopping list: *Arden hand lotion, white socks for Knight, birthday for E., two curtain rods for back bedroom, call Mother about platter.*

He brushed it all to the floor and pulled back the sheet. There was a note scribbled on a page from a calendar: *Everett darling I'll try to make everything all right. Please. L.* Well, no one could say Lily had not hit her stride with this one. Notes under the sheet.

He crumpled the note and dropped it, then bent to retrieve it because he did not want China Mary to find it when she came to clean in the morning. He sat then on the edge of the unmade bed and absently rubbed the satin tie of Lily's nightgown across his face and listened to the faint sound of the phonograph from downstairs.

> *Give me land, lots of land*
> *Under starry skies a-bove*
> *Don't fence me in ...*

151

Well to hell with Martha. Let her make her own bed. With a goddamn radio announcer.

16

Keep me baby please keep me, she had said that night with the fire down low and her hair still wet with the lake water: touched, Everett had accepted it as a trust. Or anyway he had wanted to, had longed to believe that she meant it, even as he knew that it was something women said; even as he remembered others who had said that or almost that.

Not that there had ever been, for Everett, that many others: the first had been Doris Jeanne Coe, Doris Jeanne of the glass-blue eyes, the lank blond hair, the bad teeth, and the smile that seemed to Everett at sixteen infinitely perverse. Two years older than Everett, Doris Jeanne was behind in school not from native inability, which had never held anyone back in the county consolidated school system, but simply because she had stayed out of school two years when her family moved out from Oklahoma in 1933. Her mother was tubercular and Doris Jeanne, the oldest child, stayed home to help with her brother and four sisters; their father used to be a farmer but now, according to Doris Jeanne, he fixed things, and Doris Jeanne thought California was strictly a drag.

Everett met her the week she enrolled, when they were assigned to debate the topic "John C. Frémont: Opportunist or Patriot?" She was wearing, he would remember always, a fuchsia-pink sweater with a harp embroidered in gilt threads over her left breast, a tight black gabardine skirt, and a coat which made Everett forever uneasy about Doris Jeanne, the coat about which Lily later said, when he told her about it one night in bed, "Didn't it make you cry? Didn't it make you want to cry for the world every time you looked at it?" Although he had laughed at Lily, there was little doubt in his mind that the coat had indeed lent his entire relationship with Doris Jeanne Coe certain aspects of a social passion play. A hand-me-down from someone for whom her father worked, it was a camel's-hair polo coat with an I. Magnin label, and she let it out of her sight so rarely that two of the buttons were missing and the pocket bore a year-old Coca-Cola stain.

After class, Everett had stopped Doris Jeanne and asked her which position she preferred, a phrasing which afforded her a great deal of unconcealed delight. When Everett explained, blushing, that he meant did she want to argue John C. Frémont was a Patriot or did she want to argue John C. Frémont was an Opportunist, Doris Jeanne looked at him a long time, slipped the polo coat off her shoulders, removed from her large red shoulder bag a blue vial of *Evening in Paris Eau de Cologne*, and dabbed the stopper behind her ears and in the crooks of her elbows. Then she replaced the vial, snapped the bag closed, and asked Everett who John C. Frémont was. After he had told her, she smiled crookedly, arranged the bag on her shoulder, and said, "It don't make me no never-mind, honey."

Mostly because he would have preferred it himself, Everett offered Doris Jeanne the "Patriot" position, and she eventually stood up before the class with her polo coat on, daintily applied *Evening in Paris* to her wrists in full view of twenty-four entranced students and Mrs. Nalley, the English teacher, and presented an original defense in which Jessie Benton and John C. Frémont emerged curiously as refugees from some early-day phenomenon not unlike the Dust Bowl. Although she had taken a clear fancy to the Frémonts, she could not escape the impression that they had first entered California in a secondhand Ford, and the entire exercise left Mrs. Nalley so unnerved that she excused her classes for the rest of the day.

The debate was otherwise without incident, and Everett did not speak to Doris Jeanne again until the class picnic, when her brother, who played baseball with Everett, urged him to sneak off to the river and share a half-gallon of valley red with him and Doris Jeanne, who was included in the first place only because she had negotiated the purchase. After a while Alfred Coe went to sleep over beyond an Indian mound, and Doris Jeanne, with lifeless dispatch, took care of Everett. A few days later she cornered him in the hall at school, pressed up against him as he stood backed against his open locker, and began playing lovingly with his collar; she wanted to do it again out behind the backstop during seventh period, when there were no teams on the field, but Everett hesitated, and Doris Jeanne said he was strictly a drag and could stew in his own juice. Later that semester, after the intercession of her brother, Everett wrote a term paper for Doris Jeanne on the subject "Will Semple Green: Father of Irrigation in the Northern Valley." Unhappily neither Mrs. Nalley nor the vice-principal who was called in as arbitrator could be persuaded that "Will Semple Green: Father of Irrigation in the Northern Valley" was entirely Doris Jeanne's work, and in the pressure of this controversy Doris Jeanne quit school. That she never named Everett made him admire her, and feel obscurely guilty that he had failed to do a more convincing job for her. Several years later he saw a picture of her in the *San Francisco Examiner;* described as a "curvaceous model and sometime waitress at an

El Camino Real supper club," she had instituted a paternity suit against a football player with a Polish name. Although she had changed her name to Dori Lee, Everett recognized the picture, and wondered if she would remember him. He thought not.

After Doris Jeanne it had been nobody: necking in cars on hot summer nights with the back doors open so you could lie with your legs out and sometimes even lying almost naked and covered with sweat, but never doing it; once or twice or three times even lying in somebody's bed at parties given by boys whose parents were away, lying naked under the sheet with girls who had been drinking bourbon and Seven-Up and wanted to go to sleep, lying there for hours and kissing girls who probably would have done it had anyone insisted, but Everett never insisted; it was not, as Lily would have said, much his style.

Then there had been, at Stanford, a couple of girls who required less insistence: Annis McMahon, whom everyone else called alternately "Annie" and "Pooh" but whom Everett always called Annis, wishing upon her the dignity implied by her tall, cold, blond good looks. He liked to watch her play tennis, and long before he knew her he developed the habit of walking back to the Deke house from his eleven o'clock class by way of the courts where she played every noon. When it reached a point where he thought he wanted to watch her play tennis for the rest of his life, he asked Clark McCormack to introduce him to her. Once introduced, he called her three times a day, played tennis with her every afternoon, took her to the movies every Sunday night, and in May of his sophomore year, still determined that she should be the girl he had hoped she would be in the face of mounting evidence to the contrary, he drove Annis McMahon down to Santa Cruz on two successive weekends. (On the third, he found out later, Clark

McCormack drove her down to Santa Cruz.) They lay in a motel room with a mission tile table and a framed color photograph of Bridal Veil Falls at Yosemite, and she told him in the high nasal voice which had been his first disappointment about the difficulty she was having arranging her courses to obtain her teaching credential at the same time she received her degree in physical education and therapy. She got up from the bed every time as if she were getting out of a shower, ready, in a companionable way he found dispiriting in the extreme, to discuss it; stretched her incredible golden arms, lit a cigarette, opened all the blinds, and wrapped herself in his shirt, a gambit which might have seemed more winning had his shirt not fit her almost perfectly.

The next year there was Naomi Kahn, a Jewish girl from Beverly Hills whose grades were good, whose clothes smelled always as if they had just come from Bullock's-Wilshire boxes (as a matter of fact they had not: Naomi ordered all her clothes from Bergdorf Goodman in New York), and whose mother and father were both, as she put it, in the Industry. She told Everett that her deepest wishes for her mother and father involved their abandoning screenwriting in favor of writing something like *Winterset*, and when that day came she would be more than happy, in answer to Everett's query, to stop ordering her clothes from Bergdorf Goodman in New York, although for Everett's information, Maxwell Anderson was not exactly on the relief rolls. Everett ought to get around more. Once the Kahns came up to Stanford to visit Naomi, and Mrs. Kahn later wrote that she considered Everett divine, an honest-to-Christ set piece, whereupon Naomi's ardor for Everett began to cool. One night toward the end of their junior year she announced that she was driving to Reno the next day to marry a Berkeley graduate student who was active in the Young Communist League; the Kahns, after getting the marriage annulled, transferred Naomi to Sarah Lawrence. Although Everett never knew what happened to Naomi after that, he noticed the Kahns' names from time to time among the credits on B comedies, and years later he read in *Time* that they were up before the Tenney Committee for having participated in the October 1943 Writers' Congress at UCLA. They were listed as members of several oddly named organizations the function of which Everett did not entirely understand, were later indicted in Washington for contempt of Congress, and Everett reflected that Naomi, wherever she was, must have approved at last.

Actually Everett had liked Naomi Kahn: he had liked the way her clothes smelled and liked the slightly derisive way she went to bed; she did it exactly the way she wrote out a midterm or drove a car, with a style and efficiency he had never observed in any of the girls with whom he had grown up, and he loved it. He sometimes thought he even loved her, usually when she had gone to spend the weekend with her parents in Palm Springs and he was left with the alternatives of sitting around the house drinking beer or calling up somebody like Annis McMahon. Palo Alto the winter of 1939 seemed full of girls like Annis McMahon, and Everett's appreciation of Naomi's singular virtues grew until he actually regretted, for something like four days after she eloped with the Young Communist from Berkeley, that he had not asked her to marry him.

Nonetheless, Naomi Kahn had not been, any more than Annis McMahon or for that matter Doris Jeanne Coe had been, someone with whom he could have lived on the ranch. During those four days when he wished he had married Naomi he never once thought of living anywhere with her: they were always driving someplace together, or he was putting her on an airplane, or they were registering at the Fairmont in

San Francisco and she had on a black hat with a veil.

In the end Naomi had been just like Annis Mc-Mahon and a dozen or so girls he had known not as well: something he had tried and abandoned, before the effort became too strenuous, and none of it had to do with Lily. Even as he imagined himself registering at the Fairmont with Naomi Kahn, Everett knew without thinking that what he would do was live on the ranch with Lily Knight, knew it so remotely that if he had heard, during the years he rarely saw her, that she had married someone else he would have wished her well and gone on thinking about Naomi Kahn at the Fairmont, and only somewhere in the unused part of his mind would he have begun wondering, with an urgency he would not have understood, what he was going to do with the rest of his life. Lily required no commitment: Lily was already there.

It had not occurred to him that he could lose her (had not occurred to him even that he wanted her) until the week he came home from Stanford and saw her sitting on her father's terrace in a faded pink dress, the late afternoon sun on her dusty bare feet and a large safety pin in place of a missing screw on her sunglass frames. It had seemed to him then that to risk losing her would be to risk losing Martha and Sarah and himself as well, that she alone could retrieve and keep for him the twenty-one years he had already spent. Convinced that he could ill afford to leave her untended for even that one night, he fell asleep finally with his clothes on, a cigarette still burning in the ashtray on his bedroom window sill, and when he woke in the morning he set out immediately to secure for himself the haven of her faded pink dress, her bare feet, the safety pin in her sunglasses.

As far as the safety pin went, it remained in her
sunglasses until the summer she was pregnant with
Julie, when he told her one night, irritated partly because she had just uncovered a grocery bill she had
lost three months before and partly because she had
dragged a sheet down to the sun porch the night before and slept there until ten o'clock but irritated
mostly because it had been 105° for three days and
she had accused him of not loving her as her father
had loved her, that the safety pin in her sunglasses
summed up all her unattractive habits, her sloppi-
ness of mind, her inability to accomplish the routine
tasks that could be done with one hand by any of
the girls he had known at Stanford. She had gone upstairs without speaking. When he came to bed she
had pretended to be asleep, and she had gotten up
at seven the next morning to drive into Sacramento.
She returned at noon with a new screw in her sunglasses and with, as well, a book called *The Man-
agerial Revolution* in which she later read the first
and last chapters (she pretended to have read it all
but he read it himself and saw that she had not), an
album of French language records which as far as
he knew she never played, eight dollars' worth of
closet bags and boxes, and a large account book in
which she wrote down, for two weeks, the exact
amounts both she and China Mary spent on food and
household supplies. The book was in fact labeled
"Food and Household Supplies," and she had shown
it proudly to Martha. The first day's entry, Martha
reported with a degree of admiration, began with an
itemized list showing the unit prices, the amount
saved by buying in quantity, and a tax breakdown
wherever a tax was involved, on twenty-four bottles
of beer, twelve cans of mixed carrots and peas, twelve
cans of puréed liver, four quarts of milk, two cartons
of Lucky Strikes, six tins of smoked oysters, and fifteen cans of Campbell's Soup; five consommé, five

vegetable-beef, five cream of chicken. Totaled, these items came to $18.53, and were followed by an entry which read "Etc.—$27 (about)." When Martha asked what the $27 represented, Lily, absorbed in contemplating the neatness of her figuring, had shrugged. "You know. A mop handle. Things." After Lily had abandoned "Food and Household Supplies," Everett tore the entry from the book, carried it around with him for a couple of weeks and finally put it in a drawer where he kept his Stanford diploma, a clipping about a no-hit game he had pitched in high school, and a letter from Martha describing the only 4-H meeting she ever attended.

The truth was simply that he would not have known what to do with a wife who knew what to do with a book labeled "Food and Household Supplies": it was not Everett's idea of a wife's function. Although he was not sure what his idea of a wife's function was, he knew that Lily had been closest to fulfilling it when she had been trying least. She simply did not know how. She would concentrate upon the details while the essence eluded her, unable to see that one entry in the Pillsbury Bake-Off did not make a Mrs. America.

There as everywhere, Lily failed, even as she tried with pathetic concentration, to apprehend what was expected of her. The most insignificant social encounter was for Lily, as Martha had pointed out at dinner one night this spring, fraught with the apprehension of possible peril.

"I mean Lily can't say simple things like 'thank you' or 'I'd rather not' or 'please may I have more coffee,'" Martha had added, turning then to Lily. "I don't know what's wrong with you but you can't."

"Nothing's wrong with her," Everett said, although he saw Martha's point. He had only a week before learned that Lily was allergic to strawberries, which he had seen her eating with apparent delight innumerable times. "I thought your father liked them," she said, in explanation.

"Everett, it's *true*. I'm not being mean to Lily, I'm only observing something interesting. Somebody holds the door open for Lily in a hardware store, and she thinks she has a very complex situation on her hands."

Martha poured the rest of a bottle of wine into Lily's glass and sat back, watching Lily. "First Lily says thank you. Then she wonders: did he hear her? If he didn't, was he thinking how rude she was? Assuming that he heard her, was just 'thank you' enough? If not, what more? On the other hand maybe 'thank you' was too much. Maybe she should have just smiled. Maybe he thought she'd been forward. In fact maybe she'd been mistaken in thinking he was holding the door for her *at all*. Possibly he'd been holding it for someone behind her, his wife, or an old lady. If that was the case, thanking him made her look *a perfect fool*, and now she can't remember why she came to the hardware store in the first place, and every now and then all day she thinks about how she might have handled it. I mean the *crises* Lily faces from day to day."

Lily had blown out the candles on the table and transparently misunderstood Martha: "I don't think good manners are ever amiss," she said. But later, when she was brushing her hair and he was working at the card table he had covered with tax records, he looked up and saw that she was crying, crying and brushing her hair as if she wanted to brush it out. He had put aside the depreciation schedule and picked her up in his arms, the hairbrush still in her hand. Her voice muffled against his shoulder, she explained that she wanted to be like other people, wanted to be able to talk to people. "You're shy," he said. "There's nothing wrong with being shy." There was, Lily sobbed, something wrong with being shy when

you were going on twenty-four years old, and anyway she was not shy, she was simply no good around
people and that was that. He had lain on the bed with
her and the hairbrush and told her that she was not
to talk that way, that she was not other people. She
was, he added, turning out the light, his baby. It occurred to Everett later that he had in that commonplace endearment put his finger on some of Lily's
virtues and certain of her failings.

17

Lily came home from San Francisco on a Greyhound
bus crowded with Mexican pickers and sailors. From
San Francisco to Vallejo she sat next to a sailor who
was going to meet his girl in Salt Lake City. She
lived with her folks in Salt Lake but Frisco, he explained, was their lucky town. They had met there,
in a gin mill on Market Street, four days before he
shipped out in 1943. When she promised to wait had
been the A-1 moment in his life, and the second A-1
moment had been a week before on the U.S.S.
Chester when he got his first sight in two years of the
Golden Gate Bridge. There had been fog in the morning and when the fog broke he saw it there, shining
way off in the distance like it wasn't attached to anything. The band on the well deck had started in on
"California Here I Come" and everybody had belted
it out along with the band and it might sound cornball to her but it made him want to sit down and
bawl like a baby. Lily began to cry, struck by the
superiority of his appreciations to her own, and the
sailor said wait a minute, hold your horses, it wasn't

sad, honey, it was like women crying at weddings.
She looked to him like the kind who cried at weddings. It was like that. When the sailor got off at
Vallejo to wait for the Salt Lake express Lily wished
him good luck and watched him covertly through the
window. He was sitting on his duffel bag reading a
comic book and eating a Milky Way, and she wanted
to get off the bus and give him her garnet ring for
his girl, but did not know how to go about it. It was
not until the bus had rolled out of the station that
Lily remembered that at any rate the garnet ring
had been Everett's grandmother's and was therefore
not in the strictest sense hers to give.

From Vallejo to Sacramento she sat next to a woman who was a part-time cashier at a drive-in across
the highway from Hotel El Rancho, west of Sacramento. The woman had been in Vallejo visiting her
daughter, who had a nice place, not large but fixed
up cute, above a florist's shop on Tennessee Street.
No doubt Lily knew the florist's shop. No? The woman had thought surely she would because they did all
the society weddings in Vallejo, it was very well-
known.

Regretful that she had not pretended to recognize
the florist's name and anxious that the woman not
think she had been trying to snub her, Lily hurried
to surmount what seemed to her an impasse by asking if the daughter were married. Well, not exactly.
It seemed that Sue Ann's husband, a seaman first
class but a bastard from the word go, had got his at
Okinawa—Sue Ann had been just about set to blow
the whistle anyway, as far as that went—and Sue
Ann was now supporting their six-year-old son, Billy
Jack, by car-hopping at Stan's off U.S. 40.

The woman paused, and Lily quickly assured her
that she knew Stan's. (As it happened, she did, because when Everett first went away she had listened
nights on the radio to *Stan's Private Line*, and had

even wondered academically from time to time
whether or not she could have made the grade among
the leather-jacketed *jeunesse dorée* who gathered
nightly at Stan's to eat Double-Burgers and dedicate
songs to one another.) The woman ignored her. Naturally Sue Ann got asked on a lot of dates—she was
about Lily's age but a real doll, built like Rita Hay-
worth. You could hardly tell them apart except for
the hair, and nobody would ever convince her that
Rita's was natural anyway. But don't get her
started on that. So Sue Ann had been playing the field,
but now she had a once-in-a-lifetime opportunity
to marry a young fellow who in turn had a once-in-a-
lifetime opportunity to wrap up the Kirby Party fran-
chise for the entire Greater Vallejo area. You know,
Kirby Parties. You invite a congenial group to your
home and serve a little something, doughnuts and soft
drinks, and then the Kirby representative comes and
demonstrates the vacuum cleaners and all. You get a
bonus gift for getting a certain number to come and
you get in a little girl-talk besides. If Lily wasn't on
to Kirby Parties she ought to take Fred's number and
call him the next time she was in the area, providing
his deal went through. Anyway. The only catch was
that Fred didn't know about Billy Jack. Or rather he
knew about Billy Jack but believed him to be Sue
Ann's little brother. She had warned Sue Ann it was
a crazy mad thing to do, trying to pass off Billy Jack
as her own mother's change-of-life baby, but what
could you do. Sue Ann had her right to happiness as
much as the next one. What did Lily think.

As the bus rolled out of the Coast Range and
into the heat of the Valley, Lily stopped thinking altogether, lulled by the even rhythm of the telephone
poles against field after dry yellow field, by the
regular rise and fall of the woman's voice, by the
grinding and shifting of gears as the bus swung off
the highway and down the streets of towns in which

she seemed to have spent her life: Fairfield-Suisun,
Vacaville, Dixon. Although she did not suppose
that she had driven through any one of the towns
more than on the outside twenty times, they had
about them an imprint which to perceive once,
especially if that once was on an August afternoon
when the streets looked abandoned and the frame
buildings as fragile as tinder, was to possess forever. She could close her eyes and tick it off: the
Bank of America building, the W.T. Grant store,
the Lincoln-Mercury agency; the lone woman in a
shapeless dress and flowered straw hat, sitting on
the porch of the hotel until her husband was through
in town. Off the main street there would be a few
blocks of houses, three-storey houses in need of
paint, each fronted by a patch of dry grass, maybe
a tricycle overturned on the cracked concrete walk.
The blinds would be drawn and there would not
be any people, anywhere. The afternoon heat could
bleach those towns so clean that the houses and the
buildings seemed always on the verge of demateri-
alizing; there was the sense that to close one's eyes
on a Valley town was to risk opening them a moment later on dry fields, the sun bleaching out the
last traces of habitation, a flowered straw hat, a
neon advertisement which had blinked a moment
before from a wall no longer visible: *More Yield
from Every Acre with Seeds from Northrup-King.*

It was a great comfort, watching the towns come
and go through the tinted window of the Greyhound
bus. The heat drained the distinctions from things—
marriage and divorce and new curtains and over-
drafts at the bank, all the same—and Lily could not
at the moment imagine any preoccupation strong
enough to withstand the summer. At least any preoccupation of hers; Sue Ann, now, was another
case. There would be nothing ambiguous about Sue
Ann's responses, nothing ambivalent about her wants:

Sue Ann would have kissed Joe Templeton goodbye with no second thoughts. Sue Ann's problems, unlike her own, offered the compression, the foreshortening of art; her own were inadvertent, makeshift affairs at best, and there with her head resting against the bus window she could not think why she had gone to San Francisco or why she had caused a scene with Everett or how she had gotten pregnant in the first place by somebody she did not much like or why, the heart of the matter, she had thought it made any difference.

When the bus arrived in Sacramento at six o'clock, however, she emerged as if from a darkened theater into the sudden glare, the sudden presence of pople, and the sudden recollection of why it made any difference. Standing on the loading platform, holding her raincoat and her overnight bag, she could remember just about everything except why she had chosen a four-hour bus ride over two air-conditioned hours in a Southern Pacific club car. For reasons now lost to her, it had seemed in San Francisco the thing to do; had seemed the way of the Cross.

I've been worried, Joe said when she called him from the bus station. There seemed to her reproof in every syllable.

"I'm sorry. I just got into town." She did not want to talk to Joe and did not know why she had called him, except that she had promised to.

"I worried," he repeated. "I couldn't sleep. I yelled at Francie."

"You yelled at Francie." She leaned against the wall of the telephone booth and tried to open the glass door with her foot, succeeding only in catching her heel between the door and the jamb.

"How are you?"

"I'm all right." Working her foot free, she let the shoe drop. "I'm fine."

"You sound pretty good."

"How did you expect me to sound?"

In the prolonged silence which followed she reached to retrieve her shoe and saw that she had snagged her stocking on the lock of her overnight case.

"*Damn it.*" She jammed her foot into her shoe and brushed her damp hair from her face.

"What's the matter?"

"Nothing's the matter. I was just putting my shoe on."

"Putting your shoe on? Why did you have your shoes off?"

"No reason, Joe, no reason. I'm just down here in the Greyhound bus station barefoot, see."

"Cut it out."

"I'm sorry."

After a silence Joe said tentatively: "You saw the doctor?"

"Yes."

"How did it go?"

"It was fine. Everything was just fine."

"I told you it would be."

She did not say anything.

"He didn't charge you any more, did he?"

"No. It went all right."

"I told you it would. He didn't want any more money?"

"*No,* I said." She was irritated by his preoccupation with the money; it had been her five hundred dollars in the first place. To get the cash she had sold ten shares of an oil stock her father had given her as a wedding present, and she did not like to be reminded of it. Although she had not thought of it before, there was something about Joe's inability to put his hands on five hundred dol-

167

lars without Francie's knowing about it which summed up all his rather aggressive weaknesses.

"I would have cut off my right arm if I could have gone down there for you."

"Now you cut it out," she said, and was immediately touched with remorse: if he was dishonest so was she. If she were honest she would not even be talking to him on the telephone.

"There was nothing you could do," she added, ashamed.

"It's been pretty bad. You know how bad I felt about it." He paused. "Maybe I could see you tomorrow."

"No," she said rapidly. "I mean I can't. I have to rest."

"I guess you better." He sounded relieved. "I just thought you'd want to talk to someone."

"Oh Christ. No. I don't want to talk to someone. I don't want to talk to anyone."

She clicked off the connection with her finger and dropped the receiver in her lap. Her silk suit was damp with perspiration and stained not only with dust but tea, spilled at the counter in the San Francisco bus station. She should have let the waitress sponge it off but her bus had already been called and she had not wanted to run; she had been afraid that if she moved too quickly the bleeding would begin again.

If she had not wanted to talk to Joe, she certainly did not want to talk to Everett. Nonetheless, she had to get home and felt incapable of explaining to anyone else what she was doing with her suitcase in the Greyhound bus station. She had meant to take the river bus out to the ranch, but the drivers had gone on strike. If it was not one thing it was another. Fumbling in her bag for a cigarette, she dropped two coins in the telephone and dialed her mother's number. When her mother answered she felt tears rising, hung up without saying anything, and smoked the cigarette down to her fingers. *I would have cut off my right arm,* she thought viciously. He knew what he could cut off. She blew her nose, snapped her bag shut, and called the ranch.

Everett answered on the first ring. "Sweet Jesus, Lily. You all right?"

"I'm fine."

"Where the hell are you?"

She hesitated. Where was she. It was the giveaway, the proof of how she felt, the evidence that she would never be the kind who could carry things off.

"At the Greyhound bus station," she said at last.

"You fool," he said softly. "You goddamn little ass."

She drank some warm Coca-Cola in a sticky paper cup and went outside the station to wait for Everett. At six-thirty everything seemed still: the traffic had already thinned out and the thick branches of the plane trees hung heavy and motionless over the street. In front of the loading platform a sailor was trying to pick up two girls; both the girls wore white peasant blouses, pulled down off their shoulders, and one had her hair tied up in a magenta scarf. When the sailor, teasing, pulled off the scarf, Lily saw that the girl's head was covered with pin curls. Snatching the scarf back, the girl struck an exaggerated pose with it, and they all laughed. They seemed to be having a very good time and it tired Lily to think that she was probably no older than they were.

Depressed, she turned her attention across the street to a parking lot where a few men, apparently late from their offices and obviously all acquainted, were picking up their cars. She reflected sadly that they would no doubt arrive home to find their well-behaved sun-tanned wives getting out of their swimming suits and dressed for dinner. It was too hot a night to cook; all over town those loving summer wives were brushing the chlorine out of their hair and putting on dresses to go out to dinner. They would be at the country club tonight, wearing their bright clean linen dresses loosely, as if they were unaccustomed to wearing clothes at all. They would talk about their diets and their children and their golf scores, display their even dispositions and their gold charm bracelets, and presently they would go home to take off the bright clean linen dresses, to lie on hot sheets and wait patiently for the day to begin again. You would never catch one of them standing around the Greyhound bus station in a tea-stained wrinkled silk suit not wanting to see her husband. You would never even catch one of them standing around anywhere in a tea-stained wrinkled silk suit. There was the kind of wife Everett should have, and look what he had instead. Martha had said it all: Lily had no right to her brother. Everett, like Sue Ann, had his right to happiness as much as the next one.

It was almost seven-thirty before Everett arrived. Unshaven and wearing a dirty khaki shirt, he double-parked the station wagon, swung himself over the rear bumper of a parked Chevrolet, and took Lily's arm. She had not at first seen him, and smiled tentatively when he touched her. He picked up her suitcase, helped her around the Chevrolet, and opened the station-wagon door without speaking. Before they were home she had fallen asleep, dry-eyed for a change, her head in the way of the gear shift.

Later he put her to bed, opened the shutters which had been closed all day against the heat, and wiped her face with a washcloth soaked in witch hazel.

"Did you get the hops finished?" she whispered, opening her eyes.

"Yes," he said. "Everything's fine. Go to sleep."

"Listen." She took the washcloth from him and laid it across her eyes. "I love you."

He looked at her for a long time.

"Stop feeling sorry for yourself," he said finally.

She took the washcloth from her eyes and threw her arms around his neck. "Everett, baby. I do. I love you. I know you and you know me and nobody else does. Everett please baby *love* me."

She clung to him while he kissed her hair, and when he moved to take her arms from his neck she tightened her hold. "Lie here with me," she whispered. "Lie here with me until it's all dark."

"Later." He stood up. "Go to sleep now, baby."

He sat with Knight for half an hour on the third floor, from where they could see the fireworks in town, for that day happened also to be the opening of the State Fair. There would be fireworks every night for twelve days, great slow bursts of white and pink and green, barely visible from the ranch. Long before the last distant sparks had showered out and drifted down, Knight fell asleep in Everett's arms, and he carried him downstairs without waking him and put him to bed in his playsuit.

He went downstairs then, wandering absently from room to room. The house was quiet: Julie was at her grandmother's; Martha had gone to the Fair with Ryder Channing. Insisting that Lily and Everett must come with them, they had waited an hour to see if Lily might arrive; Everett had gotten rid of them only by saying that the four of them would go to the Fair over the weekend. After they had gone Everett had sat in the kitchen with a bottle of beer and an

171

article Channing had brought him about what was described as a pioneer shopping center in Kansas City. The kitchen chairs were uncomfortable and Everett had found it increasingly difficult to concentrate on why some developers preferred shopping centers with mall layouts to shopping centers with cluster layouts, whatever a cluster layout was; the kitchen, however, was the only place in the house where he did not feel oppressed by the presence of telephones. Although he knew that there were only two telephones in the house and five on the entire ranch, the house had seemed, while he waited for Lily to call, equipped with enough telephones to service a handbook operation.

Now he sat down again in the kitchen and tried to finish the article Channing had given him, but after three or four more paragraphs abandoned it. For fifteen minutes he sat reading the labels on the beer bottle he had left on the table when Lily called, and finally he went outside and set sprinklers to run all night on the south lawn, an extravagance justified only by the possibility that it would cool Lily's and the children's room some. He thought automatically now of *Lily's room*, and when he went to sleep at eleven o'clock it was, for the first time of many, in his father's bed. Although during the night he thought he woke and heard voices in the driveway, first Channing's, *shut up you're almost shouting,* and then Martha's, *you think she's so interesting-looking maybe you could knock her up yourself the next time,* by morning it seemed easier to believe that he had only dreamed it.

18

There was nothing wrong with Ryder Channing, Martha observed, that could not be inferred from his habit, when he was at any house within fifty miles of San Francisco, of asking his hostess if she had at hand a copy of the 1948 San Francisco *Social Register* because he wanted to look up a new telephone number.

Actually, Martha amended, Ryder took her calling in San Francisco so infrequently that she had only once witnessed him asking for the 1948 *Social Register* to look up a telephone number, but she was certain that it had been no improvisation of the moment. It was of a piece with his routinely asking people from Cleveland where they lived in Shaker Heights.

"That's not fair of me," Martha added then with the instant contrition which tended, for a while quite successfully, to obscure the hostile edge on her voice; her standard conversational technique was that of a trial lawyer who pursues a tendentious line of questioning and then allows it stricken from the record.

"I mean that's perfectly true about Ryder and the *Social Register* but it's not fair. It's not the *whole* Ryder. I mean Ryder goes around talking about big deals that never go through and all but that doesn't mean Ryder's a phony. Ryder just wants things. That's not so bad, to want things. Is it?"

"Not at all," Lily said, virtuously knotting a thread in a dress she was making by hand for Julie's first

173

day at school. The dress was an economy measure:
Everett had said that their 1949 taxes would be
double this year's—both the riverfront and the
Cosumnes ranches had been reassessed for the first
time since the war—and Lily had resolved, without
mentioning it to Everett, to save money. She had
begun by saving the six or seven dollars she would
normally have paid for Julie's dress, instead buying
four dollars' worth of imported lawn and a sixty-
cent pattern. After three weeks of intermittent work,
the lawn was not only grimy from her fingers but
spotted here and there with blood from her pricked
fingers; it should, however, wash up very nicely.
Good fabrics, good soap, and good hats, her mother
often told her, were no extravagance.

Impressed with the fruit of her own economy,
Lily added: "Wanting things and working to get them.
It's the basis of the American way."

"*Balls.* You aren't even listening to me."

"Really, Martha." Although Lily had never known
exactly what the word meant, it did not sound conversational to her. She had for that matter first heard
it from Martha, the afternoon Mr. McClellan died in
Sutter Hospital. Because Martha was having a cigarette with one of the doctors, Lily had been alone in
the room, holding Mr. McClellan's hand, when he
woke from the coma. "You're a good girl, Miss Lily
Knight," he said, opening his eyes and squeezing
her hand weakly. "You're sickly-looking but you're
a good girl." "*Balls,*" Martha said from the door-
way, seeing that her father's eyes were again closed
and his hand fallen free of Lily's. Involuntarily, Lily
had put her hand out to shield Mr. McClellan from
Martha's voice, but ten minutes later he was dead
and possibly he had heard neither Martha's invective
nor, a minute later, her sobbing.

"I'm sorry," Martha said now. "It's only that you
were at it again."

174

"At what again?"

"You know." Martha paused. "Your dress is coming along nicely. That blue should be very good on Julie."

Lily smiled, and held the dress up for Martha's further approval.

"If only there weren't that gap between her teeth."

Lily laid the dress aside and began threading a needle. Martha had told Julie that unless her teeth were straightened immediately she would grow up to be a very unattractive little girl. For several days Julie had been inconsolable, repeatedly climbing up on the washbasin to inspect her teeth in the bathroom mirror.

"I told you before, her second teeth aren't even in." Lily finished threading the needle and inadvertently jammed it into her index finger.

Martha shrugged, her interest in orthodontia apparently ebbing.

"Ryder just wants things," she repeated reflectively. "That's exactly the thing about Ryder."

"What does Ryder want now?"

Martha looked at her a long while. "This is what they call a *mo-bile situation*, see, Lily. Ryder is what they call *up-ward mo-bile*. Or *on-the-make*. Didn't you ever take any courses? Didn't you ever read any books by Lloyd Warner?"

"There's—" Lily stopped. She had been about to say that there was nothing wrong in wanting to get ahead. She did not know what it was about Martha that inflexibly brought out in her diction the best of both Mr. McClellan and her mother.

"There's *what?*" Martha demanded.

"Nothing."

"'*There's nothing wrong in wanting to get ahead,*'" Martha mimicked. "I know you. Well there's not. But you don't understand about Ryder. He wants to *use* people."

"Martha. Don't get all upset."

"Well he can't use me." Martha paused. "I don't want anything from him. That's the reason he can't use me."

"Martha," Lily repeated.

"I don't want his *jobs*, I don't want his *favors*, I don't want anything *about* him."

What Martha did not want from Ryder Channing that morning was the job he had gotten her three weeks before on a Sacramento television station. It was the fourth or fifth such job for which he had arranged an interview; it was not only the first one Martha had taken but the first one, as far as Lily knew, for which she had even shown up for the initial appointment. The idea behind this particular job had been that Martha, after a month of answering letters from viewers and doing other small jobs around the station, would eventually work into doing both the morning interview program and the commercials during the afternoon movie, a job handled during the first year of the channel's operation by the manager's wife, now pregnant. It was, Ryder had declared, an unbeatable opportunity to get in on the ground floor of an industry with nowhere to go but up, and he had installed a borrowed television set on the sun porch so that Martha could observe the interview and commercial techniques developed by the manager's wife, Maribeth Sidell. Martha had only to consider that Maribeth Sidell was a household word the length and breadth of the Sacramento Valley to realize, he pointed out, the future in the job.

Together, Lily and Martha had watched several of Maribeth Sidell's programs, including one on which she interviewed, simultaneously, a retired disk jockey, Miss Sacramento, and two Japanese businessmen

in the United States to arrange a trade fair. When
the conversation turned to how Sacramento compared to Yokohama, Martha switched off the set and
declared that she was a natural for the job. After
avidly testing some of the products Maribeth adver-
tised, in order to get what she called "fresh insights,"
Martha drove into town, met Mr. Sidell, and reported
at dinner that he had asked her to call him "Buzz,"
had taken her to the Sacramento Hotel bar, and after
two Manhattans (for him) and two sherries (for her)
had announced that although she was no Jinx Falken-
burg she had a lot of class and for his money ($75 a
week) the ball was hers to run with. "I knew the
sherry would get him," Martha added enthusiasti-
cally. "The cornball."

Although Lily never learned exactly where the ball
had been dropped, Martha had worked only one full
week and three days of last week. On the fourth day
she had left the house as usual at seven-thirty, but
by eleven, when Sidell called the ranch, she had
not yet arrived at work.

Toward five o'clock she walked into the kitchen
through the back door, runs in both her stockings
and thistles caught along the hem of her white linen
dress. "I was sick," she explained shortly. "I drove to
Yuba City and climbed on some rocks and watched
a stretch of rapids in the Feather for a while."

"Sidell called," Lily said. "So did Ryder."

"Did he." Martha turned on the faucet in the sink
and splashed water on her face and arms. "There was
a dead rattlesnake caught in a backwater," she said
finally, reaching for a paper towel. "Bloated."

When Ryder Channing called again at seven o'clock
Martha at first said to tell him she was out, then, as
Lily hesitated, put down her drink, reached across
the table for a cigarette from Lily's bag, and took
the telephone from her.

"That's right, I didn't," she said. "I didn't feel good."

Holding the receiver with her shoulder she lit the cigarette and made a face at Julie, who was illuminating with red and blue crayons a Standard Oil brochure addressed to Everett. "I just didn't call, that's all."

"I'm not trying to do anything to you, Ryder," she added after a pause. "It's part of your *egocentricity* that you think everything I do is for the express purpose of getting on your nerves. I didn't go in and I didn't call and that's all there is to it. It hasn't got anything to do with you." She paused, turning her face to the wall. "Ryder, I was scared. I don't *know* why, I was just scared."

"All right," she said finally. "I never asked you to get me any jobs. I never asked you for anything but a little understanding and it's perfectly apparent to me that you aren't capable of giving anybody anything. All you want to do is *use* people." She put out her cigarette, and took Julie's hand, holding it very tightly. Julie looked at Lily and Lily shook her head. "I'm sure I don't *know* what advantage there could possibly be for you in my having a job. I don't know what goes through your mind. I only know there *was* an advantage or you wouldn't have pushed me into it. You are forever pushing me and using me and I'm through."

"Through," she repeated.

"Don't you get that way with me, Ryder Channing. I've heard that one before. I won't miss anything about you and most of all, first on the list of things I will not miss, most of all I will not miss that."

She hung up, picked up her drink, and walked outside.

Although no one mentioned it at dinner, Martha explained later to Everett that the job had been all right the first week but had become too difficult. The telephones distracted her and there was an enormous clock with a second hand that never stopped. Sidell insisted that letters from viewers be answered the day they came in, and frequently she did not know the answers to the questions raised. The week before she had stopped Sidell in the hall and asked him, in order to answer a letter, why the channel did not carry the program with Kukla, Fran, and Ollie. Sidell had looked at her for a long time and asked her if she had ever heard of networks and network affiliates. She had tried to tell him that of course she had—she had simply not thought of an answer so obvious—but he walked away and naturally she had not wanted to ask him any more questions. Instead she had begun putting difficult queries aside in a drawer of her desk, meaning to find out later how to answer them, but the days had gone by and the letters had not been answered and now Sidell would discover them and she simply could not go back. It would be all right if she could take the letters off somewhere and answer them by herself but there was no place in the office where you could get away from those clocks. She *knew* clocks weren't supposed to stop, don't be silly. She knew they needed a clock. But she could not work with it going every second. When it was going every second that way she could not seem to take her eyes off it, and because it made no noise she found herself making the noise for it in her mind.

Everett, who had thought the job a good idea because Martha's days did not seem to him generally constructive, suggested that possibly Martha would like to take a trip. Martha thought not.

For the rest of that week Martha had refused to answer the telephone, to look at her mail, or to leave the ranch, even for a wedding down the river in which she was to have been a bridesmaid. She was quite certain, she explained to Everett and Lily, that the four hundred guests, two flower girls, and seven remaining bridesmaids could sufficiently nerve Molly Bee to lose her cherry without any additional help from her. Everett walked out of the house then, neither speaking to Martha nor getting dressed for the wedding, and finally Lily had gone alone, late, to Molly Bee's reception, where she tried to apologize for Martha and Everett, drank nine glasses of champagne in an hour and fifteen minutes, was warned by her mother that she would end up with a well-deserved headache, and kissed two of the ushers, one of whom, Molly Bee's cousin from Tulare, insisted that she was in no condition to drive and that he would drive her home himself, later. That he would be returning the next day to Tulare lent him, when she was kissing him in the car, an air of infinite promise: she could make him want her and then never see him again, all of the possibilities still intact, neither his deficiencies nor her own ever revealed. *You make me feel good*, she whispered, and meant it.

When she arrived at the ranch not long after two A.M. Everett was sitting in the chair by their bedroom window, drinking a beer and looking at an old copy of *Life*. Although she tried to tell him who had been at Molly Bee's wedding he did not seem interested, and after he had picked up the pink silk dress she had dropped on the bed and looked first at the indelible wrinkles in the skirt and then at her and had dropped the dress on the floor and gone downstairs, she lay on the bedspread in her slip and turned out the lights: she had gone and lost him again and not for any reason, not for any good reason at all. After a while, because she had a headache from the champagne and from the gin she had been drinking in the car with Molly Bee's cousin and because she thought Everett would have to come if she told him she was sick, she went to the landing and called him. "Go back to sleep," he said without moving.

On the following Monday a letter had arrived for Martha from the television station, but Martha shoved it unopened into the back of a drawer where Lily found it after her death. It contained only a note from Sidell expressing concern for her illness and a check for the eight days she had worked.

19

At ten-thirty on the morning of December 18, 1948, while she was having a fourth cup of coffee and wishing that she had not already worked the crossword puzzle, Martha saw in the social pages of the *San Francisco Chronicle* the announcement of Ryder Channing's engagement to a Miss Nancy Dupree of Piedmont. After tearing the notice out of the *Chronicle* and securing it in the pocket of her jumper, Martha wrapped with her calling card—*Miss Martha Currier McClellan, McClellan's Landing,* let Miss Nancy Dupree figure out who it was—a silver dish which Channing had once admired. It was a small dish which had been her mother's, made to Mildred McClellan's order at Shreve's in San Francisco and marked *M.C.McC.* In a smaller box she placed another calling card, with her key to Channing's apartment in Sacramento Scotch-taped over her name.

She had both packages ready to mail by early afternoon, driving in to the main post office in Sacramento and stopping first at the library to look up the Piedmont address in an Oakland telephone book. In

the library she located as well several photographs
of Nancy Dupree in a University of California yearbook, Class of 1947. A member of Kappa Kappa Gam-
ma and Senior Class Council, she had one year been
chosen not only Soph Doll but Sweetheart of Sigma
Chi Attendant. Her major was listed as General Cur-
riculum. She appeared to be somewhat less blond
than Martha, with prettier features, and as Martha
studied first one and then another picture she remembered that she had met the girl at a party in Piedmont to which Ryder had taken her. She had simply
not remembered her name. It had been one of those
parties at which she drank too much and became
depressed, a party at which she had known none of
the people Channing seemed to know; as she once
explained to Everett, Ryder's only real vocation was
for remembering and being remembered by all the
people he went out of his way to meet. At some
point during the evening she had locked herself in
the bathroom and stared at her reflection in the mirror for a long time and not looked like herself (*Your
name is Martha McClellan,* she said again and again
to the mirror, and then cried because it did not
seem to be the Martha McClellan she had wanted to
be), and when she came downstairs again she had
told two strangers, a pretty girl and her husband who
had made a perfunctory attempt to include her in a
controversy over whether or not Ernie Heckscher
had played for the hostess's debut, that she was sick.
"Come sit down a minute," the pretty girl said, looking at Martha and then at her husband, but then Martha saw Ryder, standing by the piano singing "As
Time Goes By" with his arm around a girl in Ber-
muda shorts and a Liberty lawn blouse, and she ran
into the bedroom, pulled her sweater from beneath a
pile of navy-blue and red and forest-green blazers,
and walked out of the house. *Go ahead,* she screamed
at Ryder when he followed her out to the car. *You*

go on back in there and play whatever games you want to play. Just don't think I don't see. She could not now remember what she thought she saw, except that she had accidentally for once been right, because the girl at the piano singing "As Time Goes By," the girl in the Liberty lawn blouse who had earlier asked Ryder if she could count on him for a Scotch foursome Sunday at Claremont Country Club, had been Nancy Dupree. *Don't think I don't know,* Martha had screamed there in the driveway as Ryder tried to take the car keys from her. Although she had not screamed loudly, he shoved her into the car and slapped her. Her first thought had been that it was Everett's car and Ryder had no right to slap her in Everett's car, but then she had remembered that Everett surely cared as little for her as Ryder did, and all during the two-hour drive to Sacramento she sat rigid against the door, trying to think how to hurt them both. What she had done finally was spend the night in Ryder's apartment, an injury to Everett which, because he had assumed she was staying all night in Piedmont anyway, escaped him.

The more she remembered of the evening ("You're Ryder's best girl in the Valley," the girl had said, taking Martha's hand and smiling up at Ryder, "I've heard so much about you"), the more she resented Ryder now, and it was with a palpable knot of hatred in her stomach that she returned the yearbook to the librarian, crossed the street to the post office, and waited in line ten minutes to see that the clerk gave immediate attention to the key for Ryder, the silver dish for Nancy Dupree.

Rid of the boxes, she started back across the Plaza to the car, but because she felt both dizzy and a little silly, she stopped and sat on the edge of the fountain long enough to smoke two cigarettes and to chew, since an old man lay passed out at the foot of the water fountain, one of the phenobarbital tablets the doctor had told her to take three times a day. There were lighted Christmas wreaths strung across J Street and as the phenobarbital began to work she forgot about Ryder and began to wish, suddenly, that her father were alive, that Sarah could come home for Christmas. There was something about Christmas as managed by Lily that was not quite Christmas, although everyone tried very hard to pretend it was and although Edith Knight always came to stay on the ranch for a few days, decorating everything in sight, hanging stockings for Knight and Julie, and helping China Mary make quantities of eggnog which no one ever dropped by to drink.

A few minutes after she got back to the ranch, Ryder called her from a bar. She knew he was in a bar because she could hear the juke box.

Well, what a surprise. She wanted to offer him all her congratulations.

Oh, he said. He had called to see if she was home. He had planned to drive out and tell her himself. He had not thought of her seeing the San Francisco papers.

No, of course he would not have thought of her seeing the San Francisco papers. He had been on the ranch not more than a thousand, fourteen hundred times during the past four and a half years, and no one could have expected him to notice that they got the San Francisco papers. It wasn't a bit nice to think about how life went on—papers got delivered, papers got read, that kind of thing—when one wasn't counting on it, was it. But never mind. It was all very, very nice and she had only an hour before sent off her blessings to that most fortunate girl, Miss Nancy Dupree. Who was, she believed, the same Miss Nancy Dupree known to her friends in the East Bay Junior Assistance League as "Bugsy"? Just so. Nicknames. Cute as a bug's ear. You knew that any girl who'd call herself Bugsy had a sense of fun. There was one *little* thing. She did think, couldn't help thinking, that since his plans must have been more or *less* settled last night, he might have told her his surprise then. Of course they had been pretty busy last night, sorting his laundry, wondering where she had put the razor blades she had brought the day before, typing out his application for an extension on his personal loan at the Wells Fargo. There had been scarcely a minute for surprises, had there. Or possibly he had not known then. Possibly he and Bugsy had just decided late last night on the long-distance telephone and Bugsy had thrown on her forest-green blazer and rushed the news right over to the *Chronicle*. What a stroke of luck, deciding in time for the Valley Edition.

He did not know why he had called her at all. He should have known that she would only behave as stupidly as she was behaving now. Count on her to act like a gauche, bitchy little girl.

Oh. So he was drinking. She supposed he must be fairly proud of himself. She knew he was drinking or he would not have had the courage to call her in the first place. Drinking or not, his character was nothing to write home about. Even to his home, wherever and whatever that was. And as for that talent of which he was so proud, she could walk out the door and get it better from the first picker she came across. Without any of the games.

She could go to hell.

But Jesus Christ, baby. Anybody who'd call herself Bugsy.

Although she had torn the announcement from the paper expressly so that Everett and Lily would not see it, they would know by sundown anyway. Everyone on the river got the San Francisco papers. She had wanted them not to know because she did not

185

want Ryder's name taken in vain. In the strictest sense, which was the sense Martha prided herself upon, Ryder was not in the least in the wrong. Ryder was simply the way he was, and she had known all along how he was. To have persisted, knowing that, was to have taken the responsibility upon herself. *I'm quite old enough and more than smart enough to know what I'm doing*, she had told Everett three years ago, had told Lily before that, had told even her father although not in so many words. She had known it so thoroughly that for the past two years she had not even thought of marrying Ryder, except as a dark contract they could undertake if all else failed, an unattended ritual during which both would avert their eyes, a civil ceremony incorporating the more lurid aspects of a black mass. But despite what she knew, she had, every time he smiled and put his hand on her neck and said *whose girl*, smiled back. *Your girl*.

To avoid Lily and Everett, she sat in her room for the rest of the afternoon, knitting and trying to call up a catalogue of Ryder's virtues against the probability that someone would question his possession of any. Ryder loved small children, at least if they were clean and attractive. He delighted in giving people presents. He had once driven straight through from Los Angeles in order to be at the ranch in time for her birthday. Occasionally when he thought she was asleep he would kiss her ear and whisper that he loved her, although he rarely did either when he thought she was awake. (That, however, was not a widely employable defense, and neither was the fact that he had once at a party knocked out a drunk, someone they did not know, for pointing at Lily and saying *There goes the easiest lay in the room, I can always spot them, something scared in their eyes*. As she had explained to Ryder, she had appreciated it for Everett's sake.) He always asked her if his tie looked all right with his jacket, expressed concern about the correct length for her skirts, and had once gotten up at four o'clock in the morning and met every plane into Sacramento until noon on the off chance that she might be flying home from Carmel that morning.

Again in the strictest sense, she had thought of nothing which could be accurately described as a virtue, but by six o'clock she had thought of so many things that had at one time or another pleased or amused her that she put her head between her knees and, although she had regularly screamed at him to get away from her and stay away from her, cried for the loss of Ryder Channing.

When she saw the candles lighted in the dining room, she knew that Lily had heard. Lily would have heard and lighted the candles and brought up a bottle of wine and told China Mary to find some artichokes because Martha liked them. Lily and her mother were both great little candle lighters. The river could be in flood, the barn could be on fire, an escaped convict could be holding them hostage: you'd find Lily and Edith Knight in the dining room, lighting the candles and chatting about silver patterns, asking the convict if he would mind a dry white instead of a red with the roast. It was so pronounced an act that Lily's every gesture toward domestic gaiety or grace aroused the suspicion that disaster was at hand.

Avoiding Lily's eyes, she let Lily and Everett know, before the artichokes were on the table, that she had known for months. She had not only known for months, but she could not be more pleased. Really. It was exactly what Ryder needed. Of course she had met her. She had met her a year ago, and had hoped then that Ryder would marry her. Lily would have to meet her. They would ask Ryder to bring her out.

Lily thought, although she was not certain, that she had known the girl's older sister the year she was at Berkeley. Sally Dupree. A Kappa, lived in Piedmont off Mountain, near that circle. Would that be the family, she wondered.

That would be the family.

Money, then.

Construction money, Everett believed. Wartime. It was all mixed up in his mind with Henry Kaiser.

It had, Lily corrected him, nothing to do with Henry Kaiser. It was perhaps the same kind of thing, but not connected in any way. No *ships*. And although she was perfectly aware that Dupree Development Inc. had gotten big during and since the war, the Duprees had not exactly been on the street when she knew Sally in 1940.

Ships or no, Martha supposed that Nancy Dupree had probably come out at the Fairmont in a white dress ordered from Elizabeth Arden.

Lily was not sure. Those construction people were a little different, particularly if they lived in the East Bay. It was not as if her name were Crocker or Spreckels or something like that.

No, Martha agreed, it was not. It certainly was not as if her name were Crocker or Spreckels or something like that. What a revelation, Lily's sudden grasp on the San Francisco social scene. Was it possible that Lily had at hand a copy of the 1948 San Francisco *Social Register*?

Never mind about that, Lily said. Just never mind. Anyway. Sally Dupree, the sister, had been much the same type as that girl of Everett's who played tennis. Alice whatever her name was.

Annis, Everett said. Annis McMahon.

She had known it was something like Alice.

Perhaps, Everett suggested, Martha would like to take a trip.

A trip. Whenever Everett could think of nothing else to do with her, he urged her to take a trip. There was nothing like a trip.

She could, Everett pressed, visit Sarah in Philadelphia. Sarah could take her to New York and she could buy some new clothes, see some plays.

Philadelphia was not universally considered, or so Martha had heard, the ideal winter vacation spot. She had not heard of the smart San Francisco set—Crocker, Spreckels, names like that—wintering there in years.

Perhaps the Islands, Lily improvised. There were all kinds of people Martha knew in Honolulu right now and she could have a marvelous time. As a matter of fact she might plan to take the *Lurline* over with Francie Templeton in January.

It was all, Martha said, Del Paso Heights to her.

It was a joke, Lily explained to Everett. It was something funny his father had once said.

Speaking of funny things people said, Martha wanted to tell them something funny Nancy Dupree said the first night she met her. At a party in Piedmont. Nancy (who was, Lily and Everett should know, called "Bugsy," that's right, Bugsy Dupree) had told her that the only ships to take in the Pacific were the American President ships, because they were jammed with fascinating people—Japanese engineers, people like that.

There you were, Lily declared. She was exactly like her sister and they were both exactly like that Alice McMahon.

Annis. Annis McMahon.

Well, whatever. She would have said something like that. She would have told you about the fascinating Japanese engineers you met on the American President ships.

What was wrong with Japanese engineers, Everett wanted to know. If you were on a ship going to

189

Japan you presumably liked Japanese people in the first place.

Everett was, Lily said, missing the point altogether. There was nothing wrong with Japanese engineers. It was simply that a certain kind of girl would say that. Sally Dupree. That tennis player.

Everett did not recall that Lily had even met Annis McMahon.

Well, she had. And if she was not mistaken Martha had too. Hadn't Martha met Annis McMahon?

Martha did not know. Possibly she had.

She did not raise her eyes from her own hand on the table, as if she could scarcely summon up enough interest to answer at all.

After Lily had left the table to put Knight and Julie to bed, Martha lit a cigarette from the candles and then blew them out one by one.

"I wish we had some brandy."

"We drank two bottles of wine between us."

"That's not the same thing, Everett. Get with it."

"You drink too much."

"Now Everett. Sometimes I drink too much. Sometimes you drink too much. But neither of us quote unquote drinks too much. Francie Templeton is practically the only person you know who categorically drinks too much."

"You are tight right now."

"All right," Martha said without interest, scraping candle wax off the tablecloth with her fingernail.

"I never did like Channing," Everett said suddenly. "I never did think you should be messing around with him."

"Everett. Ryder Channing has been and is now my best friend."

She pushed back her chair and stood up. "Now you sing some Christmas carols with me."

Everett stood behind her at the piano, singing an occasional phrase of "O Little Town of Bethlehem" as she picked out the notes with her right hand.

Still playing, she said abruptly: "Remember before Sarah got married when we used to go to Carmel at Christmas time?"

"Yes," he said. "I remember."

"You remember we'd go to the graveyard first and put a holly wreath on Mother's grave, then drive on down to Carmel?"

"I remember," he repeated. "Why?"

"It was nice then, that's all."

Over and over Martha played the same phrase: *Above thy deep and dreamless sleep the silent stars go by.* Because she had not turned on the lights, the blaze from the fireplace and the colored lights on the Christmas tree flickered all around the room.

"I always think about how nice it was at Christmas, that's all." She stopped playing. "I always thought it was you and me together, against Sarah and Daddy. Because they remembered Mother and you really didn't. I always figured they thought she wouldn't have died if it hadn't been for me."

"You shouldn't have thought that," Everett said absently, letting his hand drop to her hair.

"But anyway I did. And we always took that same house out on the point?"

"It was Aunt Grace's house."

"I thought it was ours. I looked for it when I was down last year but I couldn't find it. And you always carried me upstairs to bed?"

"I'd forgotten."

"But you did." As she turned to face him his hand dropped from her hair to her shoulder. "You *did.*"

"I remember now, baby." She turned back to the keyboard and began again to pick out notes. *How still we see thee lie.*

"What about it?" he said.

"Nothing about it." She twisted her shoulder away from his hand. "This piano needs *tun*ing."

Because Everett told her that she should see some people and buy some new clothes, she did. She went to parties every night between Christmas and New Year's, and on the first business day of 1949 she went to San Francisco and charged $758.90 to her and Lily's account at Magnin's. Because she could not see that dressing like what the elevator advertisements called a Marima Shop Young Fashionable had gotten her very far in the past, she went not to the sixth floor, where she and Lily normally shopped, but to the third, where nothing was on racks and all the labels were oversized, heavy enough to stand alone, and embroidered with such intrinsically expensive words as *Traina-Norell for I. Magnin.* "Something way out," she told the saleswoman, and she came home that night with a red coat, a white chiffon dinner dress, two black lace slips, and a white silk dress appliquéd with silk butterflies the exact pale color of her hair. The dress with the butterflies cost $250 and was expressly to wear on the twenty-second of January at Nancy Dupree's wedding. Although Everett thought $250 a great deal to pay for a little dress with some butterflies thrown on it, it was all, he agreed, way out, and on the day of the wedding, when she put on the dress for the first time, he assured her that she had never looked prettier. Because Lily and the children had virus and Everett did not want to leave them, Martha drove down alone to the wedding, rehearsing out loud, in the car, things she could say. *Ryder's so lucky. She looks beautiful. I've never been busier.* By the time she reached Piedmont, however, she could remember none of them; her hands were shaking on the steering wheel and as she drove past the church she did not see how she could possibly go in. Anyway she would be late by the time she found a parking place, and anyway no one ever noticed who was at the church. She would drive around and pull herself together and by the time she got to the reception it would be all right. Although she began to feel better immediately, her hands began shaking again as she drove to the reception, and she sat in the Claremont Country Club parking lot for ten minutes, putting on lipstick and then blotting it off, trying to brush back a strand of hair which fell forward over her face, and smoking one cigarette after another. It was all right, however, once she went inside. Everyone said how marvelous she looked, and she kissed Ryder on the cheek and told him she already loved both his bride and his sister (whom she had just met and been delighted to find rather tackily dressed); she drank a great deal of champagne and danced with everyone—it was a good dress to dance in because the butterflies appeared to move—and when she left it was with a man who seemed to be about forty and who had a suite at the Claremont Hotel. She stayed there until 4 A.M., when she woke up and told him that the way he looked disgusted her, the way he talked disgusted her, and she disgusted herself, she was no better than Lily. Who was Lily, he wanted to know; *she's my sister*, Martha said, *and you aren't good enough to say her name.*

I've never been busier, she told them at the wedding, and in fact she had not been. Although neither she nor Lily had ever joined the Junior League, Martha now became a provisional member, spent every evening and most afternoons in town, and at the end of February calculated that she had received proposals of marriage from two of the boys with whom she had grown up and had gone to bed with three, counting one who was married and not counting the man she had met at Nancy Dupree's wedding reception whose last name she did not remember. (She believed he had something to do with shopping centers, but it was all mixed up in her mind, as in Everett's, with Henry Kaiser.) Since everyone else was at the moment married that just about cleaned the situation up, and when she tallied up their assets and their liabilities, the balance was, as she had hoped it would be, *nada*.

All the connections had been broken, all the bridges burned miles back in the country she had crossed to achieve this insular victory. Even Ryder was included in her pervasive contempt: he could no longer touch her. There, the battle had turned. All the others had been civilian casualties, lost somewhere beyond the front lines: Channing was her dam on the Ruhr, her Guadalcanal, her Stalingrad. Thinking herself victorious, she despised all the vulnerable: all those who liked or disliked, wanted or did not want, damaged themselves with loving and hating and migraine headaches. She imagined that she had emerged triumphant, and that the banner she planted read *Noli Me Tangere*.

20

It was a season of promise for anyone with a little land or a little money or even nothing more than an eye on the main chance; it was a season of promise for Ryder Channing, back in town with his bride after a three-week honeymoon in Acapulco; and it should be, Martha thought some nights as she was going to sleep, a season of promise for her.

The mornings were more difficult: some mornings she did not want to get up at all. Some mornings she could get up only if she had already scheduled every minute of the day, which she learned immediately to do. She went everywhere, met everyone. She met builders, promoters, people looking for factory sites and talking about a deep-water channel and lobbying for federal dams; people neither Everett nor Lily would have known existed had she not told them. She went to large parties at new country clubs, went to small parties at new apartment houses, and went, almost every afternoon, to inspect subdivisions opened by one or another of the boys she knew who were going into the real-estate business. Although Lily and Everett claimed to see no distinctions among the miles of pastel stucco houses, Martha knew better. It was, she explained, a matter of detail. Some builders used panels of redwood siding; others, an imitation fieldstone veneer around each door. In one tract ("Executive Living on Low F.H.A.") each back yard included a small kidney-shaped swimming pool, a cabaña, and a neatly framed placard listing "Pool Rules"; most subdivisions, however, had only Community Pools, sometimes known as Swimming Clubs, and in any case surrounded by Cyclone fencing. Robles de la Sierra, a tract north of town, afforded prospective buyers "a setting with the romance of An Old Spanish Land Grant plus No Sewer Bonds, 40-Gallon Fast-Recovery Water Heaters, and Sidewalks In"; at Rancho Valley, selling points included a leaded-glass window on the exterior of each three-car attached garage, for "the same gracious finish throughout, VETS NO DOWN." And if Lily and Everett wanted distinctions, they had only to consider Riverside City, the most distinctive feature of which was that it was "dedicated to the concept of Retirement." Another distinctive feature of Riverside City was that it was a project initiated by Dupree Development Inc., and another was that Ryder Channing had in February been placed in nominal charge of development, but never mind that. It was a far, far grander scheme than might be indicated by the fact that Ryder was in charge of it. Although none of Riverside City's projected 37,000 houses had yet been built, quarter-acre lots had been sold by agents all over the country, an artificial lake was under construction, and *esprit* among future citizens was renewed weekly by the four-page *Riverside City Sun,* mailed from the Dupree Building in Oakland. "QUESTION: Although we live at present in Chicago, we enjoy our subscription to the *Sun* because we intend to build a home on our lot in the near future. My question is, about the plastic lining now being installed in the bottom of Riverside Lake, won't it make our lake look peculiar? AN-SWER: *You can relax. The lining will be covered with six inches of earth, so unless you come out to inspect it now, you'll never even see it.* QUES-TION: What kind of plants grow best in River-side City? ANSWER: *We suggest you correspond with two of our pioneer citizens-to-be, the Mesdames Ada Travers and Bertha Kling, founders of the Riverside City Garden Club. They have already collected an impressive file of government pamphlets on the horticulture of the area. There are no weeds growing under these ladies.*"

Some nights at dinner Martha would announce that she planned to take some land and develop it herself and make them all rich; some nights she would sit at the table, not eating, and make Everett promise, again and again, that he and Sarah would never try to sell the ranch without her. Other nights she would not come to dinner at all, but would go instead to her room and lie in the dark with the sheet over her head, pretending, when Everett or Lily opened the door, to be asleep.

At six o'clock on the sixteenth of March, Martha was sitting in the bar at Del Paso Country Club wondering how it would feel to get laid in the rain on the golf course and listening to Sam Bradley, one of the river boys who had gone into real estate, explain how he had happened to join Del Paso: it was deductible and it was good business. Although they had been sitting in the bar an hour, Martha had seen no one she had ever seen before with two exceptions, the bartender and a gynecologist's wife whose picture was frequently in the paper in connection with the Opera Guild. "Meet a President," the pictures were always captioned. "No Stranger to the Gavel." No matter how hard you tried it was difficult to keep up with who was who now, and on the whole Martha would rather be on the golf course, but there were always too many people, everywhere.

Did Sam know any of these people, she wanted to know.

What the hell difference did it make if he knew any of these people. All he wanted to do, as he had been telling her off and on for twenty minutes, was get the hell out of here and drive up to that Mexican place in Jackson for dinner.

She *loved* that Mexican place. She had told him three times she loved that Mexican place. But Jackson was fifty miles away and it had been raining for three days and she really did not feel like driving fifty miles and back in the rain in his Austin-Healey.

They could get another car. They could get his brother's car. They could get her car. He hadn't planned to take the goddamn Austin-Healey.

Since both his brother's car and her car were approximately thirty-five miles from Del Paso and in the opposite direction from Jackson, that made it a drive of eighty-five miles each way. Besides, she did not even think the Mexican place was open week nights. Anyway there was illegal gambling there and he did not want, did he, to get caught in a raid. That wouldn't be very good business, would it.

Go to hell, he said. He would telephone ahead.

All right, she said, go find out, and as Sam got up from the table she saw Ryder Channing walk in from the golf course with a balding fat man. It was the first time she had seen Ryder without Nancy Dupree since December and she was faintly depressed to find that she still could not look at him as she looked at other people. She had seen him walking through the door and had thought *Ryder*, just as she always had, without any of the instant judgments she normally made about people she saw. She had been making judgments upon Sam Bradley from the moment he picked her up; she had already made maybe twenty small judgments upon the man with Ryder. But when she looked at Ryder all she thought was *Ryder*.

The other man was, she learned when Ryder brought him to the table, a Cadillac dealer from down the Valley who played, although Ryder had beaten him 79-88, a great game of golf.

"The rain put you off your game," Martha suggested to the Cadillac dealer.

He shrugged.

"You must have known Martha's father," Ryder said, not looking at Martha.

"Who's your dad, Marty?"

"John McClellan."

The Cadillac dealer looked blankly at Ryder. "Sure. Sure I know him. I probably run into him at Sacramento Rotary."

"I don't think so," Martha said. "Actually he's been dead since 1944."

"Well," said the dealer, "I wasn't here in 1944."

198

"How you been?" Martha asked Ryder.

"I'm fine. You look real good."

"I've been sleeping and eating a lot. I hear you're living in the old Carmelo place."

"A friend of Bugsy's family bought it and lent it to us until he decides what to do with it. We're going to build as soon as Bugsy finds some plans she likes."

"Great little girl," the dealer said. "The finest."

"I always liked the Carmelo place." Martha smoothed her gloves in her lap. "They gave a dance once on the third floor and lined both the stairways with azalea. It was about the first dance I ever went to."

"Termites," the dealer said. "Rotten with termites."

"Bugsy wants one story," Ryder said.

"Where is she?" the Cadillac dealer demanded querulously. "Why aren't they here?" He turned to Martha. "She's shopping with my wife. Mitzi said they'd meet us here at six-thirty."

"It's not quite six-thirty," Ryder said. "I saw you last week at Nancy Slaughter's. You were just leaving."

"That's right," she said. "We were there a few minutes."

"Listen, Marth." He absently transferred some change from one pocket to another. "I'm glad I ran into you. I'm going to be out the river road tomorrow. Maybe I'll stop by."

"I won't be home. But I'm sure Lily and Everett would like seeing you."

"Some other time." He stood up as Sam came back.

"Remember me to your dad, Marty," the Cadillac dealer said. "*Hasta luego* for now."

When Ryder arrived the next afternoon at two o'clock Martha was alone in the house: Lily had taken China Mary and the children to have their chest Xrays; Everett was out working on the levees. The rain had gone to the mountains and was melting the snow too fast. Although Lily had wanted Martha to come have her chest X-rayed with them ("Talk about sickly, you look tubercular right now"), Martha had refused: she wanted to lie down. She had not gotten home from Jackson until three A.M., and Sam Bradley, although she had told him it was not good business, had stayed until nearly five. *I can't abide your kind,* she had ended up screaming at him; she did not know what had happened but it was the same thing that always happened. She would have a couple of drinks or simply get very tired or sometimes just wake up in the morning despising someone, everyone. If it happened in the morning she could lie there, hating, until it wore itself out, but if it happened around people she always ended up screaming. The very presence of Sam Bradley had seemed a personal affront to her: his bow tie a monument to both his vacuity and her lack of taste; his enthusiasm for the Mexican place in Jackson an affectation so transparent that she was mortified to have abetted it (he had greeted the cook warmly as "Mamacita," and Martha had looked on with approval); his brand of cigarettes (not her own) the crushing evidence of his mediocrity, his blatancy, his subtle lack of the male principle. It had begun when Sam said that no matter what Everett said, Earl Warren was an intelligent and reasonable man; it could have begun as well had he merely said he liked her dress, or did not like a book he was reading. She had once turned viciously on Ryder for changing his shirt before dinner. His vanity. His shallowness. His carelessness. His thoughtlessness, his selfishness. Did he think the whole world existed simply to provide him with clean shirts. Even remembering it, she felt quite dizzy with loathing for Ryder.

200

"I thought you might be here," Ryder said when she opened the door.

"I'm trying to sleep." She did not ask him to take off his raincoat but simply stood there, trying for once to examine him closely, to make some final damning judgment. She remembered once seeing in his apartment a postcard from a girl, possibly even Nancy Dupree—it had been signed "XXXX and you know what, from B"—which read "Loved seeing you Saturday nite you looked so sexy in your white pants." Although "sexy" was not a word she had ever applied to anyone, she had tried to see Ryder that way for several days. But all she had seen, then as now, was *Ryder*, and when she said, the next time he wore white pants, "You look fat-assed in those pants, Ryder, they don't flatter you," it was no judgment, only response.

"What are you looking at?" he said.

"I've been trying to sleep," she repeated, defeated. "I'm not looking at anything."

Fifteen minutes later he had her down on the floor; she had refused to go near the couch.

"You want it," he said. She had her legs crossed and her face turned away from him.

"I do not."

"What difference do you think it makes now?" He pushed her skirt up around her waist. "After I've screwed you maybe four, five times a week every week for the past five years."

"Four and a half years," she said faintly; his logic remained intact.

"Four and a half years."

"I never wanted it." Recognizing immediately that this clear untruth tended only to weaken her position, she amended it: "A lot of times I only pretended to want it."

"You want it now, all right. You don't have to start acting half-assed with me."

201

After he had gone (*Whose girl? Your girl*) Martha went upstairs and lay on her bed until she heard, just as it was getting dark, the children's voices downstairs.

She found Lily in the kitchen, pulling off Julie's galoshes. "Where's Everett?" she asked.

"Still working on the levees. I don't know."

"I'm going to see if I can find him." Martha pulled on a raincoat, buttoned it briskly, and then, as if she had forgotten why she wanted the raincoat in the first place, sat down and slowly began to unbutton it again.

"You're undoing your coat," Julie said, laying her head in Martha's lap. "Where you going?"

Martha smoothed Julie's hair. "I guess nowhere. I guess I couldn't find him."

"I guess not," Julie agreed. She was the kind of child who agreed with anything said by an adult. "You coming to the parade?"

"What parade is that?"

"The Saint Patrick's Day Parade. It's Saint Patrick's Day in town."

"Who all's going?"

"Me and Mommy and Knight. Only Knight can't go if he doesn't apologize for breaking my pedometer."

"Knight broke your pedometer? However will you figure mileage?"

"That's the thing. Anyway, two of our cousins are in it."

"In what?"

"In the par*ade*," Lily said. "You aren't following this very closely. Sally Randall's children are marching and I thought we should go wave at them. We're going to have hamburgers first. Why don't you get dressed and come?"

"I guess I'm *dressed* all right. I don't guess I have to get all done up for the Saint Patrick's Day Parade, do I. You know what it'll be. There'll be a bagpipe band playing 'The Campbells Are Coming.' The Air Force

Band playing 'Loch Lomond.' And a battalion of small girls in spangled two-piece bathing suits and white plastic Stetsons doing close-order drill to 'Temptation.' *You-came-Ah was a-lone-Ah should-a-known—You were Taymp-tay-shun.*"

"*Martha*," Julie screamed, throwing herself at Martha's knees. "Stop making fun."

"I'm not making fun." Martha picked Julie up and swung her around. "I am telling you gospel. Because baby, I have seen Saint Patrick's Day before, *seen it all.* 'Temptation' will be *sung*—through a public-address system on a truck behind the small girls—by a mother wearing a rose crêpe dress with bugle beads, a short red car coat, and harlequin-framed glasses. So much for that. There will also be the Sheriff's Posse: fifteen dentists on fifteen palominos. And Julie baby, we're so wide open out here there'll probably even be the Masons."

"The Masons are not our cousins."

"That's right, baby. The Randalls are our cousins."

Lily stood up and picked up a lipstick from the shelf beside the sink. "You coming or not?"

Suddenly listless, Martha did not answer.

"If you're coming you better put on some shoes."

"What time is it?"

"Six. A little before."

"I was supposed to go somewhere. Sam Bradley and his brother were supposed to pick me up at six-thirty."

Lily blotted her lipstick on a piece of paper toweling and looked at Martha. "Then you can't come."

"Yes I can. I can come all right." Martha stood up and took from the pocket of her raincoat the dark glasses she wore almost constantly now.

"You want to call Sam before we go?"

"If I wanted to call Sam I'd *call* him, I mean wouldn't I?"

203

By the time they had driven into town ("Knight can look for Nevada plates and Julie for Arizona. That's right, there *are* more people in Arizona but you forget Nevada is closer. All right, *both* of you look for Arizona plates") and stopped at a drive-in for hamburgers ("I said hamburgers, Knight, I did not say steak sandwich and I did not say chicken-in-a-basket. All right, chiliburgers. You don't even *like* chili"), the parade was already underway: they had missed, a policeman told them as Lily was locking the station wagon, the Mayor's Cavalcade and the Knights of Columbus. "Cheer up, sweetie," he said to Julie. "There'll be more."

"You bet there will, sweetie," Martha whispered, giggling with Julie as fifteen palominos pranced into view, and then Knight was yelling *Hey Horse! Why did the chicken cross the road?* and Horse turned out to be not a horse at all but the name by which Sally Randall's son was known to his intimates; not long after Horse Randall and the Elk Grove Firehouse Five passed by, followed by a shivering blond drum majorette and a ragged line of high-school boys whistling and hooting, the rain began again, and when they looked for Martha she was gone. By the time they saw her, standing in front of the Rexall drugstore on the corner, the crowd was breaking up, going for cover, scattering into doorways and automobiles.

"Meet us at the car," Lily shouted over the idling of motors, the shifting of gears.

Instead Martha ran back down the block to where Lily stood with the children. Rain streamed down her face, across her sunglasses, down the neck of her unbuttoned raincoat.

"I was trying to call Sarah. Nobody answered."

"Sarah? In Philadelphia?"

Martha took Julie's hand and followed Lily and Knight to the station wagon. "I wanted to tell her about the parade," she said, lifting Julie into the middle seat.

"The parade," Lily repeated after her, fumbling beneath the brake pedal for the keys she had just found and dropped.

"Honestly," Martha said. "You'd think there might have been *some*body there."

"You can try her again when we get home." Lily fitted the key into the ignition with meticulous care while she tried to work the parade, the rain, and Sarah into some reasonable sequence. "By then it'll be after midnight in Philadelphia. Maybe they'll be home then."

"Oh no," Martha said. "It's only five-thirty there now. The man in the Rexall told me."

"It's almost eight-thirty here. You *know* it's later there."

"I'm sure I don't know why the man in the Rexall would have told me a deliberate *lie*."

"If he told you that he just didn't *know*. We *know*."

Martha shrugged. "I don't know. I don't know what to believe."

Lily switched on the windshield wipers but did not start the engine.

"Anyway it's too late," Martha said. "If it's midnight there, as you insist it is, it's too late."

"Too late for what?"

Martha leaned against the window and took off her sunglasses. Her eyes were closed. "I don't know," she said. "I didn't want to go home and I thought I might go there, but it's too late."

"I don't know what you're *talk*ing about."

"Sarah. *I'm talking about my sister. I wanted to talk to Sarah. If you don't mind.*"

21

They buried Martha's body beneath the cherry tree near the levee on the morning of the twenty-second of March. Everett and Henry Sears (who had been sleeping off the flu and a four-day drunk when Everett had the night before begun shouting and pounding at the door of the foreman's cottage *Sears you bastard Sears get out here*) carried the coffin: a long rope-handled sea chest, packed for the past thirty years with Mildred McClellan's linens, ends of lace, a box of jet beading from a dress, and the ivory fan carried by Martha's great-great-grandmother Currier at Governor Leland Stanford's Inaugural Ball in 1862; unpacked the night before when Everett said *I'm telling you for the last time, Lily, get McGrath out of here, get his deputy out of here, and get that son of a bitch quack doctor out of here, she's my sister, I'm going to bury her, and I'm going to bury her on the ranch.*

Lily walked behind them, her arms full of flowers. Everett had been out before dawn, pulling up every daffodil left after the rain, tearing down whole branches of camellias. When they reached the place Everett had chosen they laid the sea chest on the wet ground, and Everett spelled Sears digging the grave. Numb with the morning cold, Lily stood holding the flowers and listening to the water. Every hour now, the river ran faster and higher with the melting mountain snow: tearing at the banks, jamming together logs and debris and then smashing through the jams.

As she watched Sears dig it occurred to her that Martha's body could well be washed out by evening, the unnailed lid of the sea chest ripped open and Martha free again in the water in the white silk dress with the butterflies. (*$250, I should wear it every day, every evening, and every night to bed,* she had said last night when she was dressing for the party and Lily had warned the rain might spot the silk, *Just ask Everett if I shouldn't.*) It was not right to bury her this way: McGrath had said it (*I'm telling you, Everett, it's against the law of the State of California*); Edith Knight had said it this morning when she came in her robe to pick up the children (*I'm not talking about the law. I'm not talking about any law run through by the undertakers' lobby. I'm talking about what's right and what's wrong*); the doctor had said it; she had said it herself. *Everett baby you don't know what you're doing.* They had each said it for different reasons and Everett had listened to none of them.

"You hear it rising?" Everett said, looking up at the levee.

Sears stopped digging to fasten his jacket against the wind. "Going to crest at thirty-eight."

"When's that?"

"Near to noon. Thiel's Landing." Sears was coughing now. He wiped the back of his hand across his mouth and picked up the shovel again.

Everett put his hand on Lily's shoulder.

"You want to move into town?"

She shook her head. "I don't see any need."

Sears looked up. "There ain't no problem this far up. Downriver maybe."

"The Engineers might blast it tonight. Upstream. We'd get some water."

"They wouldn't blast a levee until they'd evacuated," Lily said. "We'd know."

Everett shrugged and took the shovel from Sears.

Because she did not want Everett to see that she was crying Lily shifted the flowers close to her face.

It would be all right, these next few hours, if she could keep her mind on the water. Where and when would the levee go, were the levee to go at all: there was the question to consider. Somewhere in her mind was a file of information, gathered and classified every year there was high water, and it was upon those facts that she must now focus her attention. At what point had they opened the Colusa Weir. How many gates were open at the Sacramento Weir. When would the Bypass reach capacity. What was the flood stage at Wilkins Slough. At Rough and Ready Bend. Fremont Weir. Rio Vista.

Obscurely comforted by her ability to remember, however uselessly, flood stages which bore no relation to this year's flood, she stood with her eyes closed and did not think of Martha for half an hour.

"All right," Everett said then, propping the shovel against the tree. "That's enough."

He took one end of the chest by its rope handle and Sears took the other; together they lowered it into the grave, already filling with seepage. Lily kneeled in the mud to drop the flowers on the chest, but Everett pulled her up.

"Not yet." He motioned Sears to stand back from the grave.

Oh Christ, Lily thought. He'll say that prayer and they'll cover her with dirt and that's all there is. *Christ in heaven*. How many people did you bury before you stopped screaming inside at the thought of that first night in the dark.

"*Gentle Jesus, meek and mild*," Everett repeated without inflection. It was the prayer he and Martha had learned as children. "*Look upon a little child. Pity her simplicity and suffer her to come to thee.*"

"God bless Martha, amen," Lily whispered.

Everett did not look at her. "Now," he said.

She dropped the camellias into the grave and stood back.

"Henry's going back to the house with you." Everett picked up the shovel. "Get him some breakfast."

China Mary was not in the kitchen: she had gone, late the afternoon before, to visit her sister in Courtland. They should have called her after it happened. They should have called and brought her home before they buried Martha; she had raised Martha. But there had been so many people last night: the sheriff, the deputy, the respirator squad, the doctor, Sears, even the children, wakened by the sirens; and by the time they were alone there was no use calling anyone because Everett wanted no one there. They should have called Sarah. They should have called maybe fifty people but above all they should have called China Mary and they should have called Sarah. *Sarah can't come, there's no reason to call her,* Everett had said. *It's too late. She left here of her own will and anyway it's too late now.* She had said *You're getting worse than your father was,* knowing that Sarah would hear about it from her, would read that her sister had drowned when the mail arrived one morning next week at her ivied brick house in Bryn Mawr, Pennsylvania, for Lily could never call her alone. She had tried to call Everett when his father died but had been unable to say it. Martha had finally taken the telephone and said it.

Lily dropped her raincoat on the table and held out her hand for Sears's jacket.

"Sit down. I'll fix bacon and eggs and biscuits. I had the biscuit batter made for Everett but he didn't eat."

"No bacon." Sears paused. "He don't seem so good."

"He's upset. That's all. All his family's gone now." She forgot for the moment Sarah, and when she did remember Sarah it did not much change the sense of what she had said to Sears.

"Got you and two kids. That's family."

209

Lily did not say anything.

"I didn't figure her that way," Sears said after a while.

"What way?"

"I didn't figure her to do something like that. She grew up on the river, she should have known enough not to take a boat like that out when it's in flood."

"I don't know."

"Where'd she think she was going to get to?"

"I don't know," Lily repeated.

She knew, she knew better than that: Everett had said it, almost shouted it, after he carried Martha's drenched body up from the dock. Down there on the dock he had not said anything much to anyone. He said nothing to Lily from the time he first shouted from the driveway *Get McGrath the hell over here with a respirator* until the time, almost an hour and a half later, he laid Martha's body on her bed upstairs. By the time she had called McGrath at home and run down to the dock, Everett was already in the water, on the end of the rope Sears was still knotting around a piling. *What happened,* she kept saying, and finally Sears said *Martha. She was holding onto the boat but I don't know how long.* In the dark (they did not have the flares until McGrath arrived a few minutes later) she could see nothing, neither Everett nor Martha, not even the boat, overturned and caught on a trunk off the far bank. If Sears had not told her about the boat she would not have known that much, because Everett, after he brought Martha in with him on the rope, said nothing. In the brilliant cold light of the flares they had watched then for an hour while the boys with the respirator knelt over Martha on the wet dock, but it was nowhere near an hour before they all knew, all but Everett and maybe Everett knew too. "Thank Christ he didn't lose his head and go out there without the rope," McGrath said to Lily after the first fifteen minutes. "You'd have lost them both." "We haven't lost anybody," Everett said flatly, looking up from where he crouched at Martha's head, staring at McGrath with confused malice; McGrath looked at his deputy and they both looked away from Lily. It had been five or six minutes later when the doctor arrived and two or three minutes after that when he pronounced Martha dead. "She's alive," Everett said. "You don't know anything about her." Thirty minutes later he admitted what they all knew: "All right," he said. "All right."

She knew better than that: Edith Knight had said it, when Lily called her to come for the children. "That little girl, that little fool," she repeated again and again. "She knew better." It was for Edith Knight that rare event, a happening in which she could not immediately perceive the providential pattern, the point, the unmistakable, however elusive, benefit. Usually she was able to make death seem the most fortunate of circumstances, an unlooked-for circumvention of further bother for the deceased; sudden death was, logically, the supreme economy. "What a blessing he went without a long illness," she said regularly of Walter Knight; "One thing, she had certainly gotten the good of her furs," she reflected with sincere satisfaction when informed that a cousin had met death in the crash of a Piper Apache over Pyramid Lake. Of Martha's and Everett's mother, she frequently observed to Lily: "Mildred went the best way to go, everything in order, and I only hope I can do as well." This observation usually accompanied the cleaning of a closet or the discarding of a memento, because what she meant by "order" was that Mildred McClellan, shortly before her death in childbirth, had cleaned two back bedrooms of the McClellan house, disposing of several cartons of snapshots, dance programs, newspaper clippings, unmatched gloves too good to throw away, sketches of the Yosemite Valley made on her wedding trip, and the souvenirs of a trip to Chicago taken before her marriage. Having one's things in order was a persistent note in Edith Knight's reflections upon death: the ideal life, as she saw it, was characterized by the continual jettisoning of accumulated debris. One could leave this world, with planning, exactly as one came into it. Possibly because Martha had accomplished so little in the direction of having her things in order, Edith Knight was pressed to find a rationale for her death, although after a few minutes she had managed to glimpse, in the fact that Martha had not left behind a husband and small babies, an interim silver lining. "A blessing," Lily had agreed wearily on the telephone, and then: "I don't know. I don't know."

She knew better than that: Everett said it, Henry Sears said it, her mother said it, and all she could say was *I don't know.* It did not seem possible that they could not see what had been happening, but then she had not seen it herself until she had looked last night at the notebook. It was not that there was anything in the pages she read that she had not known about Martha. It was only that she had not seen the pattern, and maybe she would not have seen the pattern even last night had Martha not been lying there dead. She had found the notebook in Martha's dressing table when she looked for a brush to untangle her wet hair. It went back three years, with only occasional entries, some in pencil and some in ballpoint pen, hard to read because Martha's handwriting had grown increasingly illegible. The last entry, dated *March 20 1949* and scribbled over seven pages, could not be read at all. In addition to the entries from day to day, there had been separate pages headed "REASONS NOT TO LOVE RYDER," "REASONS NOT TO LOVE EVERETT," "REASONS NOT TO REMEMBER DADDY WITH LOVE." When she heard Everett in the hall Lily had dropped the book into the pocket of her apron, and early this morning she had burned it. She had wanted Everett never to see it, even if he went on thinking the things he thought now. (He had, he told her last night, killed Martha himself. She had been in his care and he had killed her. He had let her go, had not kept her safe. Martha had been, Lily reminded him, twenty-six-years old. He could not have kept her in a glass box. He could have kept care of her, he insisted. He could have done that much. Martha had not been well, Lily said, as close to saying it as she ever came; Martha had not been well a long while. She knew better, he said again. *Christ almighty she looked like a kitten that's been dropped in water and all you see are the little bones. You saw her, Lily. You saw how she looked.*)

The notebook would have changed nothing. Everett would only have blamed himself more for not having seen before what she now saw with ineluctable clarity: the pattern there all along, worked through it all as subtly and delicately as, in a drawing she had loved as a child, the tiger's face had been worked into the treetops. Once you had seen the tiger's face, you could never again see the treetops.

At ten minutes past one Ryder Channing called and asked for Martha.

"She's not here. She died last night."

Channing did not say anything.

"She drowned in the river," Lily added in an expressionless voice, the only one she could master. "She took the boat out and drowned."

"I saw her last night. I saw her at Cassie Waugh's."

"It was later. It was after the party. I didn't see her but it was after that. She drove up in front of the house and Everett went out and she was down at the boat. I don't know what happened."

"I *saw* her. I didn't talk to her but I saw her."

"Well," Lily said, "I didn't see her but she's dead."

213

"Where is she?"

"She's *dead*."

"I mean her body."

She had known what he meant. "We buried her this morning," she said finally.

"Where?"

"Here on the ranch."

Channing said nothing.

"I'm sorry," Lily said before she hung up. "I'm sorry we didn't let you know."

I'm sorry. She was. No matter what she or Everett or even Martha had thought about Ryder Channing, none of it had been his doing. *November 18 1947: In bed all day, told E and L with flu. Ryder sent lilies of the valley, meant no doubt for L. Found field mouse in bathroom closet. Do not tell E because L will make him kill it. April 27 1948: Dinner at R's, things to remember about (1) making me bring gin (2) sleeping while I fixed dinner (3) asking if I intended to eat dinner in my slip (4) calling me slatternly (5) asking if I had forgotten how to cook spare ribs along with everything else (6) pretending to read while I finished my dinner and his too (7) difficulty of eating spare ribs and artichokes with someone watching (8) getting sick and telling him he was impotent and knowing it reached him because he hit me. July 4 1948: Told R at picnic he was a redneck, white trash, not fit to eat off E's plates. I am reaching him all the time at last. The ways to do it were always transparently clear but I was too much on the defensive to see them. Now he is on the defensive and thrashing blindly: called me "you Okie bitch." February 20 1949: E could fall down dead in front of me and I would think it was nice he didn't live to be old. I am so far away from them all it is incredible when you consider.*

At three o'clock the doorbell rang. It was Joe Templeton, the rain running off his bare head and down his rubber poncho. He had been working on the levees with Ed McGrath. He wanted to say he was sorry about Martha. He had seen Everett about noon but Everett had said nothing.

"Come in for a minute." She did not want to talk to him but could think of nothing else to say. "I'm upstairs sewing."

He followed her upstairs to the sitting room and stood by the window behind her chair. She had not seen him in three weeks and had been trying all winter to avoid seeing him alone.

"Put another stick on the fire," she said. "Everything's too wet to burn."

"I thought you'd have your mother here."

"She took the children this morning. Everett told me to send them to school but they were too upset. I tried to keep them away but Julie saw them carrying her in and started screaming and screaming and finally I gave her some warm milk with bourbon in it and she quieted down."

"I remember I saw them downtown a couple of weeks ago, Julie hanging onto Martha's hand, they looked like mother and daughter. They looked a lot alike."

"Not so much, actually." Lily knew that she was talking too much and too fast but could not seem to stop: she had been unable to talk to Everett. "Martha took her places, played games with her. Anyway Julie kept screaming 'my Martha, my Martha' and Knight was trying not to let his father see him cry but anyway." She trailed off and finished lamely: "They both loved her."

"We saw her last night."

Lily looked at her hands for a long while. "How did she seem?" she said finally.

"She looked pretty. She had on a pretty dress."

"Yes."

"We asked her to come to dinner with us. She said she would and then we all had another drink and

215

she turned on Francie. She said Francie was drunk and I was getting drunk and she didn't want to sit around at dinner with a pair of lushes."

He paused, as if demanding an explanation.

"Well," Lily said. "I guess she didn't."

"She was very rude."

"Well, then. It served her right, didn't it. *Sweet Christ.*"

Joe said nothing. Instead he walked across the room and began examining the framed photographs above the fireplace: Martha the night she took all the jumping firsts at the State Fair horse show; Everett at sixteen in an American Legion baseball uniform; Walter Knight, Lily in his lap, in the driver's seat of the Hispano-Suiza he had bought when she was very small.

She got up to close the door to the bedroom. She did not want Joe looking at her unmade bed, the sheets and blankets and her nightgown and Everett's sneakers tumbled together at its foot.

"How are Francie and the twins?" She sat down again.

"Francie still wants the divorce," he said after a while. "She was talking about it again last night."

"She was drunk. You said she was drunk."

"I said Martha said she was drunk. What about it. She brings it up cold sober."

"I told you. I don't want to talk about it."

It had been a month since Joe first told her that Francie had again decided to divorce him. Unless he filed a cross-complaint for custody of the twins she would not name Lily. She would simply say mental cruelty if he would keep his hands off the twins. Although she had made this latest decision in the Islands and in order to tell Joe immediately had flown home instead of waiting for the *Lurline*, she still had taken no action. She never did. Francie had been divorcing Joe off and on for fifteen years that Lily knew of; it was their way, although neither seemed to realize it, of periodically reviving interest in each other.

"I told you," Lily added. "If Francie files for divorce you file for custody if you want it. It wouldn't bother me."

"It wouldn't?"

"I said it wouldn't." It was a question so academic as to be absurd.

Joe poked at the fire. "Would you leave him and marry me if Francie goes through with it?"

Lily stood up without saying anything.

"I don't believe you'll ever leave him," Joe said.

"What would you give if I would? I mean *if Francie goes through with it*."

"What do you mean, what would I give?"

"Would you cut off your right arm?"

"Yes. I'd cut off my right arm. What's the matter with you?"

"That's right. You'd cut off your right arm." Lily paused. "You all would. Listen. You get out now but listen to me first: you think you've got some claim on me? You think it was some special thing that made any difference to me? Listen to me. Nothing we did matters to me. Nothing touched Everett and nothing touched me."

She followed Joe downstairs and closed the door behind him, and by the time Everett came home she had straightened the bedrooms, talked twice to Ed McGrath (*Well it's done. All I can tell you is it's done. We'll try to make it all right later*), and made soup from potatoes and onions and cream, a kind that had comforted her as a child, but before she gave it to Everett she took him to bed and held him against the night and the rain and Martha lying outside the house. When she finally went downstairs in the dark, barefooted, to get the soup, the telephone was ringing.

"You're lying to me," Ryder Channing said.

"Ryder. Stop shouting."

"You lied to me. Get her on the telephone."

"You've been drinking. Go to sleep."

"I said get me Marth."

"Ryder. Please."

"You're lying to me. Get her to the phone."

"I told you. She's dead."

"Screw you," he said. "Screw you all."

Everett sat by the bedroom window, the rain splashing from the peeling window sill on to his knees.

"Who called?" he asked without looking up.

She put the tray on the table in front of him and closed the window. "My mother," she said.

22

The third spring after Martha died (it was 1952, but that was not the way time was reckoned on the ranch) Lily asked Everett if he wanted to divorce her.

He did not. Of course he did not.

What, then, did he want.

He did not, he said, want anything.

It was the year they seldom talked. When they did talk, they talked always about the same thing, although they never called it by name, never even referred to it out loud except very late at night or when they were very tired: *You made me get it*, she would say. Over seven years, the August day she went to San Francisco by herself had become, in its manifold evidence of mutual error, the heaviest weapon

218

in both their arsenals, the massive retaliation each withheld until all else had been exhausted. She was convinced that year not only that she had gone to San Francisco *for Everett* (in a sense she had, and he knew it, and there was the lever) but that Everett had in fact robbed her of her womanhood: she had heard stories of women who after abortions could not become pregnant again, and although she did not want another child, Everett did. *You made me get it.* At such times she would pack a bag for Knight and Julie and take them to stay at her mother's. There in her own room, with the ebony chest brought from the Orient, the stacks of unread Dominican alumnae magazines, and the flowered lawn curtains she had made on her mother's treadle sewing machine the summer she was thirteen, the corrosiveness within her would subside, and she would begin to see Everett not as the blight of her womanhood but, on the contrary, as her only hold on sanity. *He had not held on to Martha but he would hold on to her.* She would imagine Everett dead then, and cry inconsolably for half an hour or forty-five minutes. *None of the others could help her. Joe could not help her and none of the others could help her, none of the one-night, two-night stands, none of the times when she had simply not known what else to do, how else to talk to someone, none of it could help her but Everett, and she would make Everett love her.* After she had stopped crying she would resolutely put on her dark glasses, kiss her mother goodbye in front of the television set (if it was an afternoon when the Dodger games were being televised, her mother sometimes seemed not to have known she was even in the house), and drive back to the ranch. Occasionally she would be gone only a few hours, and she would not then tell Everett that she had left him again.

The fourth spring after Martha died, Lily decided that it would be all right if they could go away together occasionally, leave the ranch. Again and again she asked Everett to take her somewhere, and at last they went, one weekend in June, to a party in San Francisco with some people Everett had known at Stanford. There were two views of the Bay Bridge, one of California Street, and four potted avocado trees (all the girls with whom he had gone to Stanford were now, Everett explained, mysteriously bent upon breaking the Calavo trust); there were repeated assurances that (alternately) Herb Caen or Barnaby Conrad or Dolly Fritz would be dropping by later; and there was Ryder Channing.

She had not seen Ryder since before Martha's death; she had not even talked to him on the telephone since those first few months, when he would sometimes call the house, drunk, and talk, about nothing in particular, for thirty or forty minutes. When he called during the day she had talked to him, but when he began calling late at night she had finally, without telling Everett, made a point before she went to bed of muffling the telephone so that they could not hear it ringing. After that she had only heard about him, here and there, from one or another of the few people they saw: none of the reports quite tallied but none of them were good. She would hear first that he was seen with a succession of unidentified girls in bars frequented by the very young; then that he was never seen, had become a virtual recluse. He was asking for sympathy all over town; he was rude, abusive, burning all his bridges. Nancy was leaving him; he had left Nancy. He had been taken off the Riverside City project because he was pulling some fast ones on Larry Dupree; he had been removed because he never appeared, showed no interest. Finally: he had moved to San Francisco to follow Nancy; they had moved together to San Francisco because her father ordered them to.

When she first saw him, standing by the bar and laughing, none of it seemed possible: Ryder had never looked better. Deeply tanned and wearing a blue blazer, he had about him the air of the men one saw in liquor advertisements, an air which suggested untroubled afternoons spent sailing off Belvedere, expensive steaks in good restaurants, and the smooth absence of eccentricity achieved only by the recently rich. It was not until she had talked to him for a few minutes that she saw that there was something about his face which belied the sun tan, made the blue blazer seem a kind of fancy dress. His gaze flickered around her without ever quite settling upon her; his smile was less a smile than a tic.

He had, he assured her, the world by the tail. Or just about.

"I'm glad, Ryder."

He just about had it licked, he insisted. He guessed she had heard things were rough for a while, but she could rest assured that it would be smooth sailing from here on in.

"I'm glad," she said again. She had heard that he sometimes hinted, drunk, that Martha's death had caused the disorder in his life, and wondered if he had so deceived himself. The disorder had been there always. Even Martha had seen it: *He's the kind of man,* she had once said, *who when your father's dying or you're having a miscarriage or a note's due at the bank, depend on him, he won't be around.*

"How's Nancy?" she added.

Nancy, he declared, could not be better. Nor could he. And they had been meaning to get in touch with her because—what a coincidence running into her tonight!—they were moving back to the Valley. He was going into an operation of his own, had some deals going, nothing he was free to talk about but very big irons in the fire. He'd be working his ass off but it was going to be worth it.

"That's fine, Ryder," she said; she wondered where Nancy was.

Although she heard, in July, that Ryder and Nancy Channing were in Sacramento again, she did not talk to him until one afternoon in September when he called and asked her to meet him in town. She couldn't possibly, she told him; *please,* he said, all pretense gone from his voice. *I need you. You're the only friend I've got.*

When she arrived at the address he had given her, a one-story house in a new subdivision south of town, she saw that he had been alone for days, perhaps weeks: there were books thrown on the floor (he had always been sloppy and she recalled Martha saying that he did not sleep well), dirty shorts and socks and shirts strewn on the chairs, and every flat surface was littered with the remnants of whatever he had been eating—celery stalks, stale ends of bread, the torn plastic wrappings from processed cheese. In the bathroom there were dark hairpins on the floor, distinctly not Nancy's, and the sheets on the bed where she sat with him and finally lay with him had not been changed when Nancy would have changed them. He looked as disheveled as the house did, and talked incoherently: he had clearly been drinking. Nancy was in Piedmont, he did not know for how long. The deal on which he had been working had not quite gone through, but never mind that. It would. You had to wait these things out, they didn't build Stonestown in a day.

Before she left she gave him what cash she had, about $20, and straightened the bedroom so that he could sleep.

"Don't worry," she said.

He sat slumped in a chair.

"I said don't worry," she repeated, holding his head against her.

It was apparent that he needed someone, and as she drove out to the ranch she imagined that he needed not someone but her. Whether it was true or not did not much matter: she was already committed.

23

"You can't dance at all," Everett said to her. "You never could dance worth a damn."

He said it in a motel room outside Salinas on a spring evening in 1957; they had driven down to look at a stock ranch, 840 acres for $225,000, which was, Everett thought, on the high side for a stock ranch but was $85,000 less than the eventual buyer, a Stockton syndicate, asked one year later for the eight acres of it with cloverleaf access to a proposed freeway south. (In the end, however, the joke was not upon Everett after all, since the route of the freeway was shifted five miles east.) In the motel there had been glass doors to the lighted swimming pool, Muzak piped in through the walls, and wall-to-wall tweed carpeting on which they had tried, after three drinks before dinner, to dance.

"Nobody can dance on a rug," she said.

"You couldn't dance at the Palladium."

Although she had never considered herself even a mediocre dancer, she was hurt; in the haze of three drinks she embroidered bitterly upon past hurts. A month before she had bought a red chiffon dress which he claimed not to like on her, although he knew

(in fact *because* he knew, he said it because he
knew) that she had wanted a red chiffon dinner dress
from the time she was in school and had seen one
on a girl at a dance; before Christmas, the day she
came home from two weeks in Carmel, he had not
been at home but (by a deliberate effort, she was
certain now) in Reno.

"I'm not that bad a dancer," she said, wondering
what had happened to the girl in the red chiffon
dress, what brilliant marriage she had made, what
adoring husband was even then leading her (*leading:* there was the key to good dancing) across the
polished floor of what fashionable hotel.

"I told you, you can't dance at all. You don't listen
to the beat. I don't know what you're listening to
but it isn't the beat."

"Then let's not dance." She sat down on the bed
and began brushing her hair.

He sat down, without speaking, and pretended interest in an advertising leaflet bearing a photograph
of a man identified as "The Salinas Valley's Number
One Restaurateur, a Ph.D. of Beef." There was also
a drawing of a steer wearing a crown, with the leg-
end "Where Premium Beef Is King."

"You're deliberately starting it again," she said.
"You're deliberately doing it again."

Everett said nothing.

"You do it," she added, "because you're insecure."

"Cut it out, Lily." He stood up and straightened his
tie in the mirror. "You ready to go?"

She picked up her sweater, and they did not speak
again (if you did not count queries for the benefit
of the waiter, and she did not) until halfway through
dinner, after Everett had left the table to say hello to
a cattleman he had seen in the bar.

"Eat your dinner," he said when he sat down again.
"Or is there something the matter with it?"

"I was waiting for you."

"You were."

She did not say anything.

"That'd be the first time." He picked up his drink. "That'd be the goddamn first time."

"When did you ever care?"

"That's right. When did I ever care? When did you?"

"I care right now."

"That'd be the goddamn first time," he repeated.

She saw the vein tightened on his forehead and tried to eat a bite of abalone. Everett had not touched his dinner and was on his sixth or seventh martini, she did not know which. *That'd be the goddamn first time.* What it was not the first time for, at any rate, was this scene: she supposed they said different words each time but it was always the same scene, and although she could not remember when or how it had begun, it seemed now that they were condemned to play it out together all the days of their lives, raking their memories for fresh grievances, cherishing familiar ones, nourishing the already indestructible shoots of their resentment with alcohol and with the inexhaustible adrenalin generated by what she supposed was (at least she did not know any other name for it) love. It did not seem to matter any more who had first resented whom, or for what. It did not seem to matter what either of them did any more: it could begin out of nothing. It could begin when they were trying hardest to keep it away, could tear apart all their tacit promises, could invade even the cunningly achieved anonymity of motel rooms with wall-to-wall tweed carpeting, rooms in which they had thought they might begin again; rooms in which she could feel, in the first glow of the first drink, that Everett was someone she did not know at all, someone to whom she might seem the gifted, graced, charmed woman she had wanted to be.

"Stop it," she said, putting down her fork.

He beckoned to the waiter. "Stop what."

By midnight Everett had fallen asleep in his clothes on one of the two double beds. Lily sat rigid in a straight chair on the far side of the room; to have lain on even the other bed would have implied domesticity, a truce. When he woke and told her to go to bed she turned away, turned her face toward the window which looked out on nothing but the Lincoln. She could not sleep, she said, in the same room with him. She had managed to sleep, he said, in the same room with plenty of other people, hadn't she. No, she had not. And what did it matter if she had. When had he ever cared. He had slapped her then and she twisted away, and he took her in his arms and it was all right again for a while. *It's going to be all right baby,* he said, *it's going to be fine now,* and she said over and over *Please Christ Everett keep us,* and he said *Lily, baby, we'll get through the next few months all right and then you take a trip, you take the kids on a trip, go somewhere you want to go and baby when you come home it'll be all right, you'll see.*

Later she had begged Everett to go with them on the trip that summer but he would not. Knight liked everything, liked Paris and London and Rome and New York, but Julie was homesick and wanted her father, and Lily was homesick too. Although she sent postcards almost every day to Everett and to her mother, neither wrote frequently: her mother twice, once to observe that Duke Snider had been off his game for a week, once to complain that the Wells Fargo Bank would allow her to subordinate not three hundred but only one hundred acres to the Paradise Valley All-Electric Homes people; Everett three times, each letter an exercise in the stiff, impenetrable optimism he reserved for all mailed communications. In Paris she received a cable from Ryder, asking if she could lend him five thousand dollars; she cabled that she could not, and then wondered guiltily where he would get the money.

After she was home, all she could remember of the trip at all was the fat Italian on the flight from New York to San Francisco, the Italian not from Italy but from New Jersey; she remembered him with a clarity she would have preferred to forego. He lived in New Jersey, was married to a woman who weighed 234 pounds, and had business in San Francisco: those were the only three facts she ever knew about him.

Idlewild that night had been hot and swept by fitful warm rains, everything smelling of the same sweet mildew that had always meant New York to her. The plane was delayed, and Lily sat (alone, because Knight and Julie were staying over a week to visit Sarah in Bryn Mawr) in the surgically lighted litter of the waiting room reading the real-estate advertisements in a *Town and Country* someone had left behind. She had on a white silk suit she had bought on sale the day before at Hattie Carnegie, and thought she presented rather a pleasant contrast to the other passengers, one of whom, an aging blonde, had on Capri pants; another of whom, an extraordinarily seedy minister, had stripped down to his pants, an undershirt, and a clerical bib. He was fanning himself with the *New York Daily Mirror*, and Lily hoped that he would not sit next to her on the plane, because she was quite certain that before they reached San Francisco she would be telling him, in a helpless drive to win his approval, what faith and works meant to her.

She smiled distantly at a man who had smiled at her. Apparently Italian, about her age, the man wore a suit of such deliberately obscure cut and color that it appeared to be a parody on a Brooks Brother suit. The suit was complemented by—and such would be the phrase—a narrow black string tie with a heavy gold tie clasp, an absurdly small hat, and a candy-striped shirt with French cuffs, which he shot several times as he repeatedly opened and closed the attaché case in which he had for some reason secured his ticket. It was not until after he had settled himself next to her on the plane that she noticed the cuff links, which were representations of two of the Caesars, and it was not until he accidently brushed his hand against her knee and then drew it away that she noticed the ring, which was large, diamond, and on his little finger.

It was about then that she noticed, as well, that he had been and was still drinking. *You're skinny but you're good-looking*, he announced thickly, his first words to her. Although she was taken aback she smiled, lowered her head and looked up at him and smiled. She always smiled that way at men she did not know, unable to think of anything else to do and wanting them to want her, recognize her as the princess in the tower. In this particular case, however, she smiled also because the stewardess had looked with disapproval upon the man, who was making little effort to conceal his intention to stay drunk for the next three thousand miles. The disapproval of the stewardess suggested a kind of pact between Lily and her seat mate, and she sealed it by accepting a swallow of what seemed to be very good Scotch, although she did not like Scotch, from his flask.

Perhaps ten minutes after they had left Idlewild, when the lights had been turned off and the engines had settled to a low roar, the incredible thing happened, only it did not seem incredible until later, on the ground, in the light: the man began a low, loving, brutally obscene monologue. Did she know what he wanted to do to her. Did she know what he was

going to do to her as soon as they reached San Francisco. How would she like that. He guessed she'd
like that all right. *Be quiet,* she whispered from time
to time, lulled almost unconscious by the dark, the
moan of the engines, the slight vibration of the
cold window next to her cheek, the void beyond the
window; *don't talk that way.* There was, however,
something about being at 25,000 feet in the dark that
drained her voice of urgency. Occasionally she
would even drop into sleep, waking each time to the
quiet, unthinkable monotone; he never touched her
and stopped talking only once, for about an hour,
between the lights of Denver and the lights of Salt
Lake, when he fell into deep sleep. She rather missed
the sound of his voice. He woke not only with his
imaginative powers still intact but with, for the first
time, a definite program: *You're going to love it,
baby, you're just going to give me three hours and
you're going to love it and then you'll walk out that
door and never see me again.* He saw this tryst as
taking place in the airport hotel in San Francisco. It
seemed he did not have to be into town until two
o'clock in the afternoon. *Just three hours, baby. I
can't,* she heard herself saying again and again, and
when he demanded to know why not she heard herself, absurdly, making up reasons: she had to be
here, there, her time was committed. Three hours
wouldn't matter, he declared, if she wanted it: *Do
you want it or don't you. I don't want it,* she said,
finally, almost inaudibly, trying to cover herself entirely with the blanket the stewardess had given her.

*You want it all right baby, you want it. Three hours
of it.*

She said nothing. What held her in trance was his
total lack of interest in anything else about her, his
promise of being what she had looked for over and
over: the point beyond which she could not go, the
unambiguous undiluted article, the place where the

229

battle would be on her terms. There could be no question of whether he liked her or disliked her, no question of approval or disapproval, no rôles at all: three hours he said and three hours he meant.

And if he had not passed out shortly before the plane landed in San Francisco, and if Everett had not driven down unexpectedly to meet her (given the second, she could thank God for the first), three hours it would probably, she knew with a blend of distaste and interest, have been. A few days later the incident had seemed so improbable as to be of obsessive interest, and she mentioned, tentatively, that she had sat next to a drunk on the plane. She had, Everett supposed, moved. Yes, she said. Of course I moved. She could not see then why she had not, and was moved, a few weeks later, to describe the flight in relentless detail to Ryder. Clearly impatient with her unresponsiveness to the details of a venture he had recently conceived (*a chain of espresso shops, see Lily, it's a natural*), Ryder said only that it could have happened to anyone. ("I'm not sure a chain of espresso shops would go, Ryder": that was all she said, but it occurred to her that Ryder found her as tiresome as she sometimes found him, and she reflected admiringly upon people in movies—and it was not only people in movies—who when they could not talk to each other said goodbye, had renunciations, made decisions: started fresh, apparently lobotomized. If there was one thing that she and Everett and Ryder all had in common, it was that none of their decisions ever came to much; they seemed afflicted with memory.)

24

Lily knew that she should not have been in town at all. Let alone sitting in the bar at the Capitol Tamale for two hours. Sarah and her new husband had arrived the day before on their way to the Islands; Knight had called up a San Francisco boy who would be in his class at Princeton and invited him up for dinner; China Mary had declared it unseasonably hot for June and gone to bed. Lily should be home. She had told Ryder half an hour ago that she was leaving; now she repeated it.

"Just finish your drink," Ryder said. "I want to talk to you."

"What about?"

"For Christ's sake I haven't *seen* you in six weeks."

"That's not my fault," Lily said automatically. She had not particularly wanted to see Ryder anyway, but it had not in fact been her doing: he had spent all of May and part of June in Phoenix, trying to raise money for a project she did not entirely understand. After a while all of Ryder's projects tended to look alike, and whenever she had not seen him for a period of weeks or months she was struck, when she did see him, not only by that but by his appearance: his features seemed constantly heavier, his eyes less focused. Looking directly into his eyes this afternoon, she had felt that she was looking right through them: *You depress me, Ryder,* she had said, *you're acting like everything you do is reflex.* But then he had ordered another drink and she had taken a Miltown and they had both laughed. *So you think I'm a shadow of my former self*, he had said, making fun of her, and she had kissed her finger and pressed it against his cheek.

"Anyway," she said now, looking at her watch and trying to finish a story she had begun before. "There Knight was, shouting that his grandmother reminded him more every day of something out of *The Cherry Orchard*. 'By Anton Chekhov,' he said. 'If anybody on this ranch has even *heard* of Anton Chekhov.' Which he supposed was asking *too much*. And there I was, trying to point out that Mother's passion for turning her particular orchard into Paradise Valley All-Electric Homes was not exactly what I would call Chekhovian. And so Knight said, straightfaced—I swear, Ryder, he meant it—why didn't she tear down the big house and move into one? It would save on electricity."

Although Ryder laughed she could see that he was not much interested by the story.

Dampened, she added: "And that's pretty much all we've been doing."

"Except for Everett's sister," Ryder corrected her.

"That's right." Lily had only had three drinks but felt a little reckless. "*Except* for the arrival of the prodigal sister."

"I saw them at the airport. Everett introduced me." He paused. "I would have recognized her anyway."

"Everett thinks she looks tired."

"She looks like Martha." Ryder paused. "She looks the way Martha might have looked at that age if she hadn't been Martha."

Lily said nothing.

"Listen," Ryder said at last, taking her hand. "You look good. You look a hell of a lot better than you did when I went away."

"I'm tired." Lily stood up and reached for the packages she had bought before she met Ryder. "I'm tired and I look terrible."

232

When she walked into the house, obscurely pleased that she had diverted Ryder from asking her to meet him somewhere more private than the Capitol Tamale, it occurred to her that no one had moved since noon, with the single exception of Sarah's husband, who appeared to have gone upstairs. Knight still lay on the verandah reading, Julie was still out by the pool, completely in shadow now; Everett and Sarah still sat in the living room. Not even the level of their drinks appeared to have changed appreciably in seven hours.

Sarah smiled uncertainly at Lily. "I was just telling Everett that I *recognize* how you both feel about it."

"About what," Lily said, taking off her gloves; she knew perfectly well about what. Sarah had been talking about selling since breakfast.

Ignoring Lily, Sarah turned back to Everett. "Surely we've had offers."

"We've had offers, all right. You know we've had offers."

"How would I know what we've had. Lily never writes about anything but the weather. How would I know about anything." Sarah paused. "I *do* know that what's-his-name, that man we ran into at the baggage counter last night, mentioned some Honolulu interest."

"Honolulu *interests*," Everett said. "That means Chinese investors. That's what they call Chinese money now. Honolulu interests. That guy's always got a deal going. I wouldn't bank on the money." Everett turned to Lily. "Channing," he added. "We saw Channing at the airport."

"Channing," Sarah repeated. "That's his name. Wasn't he a beau of Martha's?"

"No," Everett said.

"Ryder Channing was married for a while to one of Larry Dupree's daughters," Lily added hurriedly. She did not want Sarah moved to dwell again upon either Ryder or Martha; last night, going on about Martha, she had so upset Everett that he had not slept at all.

"Dupree Development," she added.

"As a matter of fact," Everett said, "Dupree has expressed some interest in the Cosumnes ranch."

"I don't *care* so much about the Cosumnes," Sarah said. "The Cosumnes at least brings in a little cash."

"I've been telling you for fifteen years, Sarah, a lot of the Cosumnes expenses come out of the riverfront's operating budget." Everett paused. "You thinking I'm bleeding the riverfront?"

"Everett, sweet," Sarah laughed. She stood up and walked over to the window. "The pool kills me. It looks like Pickfair."

Everett said nothing.

Sarah wandered around the room, picking up a silver platter and reading the inscription on the bottom, studying the photograph of her mother on the piano, returning to the window and looking out into the sunset, picking out, in the silence, a few notes on the piano.

When she sat down again her vivacity seemed suddenly exhausted. "Nothing's very different, is it," she said to no one in particular.

She smiled then at Everett but Everett did not smile back. " 'And it will not be a very *jolly* corner,' " she quoted. "T.S. Eliot. *The Family Reunion.*"

On the fourth Wednesday in June, exactly one week after they had put Sarah and her husband on the plane for the Islands, Knight had the accident with the Ford. Although the accident was neither serious nor entirely Knight's fault, he would almost certainly have his driver's license suspended for six weeks; he had admitted two beers to the Highway Patrol. "You're too honest for your own good," Julie observed with disgust. "They never could've proved two beers." "That's no way to talk," Lily said, but by lunch on Thursday she had begun to wish, if only for Ever-

234

ett's sake, that Knight had been less straightforward with the Highway Patrol.

It was 102° outside and Knight was not speaking to her. He talked only to Everett; except for yes and no and please, he had not spoken to her since Sunday, when he had seen her in Harrah's Club at the lake with Ryder. She had gone up alone to her cousin's house on Saturday morning (*I can't stand it, she had told Everett, I can't stand one more minute of your taking it out on me about Sarah, I can't stand your brooding, I can't stand any more scenes, and I can't stand the heat,* and she had walked out of the house—resolutely not thinking about the three hours she had spent with somebody's houseguest in a room at the Senator Hotel the night before—and driven straight to the lake); she had not even known Ryder was there until she ran into him outside Harrah's Club on Sunday. For once she had been totally blameless, but she could scarcely explain this small irony to Knight. She did not know what Knight had been doing in Harrah's Club in the first place. When she saw him she had called out and made her way past two crap tables to talk to him, but he had walked away.

"Just this one thing," Knight pleaded now. He wanted Everett to talk to someone at the Department of Motor Vehicles. "It'd be so *easy*. All you've got to say is you need me to drive the trucks. Can't you just do this one thing for me."

"It won't hurt you," Everett said.

"You might just talk to them," Lily said, mostly, she realized with shame, to ingratiate herself with Knight.

Knight looked at her coldly.

"It won't hurt him," Everett repeated.

She tried again. "Nobody said it would *hurt* him, Everett. But it might be nice if he could drive this summer."

"This is between my father and me," Knight said distantly.

"Apologize to your mother."

"I'm sorry." Knight turned back to Everett. "Just *one little phone call.*"

Everett said nothing.

"All right. Don't do it. I didn't expect you to do it. Nobody expects you to do anything."

Knight pushed back his chair and watched Everett expectantly, but Everett did not respond.

"You just sit here," Knight added, his voice rising. "Just sit here like you've always done and don't pay any attention to what's going on. Just pretend we don't exist. Just sit here while your son gets his license lifted and your daughter lets anybody on the river get her drunk and goes swimming nude—"

"Shut up," Everett said.

Knight stood up. "*Last Saturday night* with both the Templeton twins. That's *last Saturday night* while your wife was shacked up at Lake Tahoe."

Lily looked first at Everett, then at Knight; neither looked at her.

"Get out," Everett said. "You want to say every trashy thing you hear, you get off this place to say it."

"You think I want to stay on this place? You think I want one lousy acre of it?"

"Get off now."

"It's not what I hear, it's what I know. Nobody says it out loud, not around here. But you know what they call her? You know how they think of her still? They call her Lily Knight, not McClellan, *Knight.* Like she was never married at all. *So I guess you didn't count for much.*"

When Julie asked that night where her brother was, Lily said that he had gone out. "He's not coming back," Everett said. "He's disloyal." Julie looked at

236

her father and then at her mother and her large eyes filled with tears: "I don't believe that," she said in her steady voice. "I wouldn't believe Knight could be disloyal." "I wouldn't believe you could go swimming without any clothes on, either," Everett said flatly.

After Julie had gone to sleep Lily sat down in the dark by her bed. She wanted to hold Julie's hand, flung out from the striped lavender and white sheets, but was afraid that she would wake her. Instead she sat with her hands in her lap listening to Julie's even breathing, and when Julie woke and looked at her with the tears beginning in her eyes again, Lily only smoothed her hair. "Go to sleep, baby," she said, unable to explain to Julie, any more than she could explain to herself, just where the trouble had begun. "It's all right."

When Knight came home two days later ("That was absurd," Lily heard Julie telling him, "running away in your mother's car. That's childish"), Lily prevailed upon Everett to accept, as she had done, his inarticulate, embarrassed apology. He brought Lily a dozen white roses, but was ashamed to tell her that he had bought them ("This guy gave them to me," he explained. "This guy I know in a florist's shop had them left over"); he asked Everett, carefully casual, if Everett minded if he stuck around and listened when the hop broker came at four o'clock. That was the day they began to be very polite to one another, dimly aware that they had been, more than they had ever been before, vis-à-vis the complexities, the downright complicity, of family love. (*It had nothing to do with you,* she tried to explain to Ryder, talking to him about it night after night. He did not understand what she was talking about, but it was better than talking to herself.)

August 1959

25

Everett loosened his tie and unfastened the top button
of his shirt. Exhausted, he remembered for the first
time that the gun still lay on the dock.

"Sit down," Lily said. "Sit down, baby."

He let her lead him to a chair. The house looked no
different than it had earlier in the evening; he
could not think why he had expected it to.

"Wait here," she said. "I'll get you a drink."

"What time is it?"

Lily looked at her wrist. She was wearing the watch
he had given her the September of 1957, when she and
the children came home from abroad. He had bought
it the week she left and saved it until she came home
in September, telling her then, embarrassed, that she
could count it an anniversary present. Once he had
seen it on her thin wrist, he had seen how wrong the
heavy diamonds were for Lily, but in the jeweler's that
afternoon he had so wanted something which would
make irrevocable his love and determination that if
the jeweler could have worked the Cullinan Diamond
into a wrist watch (the point of a wrist watch being
that she could wear it every day) he would have borrowed on the ranches and bought it. Although he was
quite sure that Lily did not like the watch, she wore it
not only every day but so frequently in the shower
and in the swimming pool that the parts were rusted
and it seldom ran.

"One-thirty," she said. "One-twenty-five."

He looked at her. "The children," he said finally.

"They'll be a while. We have time."

She poured some bourbon into two glasses and handed him one.

"I meant to," he said. "I came here and got the gun. If I hadn't meant to I wouldn't have come here and gotten the gun. Would I."

"I don't know. That's not the point."

He said nothing.

"Listen," she said. "We're going to make it all right. I'm going to tell McGrath what happened."

"That didn't happen."

"It could have happened."

"It didn't."

"Don't you want it to be all right?"

He did not say anything.

She swallowed half the bourbon in her glass. "Everett. Listen to me. If you don't listen to me you're going to go to prison. You're going to go to Alcatraz and maybe *die* if you don't start listening to me."

"San Quentin. Not Alcatraz. San Quentin."

"*Everett.*"

He looked at her. He had been wrong about her down on the dock: she was no older, she was still the thin little girl with the safety pin in her sunglasses, and whatever had happened in the years between did not signify much. Channing did not signify much: he thought of Channing sitting there on the log smoking a cigarette, switching his flashlight toward the levee and calling *Lily?* then springing up and flipping his cigarette into the water when he saw that it was not Lily. (*You better get off, Channing, you better get off this property,* he had said, and Channing had laughed: *O.K., Coop, O.K.* He had imagined Channing maybe telling Lily, later, what had happened, imagined Lily laughing with him. *O.K., Coop,* Channing had said, *you're going to hurt somebody with that, and she's no good to you dead.*) None of it signified: whether Channing had tried to grab the gun to protect himself or because he thought Everett intended to shoot Lily; whether he had shot Channing because he had intended to all along or because he was angered by Channing's thinking he could hurt Lily; none of it mattered. Channing pitching forward over the log, his flashlight rolling into the water: they were events of equal importance. After a while it had all been quiet again and he had wondered how the shot could have been so accurate when he could not remember aiming.

He smoothed the hair back from Lily's face.

"Anyway," he said, trying to make her smile. "We call it Quentin. Or just plain 'Q.' "

"Everett." She buried her face in his sleeve.

"Never mind. Don't worry."

"Listen." She looked up at him. "You wouldn't do it now."

"No," he said. "I wouldn't."

"Then it doesn't matter."

"I think it does." He got up and walked over to the window.

"The swimming-pool lights are on again," he said. It suddenly irritated him: the pool lights left on when they were all at a party, the dock light burned out and not replaced, the waste everywhere, waste and erosion. "There's no reason to have the lights on when nobody's home."

"Julie thinks they're beautiful," Lily said faintly. "I left them on for Julie."

"Julie's not home," he said reasonably. "We can burn them all day and all night if Julie thinks they're beautiful, but Julie has not been home all evening."

"Everett. *Please.*"

"Don't worry," he said. "Just a minute."

"Sit down and listen to me."

He opened and closed the screen door, examined the hinges absently, picked up his drink and finished it.

"It's all right," he said. "I'm going to call Mc-Grath now."

She sat forward on the edge of the couch. "You're going to tell him what we planned? Everett?"

"Sure. Sure, baby."

"Let me call."

He closed the telephone book and dialed.

"Ed? Everett McClellan."

Lily crossed the room and sat down by the telephone looking up at him.

"That's right," he said. "*Once* before. I called you in the middle of the night once before. Ten years ago."

"You know Ryder Channing? That's right. No, they're divorced." He paused. "Listen. I shot him."

"*Tell him why,*" Lily whispered.

"I just shot him. We had a fight over a gun and I shot him. My gun. You get on over here and I'll tell you about it."

Everett hung up.

"*You didn't tell him why.*"

"No," Everett said. "It doesn't matter."

He took Lily's hand.

"Lily. Lily baby."

She did not take her eyes from him.

"I'm going down to get the gun," he said.

"Leave the gun. Wait until McGrath comes."

He shook his head.

"Leave me be," he said gently. "You sit here."

Holding her, her head pressed against his chest, he felt the sobs beginning in her frame and knew that she realized it was not going to be the way she had wanted it.

"Wait for the children," she said. "Julie will be here."

"I don't want to see her."

"Everett—"

"It was all right," he whispered. "It's been all right."

"I love you."

"I know that. Don't you think I know that."

"Nobody would have known it," she said. "Nobody. The way it's been."

"Known what?"

"That I loved you."

"I knew it. You knew it."

She clung to him. He could feel her ribs beneath her dress.

"Listen," he said. "You have to put on some weight. You have to start eating more and getting some rest. You promise."

"I promise."

"All right then." He kissed her closed eyes.

26

Sitting on the needlepoint chair where Everett had told her to sit she felt her hands wet, her head hurting (hurting, not aching; it had stopped aching upstairs, an hour ago, when she had first heard the shot), nothing very real. The only real thing had been the shot and she could hear it still, cracking reflexively through all the years before, spinning through the darkness between the games they had all played as children and the games they played now, between the child she had been and whoever she was now, sitting on the needlepoint chair and knowing that he was not going to let her make it all right.

Leave me be. What had it all been about: all the manqué promises, the failures of love and faith and honor; Martha buried out there by the levee in a $250 dress from Magnin's with river silt in the seams; Sarah in Bryn Mawr, Pennsylvania; her father, who had not much cared, the easy loser (*He never could have been,* her mother had said and still loved him); her mother sitting alone this afternoon in the big house upriver writing out invitations for the Admission Day Fiesta and watching *Dick Clark's American Bandstand* because the Dodgers were rained out; Everett down there on the dock with his father's .38. She, her mother, Everett, Martha, the whole family gallery: they carried the same blood, come down through twelve generations of circuit riders, county sheriffs, Indian fighters, country lawyers, Bible readers, one obscure United States Senator from a frontier state a long time ago; two hundred years of clearings in Virginia and Kentucky and Tennessee and then the break, the void into which they gave their rosewood chests, their silver brushes; the cutting clean which was to have redeemed them all. They had been a particular kind of people, their particular virtues called up by a particular situation, their particular flaws waiting there through all those years, unperceived, unsuspected, glimpsed only cloudily by one or two in each generation, by a wife whose bewildered eyes wanted to look not upon Eldorado but upon her mother's dogwood, by a blue-eyed boy who was at sixteen the best shot in the county and who when there was nothing left to shoot rode out one day and shot his brother, an accident. It had been above all a history of accidents: of moving on and of accidents. What is it you want, she had asked Everett tonight. It was a question she might have asked them all.

Leave him be. It was all she could do now, the only present she could make him. *Drive far away our ghostly foe and thine abiding peace bestow.* Christ on the cross couldn't drive away that ghostly foe. And maybe once you realized you had to do it alone, you were on your way home. Maybe the most difficult, most important thing anyone could do for anyone else was to leave him alone; it was perhaps the only gratuitous act, the act of love.

She sat on the needlepoint chair until she heard it, the second shot. When she found him, face down with his arm flung out and his head hanging over the edge of the dock, she lay down beside him on the wet boards and talked to him, telling him things for which there had never been any other words: *Remember, Everett baby once at the Fair, you lifted me onto the golden bear in front of the Counties Building and kissed me and we laughed. And remember we used to lie in bed mornings, sometimes with Knight in bed between us and I would say don't go to sleep, he'll smother, remember how it was and remember the day we took the children to the Cosumnes and it rained and we all sat drinking Cokes under the cottonwood and the rain coming through remember Everett baby remember.* She hoped that although he could not hear her she could somehow imprint her ordinary love upon his memory through all eternity, hoped he would rise thinking of her, *we were each other, we were each other, not that it mattered much in the long run but what else mattered as much.*

As she lay holding him against the dark she heard the sirens on the highway, but did not move until the two cars, one McGrath's and one the Highway Patrol, swung off the levee and down the drive to the house. She stood up then, left Everett and climbed the wooden stairs to the road. In the light down on the verandah McGrath, his pants pulled on with a pajama top, stood with two other men; another man, in a Highway Patrol uniform, waited on the lawn, looking not at the house but at the lighted pool. Watching them as she brushed the leaves from her skirt and licked the blood from the arm she had held around Everett, she began to wonder what she would say, not to them but to Knight and to Julie. She did not know what she could tell anyone except that he had been a good man. She was not certain that he had been but it was what she would have wished for him, if they gave her one wish.